The Winter Bride

Orphaned Charity Carew was 24 years old and living quietly with her retired barrister uncle when the unbelievable happened. The famous poet Martin Revesby came home from the Continent to live at his newly inherited Cornish mansion of Malmaynes and, thanks to Charity's acquaintance with Mr Pitman's new system of shorthand, he invited her to become his secretary. In an incredibly short time Charity found herself in effect mistress of the great house on the cliffs and under the spell of the handsome, gifted poet whose works she transcribed so faithfully.

But a shadow had lain over Malmaynes ever since two young women had been horribly murdered in the village some twenty years before. The murderer – a local youth – had committed suicide, but a wall of secrecy had been built round these events. No one in the village would speak of them. Charity's enquiries fell upon deaf ears. And what little she did learn was deeply disturbing, for the murderer was closely connected with the great house and had been known as the Beast of Malmaynes.

Suddenly two more women are murdered. Can the Beast have risen from the grave? Is he the sinister presence Charity has sensed lurking in Malmaynes, unknown to Martin Revesby whose thoughts are all of love and poetry? Not even a bride on her wedding morning is safe from the Beast's strangling hands. And Charity herself is soon to be a bride . . .

by the same author

The Dolphin Summer

Dark Inheritance

Mallion's Pride

The Winter Bride

Carola Salisbury

COLLINS
St James's Place, London

William Collins Sons & Co Ltd
London · Glasgow · Sydney · Auckland
Toronto · Johannesburg

For Beryl

First published January 1978
Reprinted June 1978
Reprinted May 1979

ISBN 0 00 221960 3

Set in Baskerville
Made and printed in Great Britain by
William Collins Sons & Co Ltd, Glasgow

Chapter One

I came to Malmaynes on a September's evening of the year 1856, a year of such continuous drought that South Cornwall had suffered a near-famine, with bread riots in the streets of Truro and St Errol, much misery, and the promise of full graveyards if the coming winter matched the severity of the previous one. It was the evening when the fine weather broke, and I saw the steep roof of the great house etched against the skyline, up there on its escarpment above the grey sea, with the coming storm clouds banked above it.

By chance, I had never before travelled so far westward along the southern coast; nor, indeed, had I ever heard of Malmaynes till fate directed me towards it.

My name is Charity Carew, the third daughter of Mr and Mrs Martin Carew of St Errol in the duchy of Cornwall. My poor mother, widowed early, perished in a tragic outbreak of cholera in the year of '42, together with my older sisters Faith and Hope; and I was taken into the care of my late father's brother, Mr Gervase Carew, a barrister-at-law, then retired upon the proceeds of a small annuity and residing in a modest cottage in the village of Poltewan, not far from St Errol. Uncle Gervase was a dear, kind person. Lack of success in his chosen profession had not soured the sweetness of his disposition, nor marred the serenity of his smooth, pink face with its frame of flaxen hair and whiskers. But he was, alas, greatly addicted to the brandy bottle – an inclination which had undoubtedly accounted for his undistinguished career at the Bar.

The year of 1856 found me twenty-four years of age, and,

thanks to my uncle, well schooled in all the rudiments, with an additional competence at Mr Isaac Pitman's Stenographic Sound Hand. It was the latter accomplishment which indirectly led me to Malmaynes, and it came about in this way.

I had always been an avid reader, especially of poetry and novels: and had for some years greatly admired the works of the poet Martin Revesby. His words had the power to stir my heart and my imagination; they have it still. It was in my twentieth year (and I had just completed the course in Stenographic Sound Hand at an establishment in St Errol) that I had the temerity to write to Mr Revesby, via his publishers in London, praising his work and thanking him for the pure pleasure that it constantly gave me. I hardly expected a reply – but reply there came, addressed from Brussels, Belgium, where the poet had been living for some seventeen years since leaving Oxford University. Penned by the hand of a secretary, though signed by the poet himself, the letter briefly thanked me for my encouragement and advised me that a collection of his latest verses was on its way to me under separate cover. In due course, the slim, calf-bound volume arrived. Entitled *Reflections and Recollections*, it carried on the flyleaf an inscription from the author.

There then began a sporadic correspondence between us – mostly issuing from myself, it has to be said. I told him of my doings: of the part-time employment I had obtained as stenographer to the St Errol Urban District Council; about the short vacation that Uncle Gervase and I had taken in Bath, for reasons of his health; of the various books that I had read and enjoyed. The replies were not always prompt, and, to my disappointment, were more often than not concocted and signed in the poet's absence by his Belgian secretary, M. Charles Alphonse. My surprise and delight may well be imagined when, that fateful summer of 1856, I received a letter from my idol, informing me that he was shortly leaving Belgium to take up residence on a Cornish estate named Malmaynes, which he had recently inherited. And – wonder of wonders! – would I be prepared to accept the position of his secretary, resident in Malmaynes, since M.

Alphonse's family commitments would not allow him to come to England? I replied by return, enthusiastically accepting the appointment.

Uncle Gervase received the news with a good grace.

'My dear Cherry,' he said, 'I knew that you would flee the nest, soon or late, whether for reason of matrimony or the taking up of a career. I wish you well. My blessing will go with you. You will come and visit me occasionally, I don't doubt.'

'Of course, Uncle,' I assured him, and dropped a kiss on his forehead.

He poured himself a generous rummer of brandy and shifted in his armchair uncomfortably, frowning – sure signs that he had something on his mind that was troubling him.

'Malmaynes,' he mused. 'Malmaynes – now that's the grim-looking place that stands on a clifftop above the parish of St Gawes. I have never set foot in the district, though I have many times seen it from seaward while on passage by coaster from Falmouth to Penzance and back – a mode of conveyance which I much preferred when I had a practice with the Western Circuit. The parish of St Gawes – ah, that strikes a chord of memory! There was a case heard at Falmouth before Mr Justice Cadwallader in, I think, the mid-thirties, that related to certain occurrences in St Gawes. And a mighty unsavoury case it was, as I recall. Cherry, my dear, be so kind, pray, as to pass me the relevant copy of the Law Reports.' He pointed to the bookshelf that stretched the length of our cottage living-room. 'It will be the seventh from the left. Yes, that's the one, dear.'

I watched him thumb expertly through the thick volume with its pages of close typescript, and experienced a curious prickling of the skin among the small hairs at the back of my neck and an indefinable sense of unease.

I said: 'Don't bother with those old matters now, Uncle.' And felt foolish for saying it. But he appeared not to have heard.

At length, he found what he was seeking. 'Ah! Here it is,' he said. 'And it was as I had recalled. If anything, it was worse – much worse. Here we have it: "... before Mr Justice Cadwallader. The accused, Saul Pendark, charged with the brutal and senseless murder of two females, Ruth Rannis and Emily Jane Witham, in the parish of St Gawes, Cornwall. The plea of Guilty but Insane was dismissed, and the jury finding the prisoner Guilty as charged, he was condemned to death ..." And that, my dear Cherry, baldly stated, is the termination of the career of a scoundrel who was popularly known in notoriety as "The Beast of Malmaynes".'

'The Beast of Malmaynes!' I cried, appalled. 'But why Malmaynes?'

He shrugged. 'The proximity of the great house, and its own ancient and bloody history – it was a stronghold of the Civil War, taken by the Roundheads only after a long and bitter siege and with much slaughter – led its name to be attached to that of the murderer. Some halfpenny journal coined the title, and it stuck. So much the worse for Malmaynes. However, that is all history now. The so-called Beast met his fate twenty-odd years ago. But not the fate to which Mr Justice Cadwallader had consigned him. He did not hang after all.'

'Then what happened to him, Uncle?' Morbid curiosity overcame my strange unease.

'As I recall,' said Uncle Gervase, 'and I don't have the facts at my fingertips, but I will look them up at an early opportunity – as I recall, the condemned man escaped from custody and made his way back to the scene of his crimes, to the parish of St Gawes. And it was there that he was sighted by the local constabulary. Chase was given. Rather than be taken again, he threw himself from the cliffs and perished on the rocks below Malmaynes – another circumstance, I don't doubt, which contributed to the unfortunate association of its name with that of the Beast.'

So I came to Malmaynes on the evening that marked the end of the great drought. As the conveyance that had brought me from St Errol toiled up the steep cliff road, a jagged fork of lightning rent the sullen clouds and was immediately followed by a roll of thunder that seemed to find echo in every nook and cranny of the tumbled cliff face. It then began to rain : a solid sheet of water that drummed on the roof of the carriage and shut out from my sight the old dark mansion on the clifftop. I did not see it again till the driver pulled his horse to a halt at the foot of a flight of worn stone steps.

'Here we be, ma'am,' he said.

I saw a sheer face of stonework, with dark shuttered windows and a line of narrow apertures high up, under the dripping eaves. A solitary window was lit, up there.

My driver, manfully braving the downpour, mounted the steps and tugged on a bellrope that hung by the side of a deeply recessed door, which was of blackened oak and studded all over with massive nailheads and banded with iron strapwork. The bellrope brought forth no sound, but presently a wicket opened in the door, and the form of a head in candlelight was briefly presented through the barred aperture. The wicket closed. Moments later, the door creaked open. A woman stood on the threshold, candle in hand, her face shadowed by an enveloping shawl. I got out of the carriage, my carpet bag in hand, and ascended the steps. The driver fetched the rest of my baggage from the roof.

'Good evening,' I said to the figure in the doorway. 'I'm Charity Carew, and Mr Revesby is expecting me.'

'Just so,' came the reply. 'Come this way, miss.'

She turned and, beckoning me to follow her, walked swiftly down a bare stone corridor that led out to a chamber of such vastness that its ceiling – till my eyes became accustomed to the dimness – remained beyond the limits of the candle's light. A long refectory table stood in the middle of the great room, and a place was set for one at an end. The woman laid the candle on the table, and, taking a spill, she lit from it a six-branch candelabrum. The flame illuminated her features, which were those of a severe-looking personage in her sixties, with deep-set eyes, cadaverous cheeks, and grey hair severely drawn back and parted in the centre. She turned to face me, and eyes of astonishing paleness briefly flickered over me, taking in my green serge travelling costume, plain bonnet, gloves – and, last of all, my face. Then she looked away.

'I am Mrs Challis,' she said. 'The housekeeper. The master left orders that you were to be served a meal after your travels.' She gestured to the place that was laid. 'Are you ready for it now?'

'That will be very nice,' I replied. 'Isn't Mr Revesby at home then?'

'He was called away on business,' she said. 'To Truro. But he'll be back tomorrow morning. There's soup and a hot game pie. Or there's cold smoked mackerel if you prefer it. Cider or wine. Or there's tea.'

'A little mackerel will be very nice,' I told her. 'And I would love a cup of tea.'

My driver came in, carrying my baggage which he deposited on the stone-flagged floor. He looked about him in awe as I fumbled in my reticule for money to pay him. This done, he thanked me and was gone. I heard the outer door slam behind him. During this time, Mrs Challis had vanished. I was alone.

I took closer stock of my surroundings. The chamber was a stone-built hall, such as might have been used for banqueting in ancient times. It was panelled in dark oak as high as a man, and the ceiling was of intricately carved wood, and hung with tattered banners that told of a martial past. I recalled Uncle Gervase telling me that Malmaynes had played a grisly part in the Civil War of the 17th century.

A line of three diamond-paned windows faced me at the opposite, longer end of the hall. Crossing to them, I looked out – and was staggered to see a view of awesome grandeur. Immediately below lay the grey sea, surging among the dark rocks at the foot of the steep cliff. To left and right were the jagged headlands of a wide bay. The last of daylight came fitfully through gaps in the tumbled skies, and the rain slanted down.

'Your supper, miss.' Soft-footed, the housekeeper had come back.

She was not alone. There was a grey-haired man carrying

a tray of food. He was dressed in seedy black, and his eyes were secretly shielded behind thick spectacles.

'This is my husband Challis,' said the woman.

'Good evening, Challis,' I murmured. The man bobbed his head briefly and nervously in my direction, but made no reply.

I took my seat at the end of the table. They laid before me a dish of smoked mackerel fillets nestling in a salad of lettuce and watercress, a plate of brown bread and butter, and a tea-set of silver. They took their places – the woman on my left and the man on my right – as I poured myself a cup of tea, adding milk.

'And how is Mr Revesby settling down in Malmaynes?' I asked, by way of filling the void of awkward silence. 'He must find it a great change from living in a foreign city.'

'He likes it well enough,' said Mrs Challis shortly.

'It's an enormous place to accommodate a single gentleman,' I ventured. 'But I suppose there must be a very large staff to go with it.'

'There's no one living in but me and Challis,' said the woman.

'But that's strange,' I said. 'I could swear I saw a light in one of the upper rooms.'

'There's no one in the house but me and Challis,' she repeated in a harsh voice. 'No one at all. There's two wenches who come up from the village. The gardener sleeps in his tool-shed. Me and Challis manage with all the rest.'

'I'm sure you manage very well,' I said placatingly. There was a thick rime of dust on the table top, and a sliver of old grease on the side of the dish containing the mackerel.

'You're not eating anything,' said the woman.

'I don't think I'm very hungry after all,' I said. 'But the cup of tea is delicious.'

At a signal from his wife, Challis began to clear away the food. I noticed that he had trembling fingers. I also was aware, when he came close to me, of the distinct aroma of alcoholic spirits. He fumbled and all but overturned a salt-cellar, which won him a sharp word of reproof from his wife.

When he went out of the chamber by a double door at the far end, she followed after him. They had not gone far from sight before her voice came back to me, strained and urgent, sibilant. And carrying quite clearly in the echoing space between . . .

'Then go and attend to it now. We don't want any trouble from her, or from him either. Can't I trust you to do anything properly?'

I heard each word separately, so I told myself that I could not possibly have been mistaken. With the shapes of the sounds still clear in my mind, I reassembled them. They came out just the same.

My quarters – bedroom with bathroom adjoining – to which Mrs Challis led me soon after, were on the third floor of the mansion, with a window overlooking the sea. The bedroom was quite small, panelled in oak, and, in consequence of an open fireplace in which a sizeable log was burning, extremely warm and comfortable – in pleasant contrast to the maze of chill staircases and corridors through which we had passed to reach there.

She left me with the candle. I heard her footsteps fade away in some far corner of the old house. The small sounds of the night took over: the crackle of the log in the fireplace; and, as I strained my ears even harder, the far-off sound of the waves breaking on the rocks far below the walls. I shivered in spite of the cosseting warmth of the room – and prepared myself for bed.

It was a comfortable-looking tester bed, with a canopy hung with green figured velvet, and a quilted eiderdown to match. Green, also, were the carpetings of the room, which were laid direct upon the stone flooring. Placing my candle upon the bedside table, I tried the springing of the bed and found it suavely to my liking. I had left Poltewan shortly after noon; it had been a long and uncomfortable drive, with unconscionably long waits at posting inns for changes of horses – and I was tired.

I slipped between the sheets, which smelt faintly of mothballs and felt none too well-aired. Despite the grandeur of Malmaynes and the awesomeness of its setting, there were obviously grave deficiencies in the standard of comfort. It occurred to me to wonder if Mr Revesby was very particular about his comfort, or sensitive about inadequate washing-up of dishes, dusty furniture, and – as I had experienced – milk that was slightly 'off'. I hoped he was, and that things would speedily be put right under the new master of Malmaynes.

With a sigh, I relaxed against the pillows and took up my favourite bedside book, to read a few of his verses before snuffing my candle and drifting off to sleep . . .

Suddenly, every nerve in my body was jolted, and I felt my skin prickle to gooseflesh.

What was that?

It came to me again: through the surrounding gloom; through byways and corridors of the ancient house; amplified by echoes and distorted by distance, the thickness of doors, the impenetrability of the very stone walls . . .

A peal of laughter. High-pitched as the laughter of a woman, or of a young child; but at the same time grotesquely inhuman, as if from the throat of some wild animal. Lingering, long-drawn-out.

I leapt from that bed, snatching up my peignoir and rushing to the door, throwing it open: instantly recoiling in horror, as the wild laughter clamoured more loudly in my ears, coming down the dark tunnel of the corridor outside, seemingly near at hand.

'Who's there – who's that?' I cried out.

The laughter faded away in a throaty gurgle. Gave one last loud peal, and then was silent.

I stood for a very long time, scarcely noticing the coldness of my feet on the bare stone, till a fit of ague set me shivering like an old woman. Only then did I shut the door and turn the key in the lock. There were bolts, also, at top and bottom. I shot them both into their stout sockets. Then, still shivering, I crept into the bed and pulled the sheets over my head; nor did I emerge till dawn ended one of the longest nights of my life, and I was able to sleep at last.

Chapter Two

The silver fob watch that Uncle Gervase had given me for my twenty-first birthday told the hour of nine-fifteen when, dressed and somewhat refreshed by a couple of hours of sound and dreamless sleep, I quitted my bedroom and set off to find my way back to the great hall.

With the natural resilience of a good constitution and a sceptical disposition, I had come to terms with my terrors of the previous night. Someone, I told myself, had deliberately tried to frighten me. Either that, or there was a wild animal caged within the walls of Malmaynes – a jackass, perhaps, or – I searched my slender knowledge of matters zoological – maybe a baboon. No matter what, I would seek it out – be it man or beast.

It was a very long way down to the lower floor. The journey – through bare corridors, set with dark corners that defied the thin daylight coming through grimed windows, and past rows of silent and secret doors – robbed me of a lot of my new-found resolution. By the time I regained the great hall, the skies beyond the mullioned windows were black with storm clouds, almost as if the new day was already spent. I gave a nervous start as I turned to see Mrs Challis regarding me from the door at the far end.

'Good morning, miss,' she said in her flat, expressionless voice.

'Good morning, Mrs Challis,' I replied. 'I wonder . . .'

'Miss?'

'Do you keep any animals in the house?'

'No animals, miss. Not so much as a dog or a cat. The late

master, Mr Henry Tremaine, couldn't abide animals. And Mr Revesby, he hasn't brought any with him.'

I searched her face. The deep-set, pale eyes told me nothing as they shifted their gaze and fixed themselves upon a spot somewhere at a point beyond my left shoulder.

'Mrs Challis,' I said, 'who was it laughing in the night?'

'Laughing, miss?' She sounded genuinely surprised. I felt more of my determination drain away. 'Why, who would be doing that, of all things?'

'I distinctly heard someone laugh,' I persisted. 'And it was most – unpleasant.'

The woman gave a shrug. 'As you say, miss,' she commented dismissively. 'But I never heard a thing, nor Challis either, as far as I know. Would you like me to fetch him, so that you can ask him yourself?'

I shook my head. 'That won't be necessary,' I said, defeated.

Did I detect a small malicious smile as she laid a place at the end of the table where I had sat the previous evening?

'As you please, miss. What would you like for breakfast? There's kippers and there's sausage, potato cakes. Porridge, of course . . .'

'Just some coffee, please,' I told her.

'Coffee it is, miss.'

She left me. There was clearly no point in pursuing the topic of the laughter in the night. I thought it over, later, as I sipped my quite tolerable hot coffee, and came to the inescapable conclusion that the laughter I had heard must have been that of her husband. Challis, clearly (recalling the smell of spirits on his breath) was a drunkard. Later that night he must have imbibed an additional amount: sufficient to drive him into almost a maniac state. I tried to picture that slightly-built grey-haired man with his frightened eyes behind thick glasses – and had my doubts about my theory, but it seemed the only one that fitted the case.

At ten o'clock the skies cleared somewhat, and, having enquired of Mrs Challis about my employer's likely hour of return, and learning that he was expected back shortly before luncheon, I decided to fill in the time and extend my knowledge of the local geography by taking a short walk.

I went out. Looking back, I saw Mrs Challis watching me from one of the few windows that faced the landward side of the great house. She withdrew immediately our eyes met.

Malmaynes, in the daylight, presented a stark and awesome countenance. The main part of the building was a regular-shaped, steep-sided block four storeys high. The ground floor housed the great hall, which appeared to stretch nearly its entire length. As I have said, there were very few windows on that side, and those scarcely more than arrow slits. This, I decided, must be accounted for by the fact that Malmaynes had been a fortified house in days gone past.

The roof of the main block was high pitched and covered with Cornish slate. A sullen column of wood smoke rose from one of the tall chimney-pots, and there was a seagull perched on one of the dormer windows high in the roof. It was in one of those dormer windows, I decided, that I had seen the light on my arrival.

With an eerie cry, the seagull rose, flapping, into the air, over the roof and out of my sight. I set off down the steep drive that led down to the gates. Almost immediately it began to sprinkle with light rain, and I wished that I had brought an umbrella. I pulled my good shawl more closely about my neck and felt grateful for my sensible bonnet.

Out through the gates, I came upon the main road that led inland towards Truro. There was a narrow, hawthorn-hung lane that ran steeply downwards, and parallel with the coast. A fingerpost pointed: *St Gawes village ¼m.* I took the lane.

It was a short and easy walk down. A few snake turns, a view over a five-barred gate to a meadow full of lean cows; the smell of newly-wet grass; the distant call of a rooster. I saw no living thing save a toad that hopped its lazy way across my path and vanished into the hedge. My first sight of the village was the top of a barn, and, beyond that, the steeple of a church. It was now raining quite hard. My thoughts turned towards the need for shelter, and I decided upon the church.

St Gawes was a single street lined with stone cottages of either thatch or slate roofs. The buildings all had the run-down appearance that told of the several successive years of bad harvest in South Cornwall. The look of poverty was everywhere: broken windows boarded up with scraps of wood; missing slates and rotting thatch; a few wretched hens pecking for scraps in the rutted road; a solitary child with a swollen belly who watched my progress, wide-eyed. There was no sign of anyone else in the place.

The church was at the far end of the village, and was approached through a lychgate and a path that ran between rows of gravestones set in high, unkempt grass. The whole – church and graveyard – surrounded by a ring of tall chestnut trees whose leaves whispered in the rain. I felt suddenly shut off from the world of the living.

The church door latch yielded to my touch; clacked open and brought to my nostrils the smell of must and rotting wood. In the gloom that was only brightened by the thin daylight coming through stained-glass windows, I could see a large puddle of water in the centre aisle. There was a dripping from the roof above, and streaks of green mould ran down some of the pillars of the aisle.

I removed my shawl and shook off the surplus rain, likewise my bonnet. Laying them across the back of a pew, I set off on a brief tour of inspection. As I walked, I instinctively moved on tiptoe, so that my footfalls should make less sound upon the stone-flagged floor.

The poverty of the village was mirrored in the appointments of St Gawes church. The bare stone altar had on it only a pair of cheap brass candlesticks, and they had not been cleaned for many a day, nor had the eagle of the lectern: and the leather binding of the Bible that lay there was split and discoloured. A token of a more spacious and prosperous age in the life of the village was a magnificent wall tomb, which bore the reclining figure of a man in the trappings of a medieval knight, with helmet, coat of chain mail, sword. His mailed feet were crossed in the manner which, as I knew, told that he had fought in a Crusade. My eye went to the inscription that was deeply carved – though incredibly worn by time – on the side of the tomb upon which the effigy lay.

SIR THOMAS TREMAINE, KNYGHT
OBIIT MCCXXII

Tremaine, I remembered, was the name of the late, former owner of Malmaynes, the man from whom Martin Revesby had inherited. As I continued my explorations, I saw further evidence of the Tremaines: on brass memorial plates set into the walls and floors of the church, on inscriptions, in the dedication of the large window at the east end. I also came upon the name of Revesby on a more recent memorial plate, and in a conjunction which suggested that the two families had been joined by marriage. It was while examining this latter – I recall quite clearly stepping back and adjusting my gaze, to reduce the slight reflected glare from a window – that I became aware of being watched.

It was quite definite, this impression: I knew as clearly as if I had seen the watcher that a pair of eyes had been fixed upon me a brief instant before I whirled round. But there was nobody to be seen. Only the church door, still ajar as I had left it. And no sound but the gentle hissing of the rain and the steady drip-drip of water from the ruined roof. I shuddered, feeling an immediate compulsion to leave that place of shadows and decay.

Walking quickly down the aisle, I took up my bonnet and shawl, and, putting them on, went out into the rain. The overcast had increased, so that the enclosed space, with its sentinel ring of high trees, seemed almost to be in darkness. I set off back down the path to the lychgate. In passing the east end of the building, I was suddenly shocked to see a tall figure waiting there, just out of sight of the church porch. A tall figure dressed in black, with a clergyman's twice-about collar and a rusty black tall hat which he doffed in salutation, disclosing a domed, bald pate of an unhealthy whiteness.

'Good day to you, ma'am.' His voice was of a low and

mournful quality that matched his sombre looks. He was a man of about sixty years, with eyes that avoided mine. 'I observed just now that we had the honour of a visitor to our ancient edifice, so I came from the Rectory to make myself known to you. Pray permit me to introduce myself – the Reverend Josiah Murcher.'

'And I am Charity Carew,' I told him, offering my hand, which he took in his. 'I have just come to Malmaynes, to work for Mr Revesby.'

'Just so, dear lady,' he said. 'That was what I supposed. One had heard of your imminent arrival. Er – Mr Revesby – he is well?'

'I have not yet met him,' I replied.

'Nor I, ma'am,' said the clergyman. 'Though I was well-acquainted with the late Mr Tremaine. A most worthy gentleman, who passed away peacefully after a long illness bravely borne. Ah, yes.' His eyes met mine, briefly, and swam away again.

An awkward silence lay between us.

'Well . . .' I began.

'Ah, I must not keep you here in all this inclement weather,' said Mr Murch hastily. 'I would invite you into the Rectory – ' he gestured towards a house beyond the church, whose roofs and chimneys could just be seen above the graveyard wall – 'but my dear wife is unfortunately – er – indisposed.' He met my eye again as he delivered this explanation, and I had the immediate impression of having been given a round of untruths. 'But I will avail myself of the honour of escorting you a little way,' he added.

'Thank you, sir,' I replied primly.

I do not know what drew my eyes to the two tombstones that stood side by side, close by the edge of the path and about half-way to the lychgate; certainly I had not paid any particular attention to them on the way in. They were a pair: both of the black Cornish slate, and alike as two crows on a fence. The names inscribed upon them – Ruth Rannis and Emily Jane Witham – brought no immediate response from my memory. But the other inscriptions common to both shocked me to instant recollection . . .

FOULLY DONE TO DEATH MAY 23RD, 1835

'Oh!' I exclaimed.

'Pray, what ails you, Miss Carew?' cried the clergyman.

I pointed. 'Those graves. The two women. The women who were murdered.'

'Indeed, yes,' he replied. His glance met mine, and on this occasion his eyes continued to remain steady. 'I am surprised that you have heard of that old tragedy, Miss Carew, for it has all but been forgotten in these parts.'

'My uncle, a lawyer, told me of it when he knew I was coming here,' I explained.

'I see,' he said. 'Well, you have heard of the tragedy, but perhaps not in any great detail – which is fortunate.'

'I was told about – the Beast of Malmaynes!' I cried.

The eyes slid away furtively.

'We – that is, the folk of these parts – do not care to utter that dreadful pseudonym, Miss Carew,' said the Reverend Mr Murcher in a ghost of a voice. 'Nor do we much like to hear it spoken.'

He saw me, in the event, to the far end of the village, to the foot of the winding hill that led back up to Malmaynes; and he pointedly did not refer again to the subject which I had raised; but kept up a monologue about his parish, about the poverty and hardship that the people suffered and how, if it had been in his means, he would have done so much to improve their wretched lot. I listened to him, replying only in monosyllables; and receiving the impression that he was only speaking thus, and so continuously, to prevent me from referring again to the twenty-odd-year-old murders of the two women. What was more, I decided that he escorted me clear of the village to make sure that I did not question anyone else on the matter – not that we saw a soul during our passage along the village street, not even the child with the staring eyes.

We parted company, then, at the bottom of the hill. It had stopped raining, but the clergyman's hand was moist and clammy.

'We shall meet again soon, Miss Carew,' he told me. 'Till then, ma'am.' He doffed his tall hat, bowed, and turned on his heel.

Clearly, it seemed, the village of St Gawes – at least, as represented by its rector – had drawn a veil of forgetfulness over the story that Uncle Gervase had unearthed for me. So be it: I would respect the local feelings, since I was to be one of them. Let the Beast of Malmaynes stay buried, along with his victims.

Reaching the top of the lane, I heard the clack-clack of horses' hooves approaching along the main road; and as I emerged from the lane, two horses and riders came into view, a man and a girl. He was in his mid-twenties or a little older perhaps, with fair hair and side-whiskers, a bronzed, out-of-door complexion, and dressed in a tail coat of hunting scarlet and a hard cap. I scarcely had time to take note of his companion before, seeing me, he doffed the cap and called out.

'Good morning, ma'am. Do I have the honour to address the lady who has just joined the establishment of my new neighbour?'

'That is so, sir,' I told him, and I gave my name.

'Nicholas Pendennis, at your service, ma'am,' he said. 'I called in at Malmaynes an hour since, hearing that you had arrived, to pay my respects. We see so very few new faces in these parts that a newcomer is esteemed as highly as a spring of water in a desert.' He smiled, a winning, boyish smile that showed white and even teeth. 'May I introduce my fiancée, Lady Amanda Pitt-Jermyn. My dear, this is the lady who has come to act as private secretary to my distinguished new neighbour.'

'How do you do?' said Lady Amanda coolly.

'How do you do?' I replied.

I would not have thought, from her mien, by her tone of voice, by the way her violet eyes flickered expertly over my costume from mud-spattered hem to 'sensible' bonnet, taking in on the way my somewhat over-large mouth and retroussée nose, nor missing such details as the chestnut colour of my hair and the decent state of my fingernails – I would not have thought, by the way Lady Amanda did all those things, that she was the sort of woman who would normally greet the arrival of a newcomer, particularly another woman of like age, with the delight of a desert traveller coming upon a spring of water, to use her fiancé's metaphor. Her reaction to me, I thought, was distinctly chilly. The angle of that aristocratic head, topped with sleek dark hair piled under her shiny tall hat; the set of her fine *poitrine* under the well-tailored hunting coat of bottle green; the pose of her slender, gloved fingers – everything about her hinted strongly of distaste of the creature before her.

Mr Pendennis seemed unaware of all this.

'So it's hail and farewell for the nonce, Miss Carew!' he cried, saluting me with his whip. 'But we shall meet again soon, I trust. Your servant, ma'am.'

A flourish of his car, and he cantered on, followed by Lady Amanda, whose violet eyes were fixed firmly ahead, but who gestured farewell to me by the slightest imaginable movement of one gloved hand. I watched them go from sight round the bend in the road leading towards the sea; then I made my way past the gatehouse.

A carriage and pair stood at the foot of the steps leading up to the door of the mansion – and I knew for certain that Martin Revesby must have just arrived back from Truro.

'Come in, please!'

There was a mirror immediately opposite the door of the library to which Mrs Challis had directed me with the information that my employer would like to see me there. I took the opportunity to make a last tally of my appearance, patted my chignon and arranged my lace fichu more to my taste. Then I opened the door and went in.

The poet was seated in a straight-backed chair at an eight-sided rent table in the middle of the book-lined chamber. His profile, with the wide window beyond, appeared to be framed by sea and sky. It was a regular, straight-nosed, firm-jawed profile. The brow high and clear. Hair greying at the sides, but thick as a youth's. He was clean-shaven.

'Your indulgence for a few moments, Miss Carew,' he murmured. 'I am just completing a line. There we are, now. That scans much better and has the virtue of creating an interior rhyme. How are you keeping, Miss Carew? Come forward into the light, so that I can see you.'

Heart pounding, I did as he bade me.

Taking a deep breath, I said: 'Hello, Mr Revesby. I – I have looked forward to this meeting for a very long time.'

He rose to his feet and took my proffered hand. 'And I also, dear Miss Carew,' he said. 'A poet ploughs a lonely furrow. Fame is slow to come, and ephemeral in quality when it arrives. The support of sincere admirers is rare enough, and greatly to be prized. I have enjoyed such support from your good self for – how long is it now?'

'I first wrote to you four years ago,' I said. 'And you replied, sending me a copy of *Reflections and Recollections*.'

'Quite my worst collection,' he said. 'Do you still have the volume?'

'Of course!' I cried. 'But how can you *say* that, Mr Revesby? That volume contains some of your finest verse. Why, the 'Ode to my childhood' is one of the finest poems in the English language. Lord Byron pales in comparison. As for Wordsworth and Coleridge . . .' I checked my outburst, seeing that he was looking at me with a slight, quizzical smile on his lips, head slightly on one side. Was he mocking me?

'Yes?' he said. 'Please continue.'

'I – I'm sorry,' I faltered. 'I got carried away. It was presumptuous of me to contradict you, who know best about your own work. But I *still* think that *Reflections and Recollections* is a beautiful collection!' And I added lamely: 'At least, that's my opinion.'

Suddenly, with a pang of strange emotion, I saw that his eyes – his dark and somewhat inscrutable eyes – were misted with tears. He was not mocking me. How could I have thought he would do such a thing? My clumsy sincerity had touched his heart: the heart of the 'poet, who ploughs a lonely furrow'.

He turned his back on me. Walked towards the window. When he turned again, he was completely composed.

'Well, now,' he said briskly. 'Let me bring you up to date on my present activities. Please do take a seat, Miss Carew. As I told you in my last communication, I am at present engaged upon a cycle of poems relating to the age-old theme of love and death. The central part of the work is a version of the famous medieval romance, the tragedy of Tristan and Iseult. The results – ' he gestured towards a sheaf of papers lying on the desk, and I recognized his dashing script – 'are quite promising so far.'

'I would love to read some of it,' I said.

'And so you shall,' he replied. 'And without much more ado.' He gathered up the papers and passed them across the table to me. 'What I would like you to do, Miss Carew, is to take this first draft of the Tristan and Iseult legend and copy it out in a fair hand – your own fair hand, with which I am happily familiar – leaving plenty of space between the lines, so that I can make further amendments and improvements. That is the method of work I evolved with Charles Alphonse in Brussels these many years. How does that strike you?'

'Nothing easier!' I cried enthusiastically.

'Do you think you will be able to decipher my handwriting?'

'If I have any difficulties,' I told him, 'I can always refer back to you.'

'Indeed you can,' he said. 'And one thing more before you go, Miss Carew: I should like you to write to various of my neighbours – to the Rector, Mr Murcher and his wife, and to my neighbour Mr Pendennis and his fiancée, also to Dr and Mrs Charles Prescott, of St Gawes – inviting them to dinner on Thursday next at seven-thirty p.m. . . . And, of course, Miss Carew, you are included in the general invitation. You will excuse my asking, but why, pray, are you making those undecipherable squiggles on the corner of that sheet of verse?'

'I am taking down your instructions,' I told him, holding out the sheet. 'This is Mr Pitman's Stenographic Sound Hand.'

He peered at it, and exclaimed: 'Well! Upon my word! What will they think of next? You truly are an acquisition for a hard-working poet, Miss Carew.'

That afternoon, I wrote the letters of invitation and gave them to Mrs Challis, who said that the gardener would deliver them immediately. Next – steeling my nerve for an experience to be remembered all my life – I addressed myself to the breathtaking task of transcribing a piece of original work by him whom I regarded as the greatest living poet of the English language. And I should be the first to set eyes upon it, to savour its beauty.

Naturally, I first read right through the work. It comprised four closely-written sheets, each of some thirty lines in length and divided into seven-line stanzas. There were many deletions and corrections. In some places the poet had bracketed several similar-sounding words together, and even phrases of similar meaning, as alternatives – as if he had not yet made up his mind about the final form. But, despite these superficial imperfections – and setting aside his truly awful handwriting – the glory of the poetry shone through.

As he had explained to me, he was telling the tragedy of Tristan and Iseult; and those opening verses lightly sketched in the setting of the legend and the appearance of the principal characters. It was like a lifting of the curtain and the introduction of the actors – but was so much more. Already, with the most subtle and delicate allusions, the poet had begun to weave a web of tragedy about the doomed lovers. Their delight in each other, the tenderness of their passion, carried overtones of a terrible mortality. When I laid down the last sheet, I found that my hand was trembling. It was undoubtedly the most affecting poetry I had ever read. And I – Cherry Carew, spinster, late of the parish of Poltewan – was fated to be a party, however humble, to its creation.

A midwife at the birth of a masterpiece!

I set to with a will, and carefully made three copies of the verses, retaining all the poet's alternative words and phrases by neatly bracketing them together, so that he could delete the unwanted ones. Two copies I placed in a folder which I had made up of brown paper, string and glue, with the title: *Mr Martin Revesby, his work* written on the front, and in it also I put the original manuscript. The third copy I retained for my own records in a tin box – a businesslike procedure that I had been taught at the stenographic establishment in St Errol. I then took the folder along to the library. Martin Revesby was not there, so I placed it on the eight-sided rent table, by his pens and inkwell. It was six-thirty o'clock, and the rain still slanted down from the slate-grey sky.

My employer and I had had luncheon together at one o'clock in the great hall, where he had entertained me with a most interesting account of his life in Brussels, and had very civilly consulted me about what time I preferred to dine. In fact, Uncle Gervase and I had never been in the habit of dining – preferring to take high tea at about six, and a cup of chocolate and a biscuit before retiring. Nevertheless, I was now living in a very different establishment from the cottage in Poltewan – so I had proposed eight o'clock as if it was, for me, the most natural thing in the world. And Mr Revesby had nodded assent.

But what to wear?

I possessed no formal evening costume. And the nearest thing to a 'best' dress I owned was a pretty thing of white muslin, trimmed with pink, with a shaped bodice, high in the neck, and a three-tier skirt falling over the crinoline. I had worn it perhaps three times, once at the annual St Errol Fair. Pretty though it was, one could not by any stretch of the imagination have described it as a dinner gown. But as such it would have to perform.

In my oak-panelled room overlooking the sea, I made my toilette and dressed myself for the occasion, taking stock of my appearance as I did so. My mouth and nose depressed me, as they always had the power to do; but I told myself that my hair was my crowning glory, and that my figure was not at all bad. Dressed, I went to the window and looked out. It was dusk, and the rain seemed to have slackened. Out at sea, beyond the headlands of the bay, a two-masted lugger was sailing, close-hauled, to the west, no doubt hastening to make safe anchorage in Penzance before night closed in. I heard the screech of a seagull, and remembering that they were supposed to be inhabited by the souls of drowned sailors, I shuddered.

Eight o'clock. I descended to the great hall.

Martin Revesby was waiting for me. He was in a tail coat of deepest blue, with a black neckcloth. Tall and sparely-built, he looked much younger than his years – which I put at somewhere in the late thirties. There was an indefinable air of distinction about him: he was clearly a man who was destined to be set above others. And I had the notion that he was aware of this quality; though he had not the slightest conceit or arrogance.

'How delightful you look, Miss Carew,' he said.

'Thank you, sir,' I replied.

'Shall we take our places? I believe all is ready.' He pulled a bell-cord by the fireplace and gestured for me to take my seat which was set next to his at one end of the table. Scarcely had we sat down before Mrs Challis appeared, her husband at her heels. Silently, they served us with soup from a great tureen, and then departed.

'They are not the most engaging of servants,' smiled my companion.

'I'm sure they must have a tremendous amount of work to get through in this enormous place,' I replied.

'Do you think so? I'm afraid I've scarcely given any thought to the running of the establishment. Very remiss of me.'

'But you've only been here for a short while,' I said loyally.

'A fortnight, only. But enough time to have looked about me, if I had the inclination, and put anything to rights that needed to be put to rights. The preparation and serving of the meals, for instance. Tell me, Miss Carew, what is your opinion of the soup?'

I took a sip from my spoon, and considered.

'The ingredients are fresh and excellent,' I said. 'Fresh lobster, fresh cream. It has been prepared with some care, and is very successful. But perhaps not quite as hot as it might be.'

He tasted. 'You are quite right, Miss Carew,' he said. 'Confound it – the stuff is lukewarm!'

I said placatingly: 'I haven't visited the kitchens. Perhaps Mrs Challis doesn't have the facilities for keeping things warm. I should think, also, that they have quite a way to come, from there to here.'

With the air of a man who has come to a decision, he slapped the table smartly with the palm of his hand. 'By heaven, Miss Carew,' he cried, 'I think I have the answer. You shall take stock of the domestic situation at Malmaynes, find what's amiss, and put it to rights. If we need more servants, then you shall obtain them. If the Challises need to be sent packing, then packing they shall be sent. Now – what do you think of that, hey?' He poured himself a glass of wine from a decanter, sat back in his chair, and eyed me questioningly.

'I will do the best I can, Mr Revesby,' I replied.

'And you'll have things in some order by Thursday next, the day of the dinner-party, when I entertain my neighbours for the first time?'

'I'll try,' I told him.

'There's plenty to be done, I don't doubt, Miss Carew,' he said.

I glanced down at the fork by the side of my plate. The gaps between its prongs contained fragments of old food.

'Quite a lot,' I agreed drily.

Presently the man and wife returned to take up the empty soup plates and serve the fish course. It was then that our mutual employer dropped his bombshell. He directed it at the woman.

'It is my wish,' he said, 'that Miss Carew will assume the position of châtelaine of Malmaynes. In addition to her duties as my private secretary, she will order the running of the household, and you will defer to her in all things. Is that clear?'

Mrs Challis had just laid a portion of sole upon my plate and was spooning a sauce upon it. I saw her hand begin to tremble as if in fury. The deep-set eyes never left their task, but seemed to burn with a sudden new light.

'As you say, Mr Revesby,' she said expressionlessly.

'In all things, Mrs Challis.'

'Yes, sir.'

The man Challis said nothing, in fact he showed no sign of having heard the exchange, but continued to carry the dirty dishes over to a side table and lay them upon a tray. When the woman had finished serving, they departed together. The double doors at the end of the hall shut behind them.

'Well now, that's settled,' said Martin Revesby. 'I don't doubt but that Mrs Challis will resent your being set to take charge of her but she will have to become accustomed to it. Or pack her traps and go. So much for that. Now tell me more about yourself, Miss Carew. You are Cornish, I believe you once told me in a letter.'

'Yes,' I said. 'Born and bred in St Errol.' I resigned myself to his questions, making the reservation that, at the first opportunity, I would bring the topic round to the subject of his poetry – in particular the wonderful verses I had copied out that afternoon.

'I, too, am Cornish,' he said. 'Though, as you know, I have spent some years abroad. We are a strange race, Miss Carew. Kin, as you know, to the Bretons immediately across the English Channel. As recently as the end of the last century, the Cornish language was quite widely spoken this side of the River Tamar, though it is all but dead now. The sole is excellent, don't you think? But the sauce undistinguished. Only the continentals can make sauces.'

'It's very nice,' I said.

'And what legends we have,' he resumed. 'We Cornish, with our ghosties and our ghoulies, and things that go bump in the night. Not to mention the piskies, the little people. And the horrors that we concoct about people and places. Why, there's scarcely a hamlet in the duchy that doesn't have some tale of horror woven into its history, nor a patch of moorland nor a lonely crossroad – and most of it pure legend, lightly overlaid with fragments of truth. I shouldn't wonder if there isn't a grisly tale connected with this very place.'

I said: 'Well, there's the Beast of Malmaynes, of course.'

He lowered his fork and stared at me in some surprise. 'I beg your pardon, Miss Carew. Would you please repeat that observation?'

'The murderer,' I said, surprised. 'Surely, Mr Revesby, you've heard about the condemned murderer who escaped and threw himself over the cliff below here.'

'And they gave him that name – the Beast of Malmaynes?'

'Didn't you know?'

He shook his head. 'What you have to bear in mind, Miss Carew,' he explained, 'is that, till by an accident of birth I succeeded to the estate of my distant relation Henry Tremaine, I have never had the slightest connection with Malmaynes, nor with this part of Cornwall. I was born near the border, in Liskeard. The Revesbys had no connection, no correspondence, with the Tremaines in my lifetime. There was murder here, you say? In Malmaynes?'

'Not in the house itself. In the village.'

'And when was that?'

'About twenty years ago. In eighteen thirty-five.'

'It never came to my ears,' he said. 'Was the case widely reported? Who told you of it?'

'My uncle,' I said. 'But that doesn't signify that it was widely known. He remembered the case because of his legal connection with the courts of the West Country. And even he had to look it up in an old law book.' I then told him the story as I knew it, ending by describing the graves of the victims that I had seen down in the village cemetery.

'How very interesting,' was Martin Revesby's comment. 'I really am most grateful to you, Miss Carew, for bringing this old affair to my notice. Though, of course, I would have heard the story, sooner or later.'

'I have an idea that the local folk don't like to speak of

it.' And I cited the instance of the Reverend Mr Murcher.

'We'll see about that,' he said. 'Wait till the Challises come in again. We'll see if the tongue of local gossip can be loosened in regard to the Beast of Malmaynes!'

He grinned across at me: a boyish grin that belied his greying temples and seemed curiously at odds with a man who could write poetry of such delicate sensibility. But then I reminded myself of the adage that all men are boys at heart.

Only – I wished that he would not probe the past and unearth any more of the horror surrounding the doings of the long-dead killer. Some sixth sense whispered that such a course might bring nothing but ill to him and to me.

By the time the Challises returned, I had managed to change the topic of our conversation to that of his poetry. I tried – stumblingly, imperfectly – to express some of the delight that the new verses had given me that afternoon. Martin Revesby was proud and grateful – and did not let false modesty prevent him from showing it. I liked him for that. He was launched upon his plans for the development of the Tristan and Iseult theme – and had quite lost me, so involved and convoluted were his arguments – when the man and wife came in with the next course.

The poet paused for a moment, as Challis took away his plate. Then he resumed his discourse. 'You must realize, Miss Carew, that the plot and counterplot of the traditional legend quite obscure the essential simplicity of the relationship between the two lovers. In my version, the theme of love and death is . . . ah, what have we here, Mrs Challis?'

'There's lamb cutlets, sir,' she replied, 'or there's stuffed shoulder of veal. And there's a cold collared calf's head over on the sideboard.'

'I see Miss Carew has chosen the cutlets,' said Martin Revesby, 'but I will settle for the collared head.'

'Carve Mr Revesby some collared head, Challis,' ordered the woman. And her husband obediently moved over to the sideboard.

The master of Malmaynes poured himself another glass of

wine: I had not touched my own. Mrs Challis laid a silver dish in front of me and took off the lid, disclosing potatoes in their jackets. I noticed that her fingernails were none too clean.

'Tell me, Mrs Challis,' said Martin Revesby abruptly. 'Were you ever acquainted with the gentleman known by the unfortunate sobriquet of – the Beast of Malmaynes?'

There was a muffled cry from the direction of the sideboard, followed by the crash of a falling dish. This distracted my attention from the woman: I turned my head to see Challis on his hands and knees and scrabbling to pick up a large roll of pressed meat that lay on the flagged stone floor amid the shards of its shattered dish. When my gaze returned to the man's wife, whatever initial shock she might or might not have received from the sudden question had been obscured by fury at her spouse's action.

'Look what you've done!' she cried. 'No use thinking you can serve that collared head now it's been on the floor. And Mr Revesby particularly asked for the collared head.'

'It was merely a caprice,' said Martin Revesby mildly. 'I shall be perfectly satisfied with cutlets. You did not answer my question, Mrs Challis.'

I could only see a part-profile of the woman's face, which was turned away from me and towards her master, and her deep-set eyes were hidden from me. But I saw her hands – big, capable hands – clasped so tightly together that the knuckles showed white.

'I – I don't rightly get your meaning, sir,' she said hoarsely.

'The so-called Beast of Malmaynes, Mrs Challis,' replied the other. 'I understand from Miss Carew, here, that his name was Saul Pendark. I asked you if you knew him, or of him, when he was alive. Did you?'

'It – it were many years ago, sir,' said the woman.

'Just over twenty to be precise,' he said. 'You would have been somewhat younger than you are now. However, as you informed me when I arrived here, you have lived in the parish of St Gawes all your life, so you must have been here when the murders were committed. I repeat: did you know

Saul Pendark? I am merely curious.' He smiled at her reassuringly.

She nodded. 'I – I knew him, sir.'

'Did you know him well?'

'Well enough.' In almost a whisper.

'What manner of creature was he, who would slay two women, senselessly, brutally – as I am informed? Was he insane?'

'Some said he was insane. But it didn't save him. They said he was to hang.'

'Ah, but he did not hang, did he? I am informed that he escaped from custody and came back to St Gawes; that he was finally cornered up here on the cliffs, where, rather than face the noose, he hurled himself over and perished. Did you know all that, Mrs Challis?'

'Yes, I knew all that – sir,' she replied harshly.

'It is certain that he perished?' demanded Martin Revesby. 'The body, I take it, was recovered?'

The woman nodded. 'Yes.'

'And safely buried?'

'Yes.'

He smiled across at me. 'I am sure you are as relieved as I am to hear that, Miss Carew,' he said. 'The idea that some mistake had been made: that the Beast of Malmaynes had not perished after all; that he is still alive, lying low somewhere, perhaps, waiting to strike again – that would have been disturbing to the extreme, would it not?'

'It would!' I exclaimed feelingly.

'Having settled that point,' said Martin Revesby, 'I should now be grateful, Mrs Challis, if you would please serve me with a couple of those splendid-looking cutlets.'

We rose from table at ten. I said good night to my employer, and, taking a candle, I set off, through the stark corridors and stairways, for my room on the third floor. With every step, the candle flame sent my shadow flickering across the lofty walls all about me, following after me like a giant wraith from which there was no escape. My heart was pounding, and my mouth dry with fear, when I shut and bolted my bedroom door against the night.

I went to the window to close the shutters. The full moon was riding through a sea of broken clouds. The rain had stopped. Far out on the horizon, I could just discern the lights of a passing ship. Below, white waves broke ceaselessly among the rocks. I shuddered, and drew the shutters close.

So ended my first whole day at Malmaynes. It had not been without its merits, for, in addition to becoming involved in the creation of a masterpiece of English literature, I had been appointed to take charge of the great mansion: though the latter, I had to admit to myself, could well present me with more kicks than halfpence. Mr Revesby had shown considerable prescience in predicting that Mrs Challis would resent my new authority: if I was any judge of another woman's character, I guessed that plenty of trouble lay in store from that direction. Nevertheless, I meant to succeed. Malmaynes should become a gracious home, fit for England's greatest living poet. A place where, later – when showered with the honours that would undoubtedly be his – he would be able to entertain the highest in the land.

'Châtelaine of Malmaynes' – that had been his phrase. Composing myself for sleep, I smiled at the thought, all fear forgotten. Châtelaine of Malmaynes: it had a splendid ring.

I drifted into sleep. It could not have been very long before I awoke with a start. Something – a sound – had disturbed me.

I sat up in bed. Nothing to hear, now, but the pounding of my own heart and the far-off sound of the breakers at the foot of the cliffs.

And then to my ears came a tiny sound that might have been a rat scrabbling in the wainscot.

Or, again – to the mind of a woman suddenly shocked into terror almost beyond imagining – it might have been the tip of a fingernail trailed softly, almost caressingly, across the panels of my door!

Too terrified to cry out, too bemused to come to grips with the possibilities, I simply crouched, staring into the darkness, waiting to hear the sound again.

It was not repeated. I must still have been crouched there when sleep returned, taking me unawares. Nor did I wake till the daylight showed through the cracks in the shutters, and I found myself propped upright against my pillows.

The new day restored my spirits. A day of cloudless blueness, with sea as calm and unruffled as a sheet of coloured glass; while a breathless quiet lay over everything, and not a blade of grass stirred, nor a leaf in a high tree. The perfection of late summer. Who could imagine ill on such a morning?

Dressed, I opened the bedroom door and looked out into the corridor. It was dark and gloomy there – yes. The ancient stonework of the wall felt damp to the touch, and the bare, flagged floor was pitted by time and marked with ancient stains. For all that, it was hard to imagine that someone – something? – had stood there on the previous night, by my door: listening, perhaps; or waiting. I shook off the thought and went downstairs.

Mrs Challis was in the great hall, where the table was laid for one. Mr Revesby, she told me, had breakfasted early and was already at work in the library. The postman had called, she said, and there was a letter for me. It lay by my place at the table. I rejoiced to see it was addressed in Uncle Gervase's spiky, legal hand.

The woman brought me a fresh pot of coffee. As she left, I called after her.

'If it is convenient to you, Mrs Challis, I should like to inspect the domestic arrangements later this morning, commencing with the kitchen.'

'As you say, miss,' she said expressionlessly.

'Will ten o'clock suit?'

'Any time at your convenience, miss.'

'Ten o'clock it is, then. One other thing . . .'

'Miss?'

'The third floor, in that part of the house where I sleep – does anyone else have a room there?'

Did her eyes waver at the question? Did I see those large

hands tighten convulsively, one clasped in the other?

'No, miss,' she said. 'The master's on the second floor. Me and Challis, we've rooms in the servants' wing. Will that be all, miss?'

I nodded, poured myself a cup of coffee, and opened Uncle Gervase's letter.

After a fond and extended expression of how much he was missing my company in Poltewan (which could have had me moping and in tears but for him letting drop that he had joined a gentlemen's chess and dining club in St Errol, and had also made the acquaintance of a Mrs Parnes – a handsome widow lady, he said, who had recently taken up residence in the largest of the rather splendid houses above the quay at Poltewan – and she had invited him to tea), Uncle went on to the main theme of his letter, which was to give me further information about the Beast of Malmaynes. Despite my revulsion, I felt a strange prickle of anticipation as I started to read his next paragraph . . .

> I made the matter an excuse to call and see my friend Joseph Shearer, QC (who is your godfather, remember?) Twenty years is a long time, but Shearer recalled many details of the Pendark case, since he was retained by the Crown, as junior to the late Sir Herbert Fotheringhay-Knight, QC, who led for the prosecution against Pendark.
>
> Some interesting facts emerge. One thing that had slipped my mind was that Saul Pendark was little more than a youth at the time of his trial: a mere 18, though mature, in all respects, for his age, and – as Shearer put it: far gone in depravity, with the cunning strength and viciousness of a jungle predator. The defence was 'insanity', and evidence was brought to support the plea. Have you yet met a certain Rev. Mr Murcher, then Rector of St Gawes, who may still be alive and incumbent? Well, this reverend gentleman testified to having wrestled on two occasions with the Prince of Darkness for the immortal soul of Saul Pendark. It appears that Pendark's mother

sent for the Rector, telling him that her son was possessed by demons, and would he, Murcher, exorcize them? So appalled was Murcher by the appearance and behaviour of the youth that he agreed to perform, there and then, a simple form of exorcism. It seems to have worked tolerably well, for Pendark was calmed, and addressed his mother and the clergyman is something like rational terms. However, the cure was not complete. Some days later, Pendark gave indication of what were to be his ultimate acts, by attacking a young woman, and was only with difficulty restrained from strangling her. Once again, the Rev. Mr Mucher tried exorcism – again at the mother's frantic request – and this time with the full panoply of bells, incense, laying on of hands, incantations, etc., etc. . . . And a week later, Pendark committed double murder – by manual strangulation – of the women Rannis and Witham.

Murcher gave all this evidence at the trial, in support of the plea of insanity; but, as we already know, the plea was dismissed. There was little else of interest that Joe Shearer was able to give me (and, by the way, he sends his godfatherly regards); but I was prompted by the lively interest that this case has stimulated in me to make enquiries at the offices of the *St Errol & District Advertiser,* where I was given permission to peruse the file volumes of the back issues relating to the period of the Pendark trial and its aftermath.

Not surprisingly, an obscure murder case at a remote end of the duchy gained little prominence in the St Errol journal (it was also the year of the Sixth Kaffir War, Halley's Comet, and the opening of the St Errol to Truro railway line, so there was considerable competition for newsworthiness). There was a bald account of the trial and sentence. Pendark's escape and subsequent death received a little more prominence, but not much more. One gobbet of new information emerged in the very brief report of the inquest following the discovery of Pendark's body, some three weeks after his fall, when it was washed up on the beach below St Gawes. Evidence of identity was given by Mrs Edith Pendark, mother of the dead youth, and (again he comes into the story!) the Reverend Mr Josiah Murcher, Rector of St Gawes.

And that, my dear Cherry, is all I have for you on the Beast of Malmaynes – for the present. But there are other sources of information which I intend to pursue, for the unfolding of this long-forgotten case has – by reason, I don't doubt, of the fact that you are presently at the scene of the crime – become something of an absorbing interest to me. And so, kind reader, it is here that we must (in the phrase of the penny weeklies) leave our dramatic serial till the next instalment...

Uncle Gervase concluded with a reaffirmation of his despair at my absence, coupling this with an assurance that he was coping tolerably well without me – of which I had not the slightest doubt.

The substance of his letter gave me plenty of food for thought that morning – and afterwards.

At ten o'clock, I sought out Mrs Challis and found her waiting for me in the hall, from whence she conducted me to the kitchen. As I had guessed, this was a very considerable distance from the place where the main meals of the establishment were taken – a matter of at least a hundred and fifty yards' walk along an exceedingly chilly passage and down a flight of stone steps to a basement.

The kitchen was medieval in construction and must have dated from the time when meats were cooked with the whole carcass upon a spit. Some evidence of the ancient fireplace remained behind a quite surprisingly modern kitchen range, which I immediately recognized (because my business studies at the St Errol establishment had also included classes in household management) as the last word in such appliances: the *Improved Leamington Kitchener – First Class Prize and Medal in the Great Exhibition of 1851* – so it announced itself in raised ornamental lettering upon one of its oven doors; possessing a hot plate, wrought-iron roaster with movable shelves, draw-out stand, meat stand and double dripping-pan; as well as a large iron boiler with a brass tap and steam pipe, to provide constant hot water throughout the day. With such a superior appliance, the running of a home – even one as large and demanding as Malmaynes – should have been greatly simplified.

Mrs Challis saw me looking at the Kitchener range, and must have guessed my thoughts.

'Mr Henry Tremaine,' she said, 'he saw it at the Great Exhibition when he was there, and ordered one right away from the makers in London. Very forward-looking was Mr Tremaine, and a gentleman who liked his food.'

'You are certainly well-equipped here,' I said, looking about me. All round the kitchen, neatly stacked or hung on the walls, were the most up-to-date utensils obtainable: saucepans, stewpans and steamers in copper and iron, all graduated from the smallest to the largest in size; bread moulds and jelly moulds, colanders and chafing-dishes, cheese rasps, bread-graters, fish kettles and frying-pans; and whole rows of kitchen knives, forks, spoons, and ladles – all new, all of the very best quality. But none of them bright and shining.

I touched the top of the long preparing table: there was a suspicious stickiness on the surface. The thing had been wiped clean after use, but not scrubbed. And the splendid Leamington Kitchener had not seen the black lead brush in many a long month.

'Mrs Challis,' I said, 'you are attempting too much in this house, with not enough hours in the day to get through the work. You need a kitchen maid, if not two. And a scullery maid. And at least two housemaids to wait at table. Yet you are trying to cope with – what? – two girls who come up from the village. And where are they now, pray?'

'They only come three days a week,' she replied sullenly. 'And today isn't one of the days. I manage well enough,' she added.

'But how much better, Mrs Challis,' I pleaded, 'and how much more pleasant and easy your existence would be, if only you had adequate assistance. See here – Mr Revesby has given me a free hand to bring in as many extra servants as are needed. I don't want to burden you with people of my choosing; I leave it entirely to you to select your own staff.'

The deep-set eyes grew suddenly cunning. 'There's no help to be had in these parts,' she said. 'And them as are to be had, they don't want hard work.'

'Oh, come, Mrs Challis,' I said. 'I've been down to the village and seen the poverty there. You're not telling me that we can't secure five or six girls or women who wouldn't leap at the chance of a roof over their heads, four square meals a day and good wages.'

'What wages do you have in mind?' she demanded.

This left me something at a loss. What was the scale of pay for domestic staff in the West Country? Desperately I sought to remember my notes from the household management classes.

'What are you paid, Mrs Challis?' I asked.

'Eighteen pounds,' she said.

'Then I think that we could offer – let me see – ten pounds each to the housemaids, and for that you must obtain clean, well-mannered girls of good appearance. Eight pounds for the kitchen maids; and, say, four pounds for the scullery maid.'

She gave a short and scornful laugh. 'Ha! Mr Revesby must be made of money if he's going to agree to that!'

I felt my hackles rise. This woman – for reasons best known to herself – simply did not want to be helped. My goodwill, my tact, were being repaid by a lightly veiled insolence.

'Mr Revesby's financial state,' I said icily, 'is no business of yours. It may very well be that he will consider something like – let me see – an extra forty pounds a year too much to pay for his added comfort and convenience. In which case he will say as much – to me. You, Mrs Challis, will not be consulted on that score.'

A dark flush appeared on her cadaverous cheeks, and I knew that my words had struck home. I had demonstrated that behind the goodwill and the tact was a person who meant to carry out the task that she had been given. The woman was not looking at me, but I knew that I had possibly made an enemy of her. It occurred to me that it might be politic to find something for which to praise her, to soften the blow that she had just received. With this in mind, I approached the Kitchener range once again. There were three covered pans simmering on the big hot plate, and the oven gave out an appetizing smell of roasting meats.

'I should like you to make arrangements for getting at least some of the new staff in time for the dinner-party next Thursday,' I said calmly. 'And, by the way, I should like to discuss the menu with you later. Mmmm – this smells delicious. What are you preparing for luncheon, Mrs Challis?'

'There's roast saddle of lamb,' she said sullenly and with some reluctance. 'And baked beef. Then there's cold cuts.'

'Excellent,' I murmured. 'Excellent. As I said before, I think you manage extraordinarily well under the circumstances. It's nothing short of a miracle the way you cope . . .'

By this time I had moved in the direction of the earthenware sink that stretched the length of the window wall, which looked out on to the kitchen garden. It was there that my words of praise began to ring rather hollowly in my ears, for here was evidence enough that, in some particulars at least, the housekeeper and her husband were demonstrably not coping at all well. The long sink, and the draining-boards at either end, were piled with dirty dishes, plates and cooking utensils. Furthermore, from their particular state, I recognized some of them as remains from luncheon on the previous day.

But it was while I sought in my mind for some way of showing disapproval without further antagonizing the woman that I saw something which stood apart, in every respect, from the pieces of elegant bone china, the good ironware, the silver, copper and glassware . . .

On a plain wooden tray that stood upon a draining-board was set the remains of a meal for one. It comprised a gravy-stained pewter plate, with a fragment of gnawed bone; a pewter mug half-filled with what looked like small beer; and there was one eating utensil – an ordinary kitchen spoon.

I heard the woman moving behind me. She was crossing the room and coming in my direction. At that moment she could scarcely be aware that I was looking at the tray and its contents. I had seconds only in which to speculate. And it was not long enough.

When she stood beside me, I said: 'Whose is this tray, Mrs Challis?'

'Tray, miss?'

'This tray here. There's only one.' I found my voice to be over-loud, with almost a touch of hysteria, and it shocked me to hear it. 'And there's no knife or fork on the tray – but surely neither you nor your husband eat lamb chops with your fingers. Then who . . .?'

'Why, 'tis Jabez's breakfast tray, miss. What use giving the likes of him a knife and fork? He wouldn't know what to do with such.'

'Who,' I heard myself say in a small, tight voice, 'is Jabez?'

'The gardener. I told you about him the night you came.' She pointed towards the window. 'There he be, over by the raspberry canes.'

I followed the direction of her pointing finger. At the far end of the kitchen garden, by a tall and ancient wall that entirely enclosed it, a massive figure was stooping by a line of fruit bushes. His back was turned to us. I had an impression of an almost animal presence: great limbs, disproportionately assembled, with stocky legs and over-long arms; a domed head rising from the top of a barrel-like torso with scarcely the benefit of any neck. The apparition wore ragged shirt and breeches, and was barefoot and hatless.

'He's a deaf-mute is Jabez,' said Mrs Challis, 'but a wonderful way with growing things.'

Almost as if he had heard, the gardener paused in the slow and deliberate movements of his hands, and, without straightening up, turned his huge head to look towards the kitchen window.

The face was a travesty of the human state, as if a mad sculptor had assembled it blindfold from fragments of his previous failures. A bulbous nose, set off-centre, overshadowed a slash of a mouth with a pendulous lower lip. But it was the eyes – small, bright and questing – that struck sudden terror in my heart. They seemed, to me, to be the eyes of a predator.

Chapter Three

The days that preceded the dinner-party were among the most diverse and busy I had ever known. I hardly saw anything of Martin Revesby, who wrote in the library from morning till night, eating his lunch at his work table. Every evening, punctually at six, he handed me the folder containing his day's labours: never less than four pages of verse, sometimes more. These I transcribed the following morning and saw to it that my 'fair copies' accompanied his luncheon tray into the library. Over dinner, which we took together, he was always full of gratifying praise about my transcriptions: how the clarity of my handwriting and setting-out permitted him to read his work with, as it were, a new eye. One evening he brought out some of my transcriptions, upon which he had done some further rewriting. Of these I made yet another copy. In this way the masterpiece progressed.

The quality of the poetry was beyond any words of mine to express. The tragic saga of Tristan and his forbidden love for Iseult took shape, in Martin Revesby's verses, with a growing intensity of feeling that reminded me of nothing so much as an approaching thunderstorm which, on a summer's day, may be heard faintly and far away, no more than a distant rumble and a slight darkening of someone else's sky; next, the inevitable approach, the nearer rumbling, the sudden and startling flashes; finally, the total and overwhelming fury of sound and fire, where one runs for safety, hands over ears to shut out the terror from which there is no escape. So did our greatest living poet conjure up the destructive love of Tristan and Iseult.

The remainder of my duties as private secretary were slight. Engaged, as he was, on a major work, my employer had little time for commonplace business and social matters. He gave me *carte blanche* to deal with anything that came by post – and there was little enough of that: a few bills, a note from his bank in Truro giving the total of his credit on current account (a staggering sum to my eyes), an invitation from the local Tory party headquarters inviting him to subscribe to party funds, ditto from the Liberals. I apprised him of these matters over dinner, and dealt with them according to his wishes.

He asked me how the preparations for the dinner-party were progressing and I was able to inform him that things were going well. The guests had all accepted their invitations by notes of hand. Mrs Challis had managed to secure the services of two women to act as kitchen maids (though not on a living-in basis), and spoke of two more who might be suitable for training to wait at table during the dinner-party: it would be a disaster, I knew, to entrust the task to untried country lasses. As to the menu: I was satisfied that the *cuisine,* on that notable occasion of Martin Revesby's first social venture, would be something that would not soon be forgotten in the parish of St Gawes (and might even cause the insufferable Lady Amanda Pitt-Jermyn to raise an elegant eyebrow!).

Meanwhile, the fair weather continued, with continuous, day-long sunshine that almost – but not quite – softened the grim, grey outlines of the ancient mansion itself. I found myself warming to Malmaynes, despite its uncompromising bleakness, its bewildering vastness, its chill dankness even in the most clement weather. The forbidding corridor outside my room and the empty corridors and staircases that led down to the great hall I enlivened with bowls of wild flowers which I myself picked and arranged. There were cultivated flowers in plenty in the formal gardens between the windows of the great hall and the edge of the cliff – but I never went there for fear of encountering the forbidding

Jabez, who had assumed the role of a nightmare figure in my mind.

It was on the morning of the dinner-party that I received another communication from Uncle Gervase.

Rose Cottage,
Poltewan.
Sept. 23rd, 1856

My dear Cherry,

A brief postscript to my last. I overlooked to tell you that Joe Shearer had two more pieces of information. Firstly, that Saul Pendark's mother was 'Mrs' Pendark only by courtesy – in short, she had the child out of wedlock. Secondly (and I hesitate to give you this, for fear that you will have nightmares), when Pendark was asked, prior to sentencing, if he had anything to say, he was most loquacious, declaring, *inter alia*: 'Kill me, but you will not destroy me. Listen for me in the dark hours of the night and you will hear me. And for many, it will be the last thing they ever hear!'

A macabre little postscript, I am afraid, but not one which will greatly disturb a sensible person like yourself.

Tomorrow I am to take tea with the handsome widow. I fear that she has designs on me; but she has left it a little late to come knocking on this creaking door.

More news – and information – as available.

With fondest wishes, my dear Cherry,

Your aff.
Uncle G –

I had little time to dwell upon the contents of the letter, for the whole establishment was in a turmoil of activity. The two new kitchen maids had arrived, together with the regular daily girls, and all were at work preparing for the evening's event. And there were few enough hands to cope with all that had to be done – what with all the silver to be polished, and a fine Worcester dinner service of a hundred pieces to be taken out and cleaned till it shone. This is not to mention a menu of three courses with *entrées*, each course comprising a choice of four main dishes and two removes. The cold fare had been prepared, by Mrs Challis, earlier in the previous week. The roasts had gone into the oven at first light of dawn, and the vegetables cleaned, peeled, chopped, etc. likewise. The kitchen presented a scene of frenzied activity, and I was tactful enough to keep well clear – the less to fluster Mrs Challis, who was already showing signs of strain. To make myself useful, I decided to attend to the floral decorations for the table and for the great hall generally, where one of the girls was scrubbing the huge flagged floor from end to end, while another was waxing and polishing the long refectory table.

Through Mr Challis (to avoid contact with Jabez), I had ordered a supply of cut flowers from the garden: chrysanthemums and late roses and I thought to fill these out with some of the delicious autumn wild flowers and foliage that abounded in the hedgerows about Malmaynes. Throwing a shawl over the shoulders of my warm green woollen dress (for, though sunny, there was quite a keen wind that late September day), I set off with my basket.

There was a wide sward sloping down to the gates, its grass kept close-cropped by sheep; and this was bounded by an ancient drystone wall that was all but hidden by a hedgerow of tremendous age and complexity, being made of blackberries, holly, beech and blackthorn – a treasure store for the floral decorator. I began gathering, and had scarcely filled one end of my basket, before a girl's face bobbed up from the other side of the hedge and stared at me in alarm: green eyes open wide, thin cheeks flushed. All round her mouth was smeared with blackberry juice. I judged her to be about seventeen years of age.

'And who are you?' I asked, smiling.

'Alice Witham, begging your pardon, miss,' she replied fearfully. 'I've only had a few of the berries, I promise, and it shan't happen again.'

'Eat your fill,' I said. 'There's plenty. Are you from the village, Alice?'

'Yes'm,' she replied.

She was pitifully thin, and clearly half-starved. But her cheap cotton dress, though patched and cobbled at every seam, was quite clean.

'Do you have any employment, Alice?' I asked her. 'Do you work for anyone?'

'I helps with the haymaking,' she replied, 'and at harvest time.' Every child of every peasant family in the West Country did likewise: she had no regular employment.

'Would you like to work at the big house?' I asked, pointing to the grey bulk at the crest of the greensward.

'At Malmaynes?' Her eyes widened again, and not only in surprise; did I not discern alarm there, once again? 'Mrs Challis wouldn't have the likes of me working there, miss. Not she.'

'Mrs Challis will be very grateful to have you today,' I assured her. 'Go round to the kitchen door right away, Alice. Tell Mrs Challis that you've spoken to Miss Carew and I've said it will be in order for you to begin work right away.'

The girl looked doubtful, but she moved away, and presently appeared through a gap in the hedgerow. Her thin feet were bare – as bare they had almost certainly been all her life, winter and summer.

'Off with you then, Alice,' I told her. And when she started for the house, 'Have you had any breakfast?'

She answered almost with puzzlement. 'Why, no, miss.'

'Then tell Mrs Challis to give you a bite. Away you go, Alice.'

I watched her slight figure bound swiftly up the sward and disappear behind the wall that led to the kitchen quarters, then returned to my task. And something was nagging at my mind: something I had heard, quite recently; a word that had conjured up a strange feeling of sudden disquiet. A name . . .

'Witham!' I said it aloud. 'Alice Witham – she must be related to the woman buried in the churchyard. One of the victims of – the Beast of Malmaynes!'

At six-thirty, before going up to dress for dinner, I set off on a brief tour of inspection. Mr Revesby had given me his day's writing and had himself gone to get ready.

The great hall, and the long table with its richness of silverware and napery, presented a splendid sight – and would look even grander when whole battalions of candles were lit shortly before the arrival of the guests at seven-thirty. Nor, I told myself, were my floral arrangements to be sneezed at: the contrast between the formality of the cut flowers and the rugged plants of thc hcdgerow provided a certain drama.

The table was laid to receive the first course of soups and fish dishes. I checked every knife, fork and spoon for cleanliness, and could find no fault. I had just finished doing this when I was aware of the presence of Mrs Challis. It was obvious that the housekeeper had been watching me.

'Very nice, Mrs Challis,' I told her. 'Very commendable. Is all well in the kitchen?'

'Yes, miss.'

There was a surly look about her thin lips and the deep-set eyes avoided mine, as ever. I decided that I had offended her by inspecting the silver.

'And you're sure that you and Challis can cope?'

'Two of the women will help bring the food from the kitchen to the table,' she said. 'And I'm satisfied that one of the others, Janey Pinner, will manage to remove the guests' empty plates.'

'See to it that she's neat and tidy,' I said. 'And do please inspect her hands and particularly her fingernails.'

'Yes, miss.' A spot of angry colour appeared on the woman's thin cheeks. She cast a guilty glance down at her own hands, then clasped them together, hiding the nails.

'Well, I will go and get ready,' I said. 'By the by, how are you finding Alice, the new girl?'

'Her – humph!'

'What's wrong, Mrs Challis?' I demanded. 'She struck

me as being a clean, bright child. Isn't she giving satisfaction?'

The dark eyes probed here and there, ever avoiding mine. She seemed to be searching for words. It suddenly dawned on me that I had stumbled upon the real reason for her ill-humour: it concerned the girl whom I had employed without consulting her.

'Comes from a bad lot, she does,' she said presently. 'An idle bunch of good-for-nothings. And the father drinks.'

'We are not employing the father,' I responded tartly. 'And if Alice doesn't work hard enough, you will simply discharge her. But, surely, any pair of hands is welcome today.'

'As you say, miss,' came the sullen reply.

And then I remembered. 'Mrs Challis, is not that girl Alice related to one of the women who was murdered all those years ago – or is the name Witham very common hereabouts?'

'It isn't common,' she said. 'They're foreigners. Hail from Somerset, or even further. And, yes, Emily Witham was sister to Ned Witham, he being Alice's father. Will that be all, miss?'

'Yes, thank you, Mrs Challis.'

I went upstairs to get ready.

My white and pink muslin had to serve for a dinner gown yet again. Washed and newly-ironed, and with a corsage of fresh roses, it looked not too bad. At least, Martin Revesby's eyes lit up with gratifying admiration when I descended into the great hall at seven o'clock. He was standing by the fireplace, a tall glass in his hand.

'You present a vision, Miss Carew,' he said. 'May I offer you champagne?'

'Thank you, Mr Revesby.' I took the glass from his hand, noticing as I did so that he wore a narrow strip of maroon ribbon on the lapel of his coat, from the buttonhole to the outer edge, and I asked him what it meant.

He shrugged. 'It's a not very senior decoration awarded to me by the Kingdom of Belgium for services to European letters,' he said. 'But I'm grateful to have it, since my own country has never seen fit to acknowledge my small efforts in that direction.'

'Oh, but they will, Mr Revesby!' I cried. 'They will! Wait till your new masterpiece has been published. There's been nothing like it in English literature since *Childe Harold's Pilgrimage* took London by storm.'

The dark eyes softened. 'And you think, do you, Miss Carew, that my little cycle of poems will have a similar effect? You think that I shall be lionized by Society, as Lord Byron was?'

'I'm sure of it!' I affirmed. 'If only you knew how those wonderful lines go straight to my heart, uplift my spirit . . .' I broke off, feeling suddenly awkward and gauche before his steady gaze. 'At least, that's my opinion,' I added lamely.

He smiled, and the rim of his glass touched mine. 'Thank you, dear lady,' he said. 'We will drink to that. I give you the toast: to the success of *The Saga of Love and Death.*'

'You've given it a title!' I cried. 'I like it. To *The Saga of Love and Death.*' We touched glasses again and our eyes met over the rims as we both sipped at the tangy wine. Unaccountably, I felt my heart begin suddenly to beat faster.

'Carriage coming up the drive, sir,' Challis called from the door. He was smartly turned-out in tail coat and a white neckcloth, white gloves. A passable butler. I only hoped that Mrs Challis had managed to keep her spouse from the bottle, and would continue to do so for the remainder of the evening.

'Usher the guests straight in, Challis, announcing their names at the door.'

'Very good, sir.'

The interruption gave me the opportunity to turn away and compose myself. I felt most strange. My heart was pounding and I was certain that my cheeks must be flushed. It must be the heat of the fire, I told myself. Or perhaps the champagne. Surely no other explanation would fit the case. Surely, the mere proximity of Martin Revesby's thoughtful dark eyes did not hold the power to affect me so? It was all very puzzling – and not a little disturbing.

'Lady Amanda Pitt-Jermyn and Mr Pendennis,' intoned Challis from the doorway.

'Good evening. How very nice to see you.' The object of my speculations moved forward to greet his guests – the perfect host.

The dinner was going well. Janey Pinner – clean of hand and neat in appearance as anyone could have wished – cleared away the empty dishes of the first course, while the Challises laid the *entrées* down the centre of the table, for the gentlemen to help the ladies and themselves – since Malmaynes did not have sufficient trained staff to cope with the new-fangled *à la Russe* method, whereby each guest is individually served, to his requirements, from a side table.

Dr Prescott picked up the menu card and read aloud the list of *entrées*. The doctor was stout, ruddy-complexioned and good-humoured. His wife, who was sitting on my right, had scarcely a word to say for herself save 'Yes', 'Is it indeed?' and 'Upon my word, you don't say so'; and spent almost the entire time gazing in rapturous admiration at her spouse, who was placed at the other side of the table, between the Rector and Lady Amanda.

'We have lamb cutlets and French beans,' declared the doctor. 'We have also scalloped oysters, fricasséed sweetbreads, and grilled mushrooms. Now, that's something like a choice of *entrées* for you. That's richness indeed.' He turned to Lady Amanda on his left. 'What is your pleasure, your ladyship? Can I help you to a nice lamb cutlet, perhaps?'

'Thank you, no,' was Lady Amanda's cold retort. 'Mr Revesby is attending to me. You were saying, Mr Revesby, that you don't have a house in London. That is a matter for some regret, which you must speedily rectify. One cannot entertain without an establishment. I must give the matter my attention and start to find you a suitable property as soon as I return to Town.'

'You are very kind, ma'am,' said Martin Revesby, who

sat at the far end of the table from me, with Lady Amanda on his right and Mrs Murcher on his left.

'No oysters for me, Mr Pendennis,' the Rector's wife was saying. She was a large woman, and her voice carried a powerful tremor of self-pity. 'Since the commencement of my illness – and it's all of thirty years that I've suffered, and not a day free of pain, nor a night of easy sleep – I have never been able to abide any form of shellfish. Isn't that right, Josiah?'

'Quite correct, my dear,' responded the Rector, from my left, dutifully, and without looking up from his plate, where he toyed unenthusiastically with a few mushrooms. He had declined to take anything in the soup and fish course.

Nicholas Pendennis was not put out. 'Come now, Mrs M.,' he boomed heartily. 'You must build up your strength. Sweetbreads are the thing. There. And a few mushrooms won't come amiss. Now – what do you say to a cutlet on top? Just a small one.'

'Oh, Mr Pendennis,' trilled the Rector's lady. 'You are spoiling me, you really are.'

Lady Amanda lowered her fork and smoothed her side hair, preening herself like some splendid bird-of-paradise. 'When you have a London establishment, Mr Revesby,' she said, 'I will see you launched upon Society. My late dear father was a patron of the arts, and though my brother, the present earl, is more inclined to matters sporting . . .'

'Capital fellow!' interjected her fiancé. 'Jack was my fag at Eton, and, though I beat the young bounder unmercifully, he never blubbed.'

'It is my intention,' continued Lady Amanda, with a chill glance across the table at her intended. 'It is my intention to follow in the footsteps of dear Father and offer every help and encouragement to art and to artists. Are you personally acquainted with Mr Alfred Tennyson?'

'No, Lady Amanda, I am not,' replied Martin Revesby.

'Or with Mr Charles Dickens?'

'No, ma'am.'

'As regards painters – with Sir Edwin Landseer, or Herr Winterhalter?'

'Neither gentleman, I fear.'

'The discrepancies will be made good.' So saying, Lady Amanda took from her reticule a notebook bound in cloth-of-gold and a tiny pencil in a holder of gold. She scribbled a few lines and replaced them in her reticule. I was intrigued to notice that Nicholas Pendennis was by now regarding his fiancée with a sullen, lowering expression, like that of a little boy whose mother is paying too much attention to the new baby and not enough to him. I smiled into my napkin as I dabbed my lips.

'That was capital – capital!' cried Dr Prescott. 'Was it not, my dearest?'

'Yes, indeed, dearest,' responded his wife.

With a rattle of plates and dishes, the *entrées* were cleared and the second course brought forth.

The final, third course was all but spent (roast hare removed by plum-pudding; grouse and bread sauce removed by Charlotte Russe; plum tart; cabinet pudding) and the talk had become more general, so that Lady Amanda was no longer dictator of the table – even though she continued to monopolize Martin Revesby's attention; and I was strangely piqued to see how a man of his sensibility and intelligence could allow himself to fall so easily under her spell; for her ladyship, notwithstanding her cool air of aristocratic patronage and her gracious condescension, was flirting with the master of Malmaynes as blatantly as the common fishergirls on Poltewan quay preen and prattle for the favours of the lads from the lobster boats. Nor was this lost on Nicholas Pendennis, who had drunk his way down two-thirds of the large claret decanter which stood at his elbow (and had taken champagne between every course), and was casting surly and resentful glances from time to time at the couple at the top end of the table.

Oddly enough, it was Mrs Murcher who disturbed the *tête-à-tête* between her host and the beautiful aristocrat. The

Rector's wife had – notwithstanding the professedly delicate state of her health – stolidly eaten her way through every course, accepting everything that Nicholas Pendennis had piled upon her plate, and helping herself to generous portions at those times when his involvement with what was passing between his fiancée and Martin Revesby caused him to forget his manners. Replete, she sat back and regarded her host fondly.

There was a sudden and total break in the conversation round the table, as will happen occasionally in a gathering. The silence was immediately filled by the strident voice of the Rector's lady.

'Ah, Mr Revesby,' she declared, 'how greatly have the people of this parish been blessed by the generosity of the successive masters of Malmaynes!'

'Indeed, ma'am?' replied Martin Revesby. 'I am glad to hear it. And it will be my pleasure to continue the tradition, I assure you.'

Mrs Murcher took a sip of her wine (it occurred to me that perhaps Nicholas Pendennis had not been solely responsible for the inroads upon the claret decanter that stood between them), and said: 'The common people have benefited, and not only they. Your predecessor – your uncle, Mr Henry Tremaine . . .'

'My great-uncle, ma'am,' he corrected her.

'Your great-uncle,' said Mrs Murcher. 'Your great-uncle, sir, was most generous to me at a time of tremendous need. Is that not so, Josiah?'

The Rector, who for the last half-hour had been sitting with his head bowed over his empty plate so that I had thought him to have nodded off to sleep, suddenly looked up. 'Quite correct, my dear,' he affirmed.

'I have heard,' said Martin Revesby, 'that Henry Tremaine was a kindly man.'

'We never met,' said Lady Amanda distantly.

'At the time of my tremendous need,' said Mrs Murcher. 'At the time of my tremendous need, when they feared for my very life, Mr Henry Tremaine came forward and provided the means for me to journey and take the waters at Baden-Baden. Were you ever in Baden-Baden, Lady Amanda? It is exceedingly fine. One meets all the best people there.'

'Indeed? No, I have not been,' said Lady Amanda.

'That would have been before my time, Mrs Murcher,' said Dr Prescott. 'When you were being attended by my predecessor Dr Hemsley, was it not?'

'Dr Hemsley it was who diagnosed my condition,' said the Rector's wife. 'He understood my case perfectly, and was the very soul of kindness and understanding.' She said this with a sharp glance at the physician opposite her. 'Yes, that would have been in 'thirty-five when I took the waters in Baden-Baden, thanks to the generosity of Mr Henry Tremaine. I shall never forget it.'

I felt my skin prickle. 1835 – again that fateful date. Glancing down the table to Martin Revesby, I met his eyes, and saw from his reaction that he, too, had picked up the significance of the year in question.

It occurred to me, bearing in mind his keen interrogation of Mrs Challis, that he would not let the moment pass without comment. Nor was I mistaken.

'Eighteen thirty-five,' he mused, with an elaborate show of casualness, glancing down into his wine glass and swilling round the dregs absently. 'Was that not the year of your notorious murders?'

The question was greeted by a dead silence. I was looking at the Reverend Murcher, who gave no sign of having heard, but continued to sit with head bowed.

It was Lady Amanda who broke the silence. 'You had murders here?' she cried. 'How exciting and intriguing. Do please tell me about it, Mr Revesby.'

'I know little enough, ma'am,' he replied, 'and that only by mere chance, the other day.'

'As I said,' muttered Dr Prescott, 'it was before my time.' The cheerful physician seemed relieved to be absolved from further part in that particular conversation.

'I was scarcely out of long frocks,' said Nicholas Pendennis. 'It was never discussed in my presence, but I overheard a garbled version below stairs, as one will. I recall that, when I asked Nanny what Cook meant by the strangled ladies, I was soundly slapped and sent to bed early.'

'Upon my word!' exclaimed Lady Amanda. 'And to think that you have never spoken of this to me, Nicholas. I am vexed with you, I really am.' She turned to her host, eyes shining with excitement. 'Tell me as much as you know, Mr Revesby, before I faint clean away with the suspense of it.'

Martin Revesby then proceeded to give her ladyship, and the rest of us, the bald outline of the occurrences, more or less as I had myself presented it to him from Uncle's information. When he had finished, his aristocratic table-companion blinked her violet eyes, and her splendid bosom heaved with emotion.

'The Beast of Malmaynes!' she cried. 'How incredibly terrible! I declare that I shall not sleep a wink tonight.'

'You need have no fear, ma'am,' said Martin Revesby cheerfully. 'The Beast is dead and buried, and the old story overlaid with the passing of years, the shortness of human memories, and – it has to be said – a certain conspiracy of silence among the local people, which I put down to the natural reticence of us Cornish. Would you not agree, Rector?'

The latter gave a start and looked towards his host. 'Ah, my apologies, sir,' he stammered, 'but I fear that I have not been attending to the conversation . . .'

'Speaking of the Pendark murder case,' repeated Martin Revesby, 'would you not say, Rector, that the affair is dead and buried, along with Pendark himself?'

'Indeed I would, sir,' cried the clergyman vehemently. 'Indeed I would – and may it remain so!'

I hesitated, seeing the clergyman's obvious distaste for the subject, and ever being one to respect other people's sincerely held points of view; but there was something about the Rector of St Gawes, something – how to put it? – disturbingly shifty – that I overcame my natural scruples and determined to probe him further, armed as I was with the information that Uncle Gervase had given me.

'I believe you knew Saul Pendark, Rector?' I said. 'Were you not called for, by his mother, to render some assistance?'

The short-sighted eyes under heavy eyebrows probed at me defensively. 'That is so, ma'am,' he murmured.

'Miss Carew's uncle is a legal gentleman,' explained Martin Revesby to the table in general, 'who has some familiarity with the case. Which is why she is so well-informed.'

I said: 'Didn't Pendark's mother complain that her son was possessed by demons?'

'Possessed by demons!' cried Lady Amanda. 'I can scarcely bear it – but please continue, Miss Carew.'

'That is so, ma'am,' he replied in his ghost of a voice.

'And that you performed exorcism – and on two occasions?'

'Exorcism!' exploded her ladyship. 'And to think that you never so much as hinted to me of all this, Nicholas.'

The Rector's eyes continued to hold mine, but waveringly. 'I did for him what I was able, ma'am,' he said. 'It was, perhaps, imperfectly done, but sincerely done. We know so little of these things. In the event, my efforts were fruitless – as we know.'

I had one last question, which I decided – considering the circumstances in which we were all gathered – to frame in an oblique manner. 'If you knew Saul Pendark so well, Rector,' I said, 'you must be well-satisfied that he has gone for good.'

Without hesitation, he replied, 'There is not the slightest doubt, ma'am. After taking his own life, that tragic creature was buried in an unmarked grave and in unhallowed ground.' The voice took on a note of earnestness. 'I, who have good cause to know this, can assure you emphatically that it is so.'

'But of course,' came the voice of the Rector's wife – a stone tossed in the pool of silence that followed her spouse's declaration, 'I was not aware of any of those goings-on. Dear Dr Hemsley, despairing of my condition, kept me in bed in a darkened room, and would not permit me to be worried by anything. Did you say you had been to Baden-Baden, Lady Amanda?'

'I have *never* been to Baden-Baden,' replied the other.

The dinner-party was breaking up. From the corner of my eye, I could see Mrs Challis motioning to her husband and Janey Pinner to clear away the spare dishes from the side table. I had made an arrangement with Martin Revesby to lead the ladies into the drawing-room, leaving the menfolk to their port and cigars – I looked to him for the nod which would be his signal, but his whole attention was upon Lady Amanda, and I observed that her fiancé was glowering at his host over the rim of his wine glass.

'You are staying in the district till when, Lady Amanda?' asked Martin Revesby.

'Till the beginning of October,' she replied. 'Then I have to return to act as hostess at our Town house, my brother – the present earl – being a bachelor. After that, we go to Suffolk for Christmas and the pheasant-shooting. Next year, of course – ' and she looked wistfully across at her fiancé – 'next year I shall be married, with establishments of my own.'

'Do you ride, Revesby?' demanded Nicholas Pendennis brusquely.

'No, my dear fellow,' replied the other with a smile. 'I'm afraid that I have never had the inclination for the manly sports. When younger, I was delicate, and inclined to be artistic.'

This won him a scarcely-concealed snort of contempt from the younger man; but a look of adoration from her ladyship.

'I must take after my father, the late earl,' she declared. 'I too have always had artistic leanings, even as a child, when my greatest delight was the collection of Gainsboroughs, Reynoldses and Romneys at Hundlesham Hall, our seat in Suffolk. Are there any notable pictures in Malmaynes, Mr Revesby?'

'Indeed there are, ma'am,' he replied. 'My great-uncle travelled extensively on the Continent and brought back fine examples of the Florentine and Venetian schools, together with paintings by the French eighteenth-century masters, Watteau and Fragonard.'

'How tremendously exciting!' cried Lady Amanda. 'You must show them to me, I beg you.'

'The pleasure will be mine, ma'am,' was the reply.

Nicholas Pendennis, who had been listening to this exchange with mounting fury, abruptly turned, and, leaning forward across his neighbour Mrs Prescott, fixed me with a tipsy stare.

'Do you ride, ma'am?' he demanded.

'Yes, I do, sir,' I replied. 'But not often.'

'I have a very quiet mare for you, ma'am,' he said. 'Which I will bring round – possibly tomorrow. We will ride out together, you and I. What do you think of that, hey?'

I was spared the necessity of replying to his embarrassing proposal by a distant hammering on the great doors beyond the hall, followed by the jangling of the bell.

'Visitors?' said Martin Revesby. 'At this hour? See who it is, Challis.'

Challis was already on his way. We heard him go down the corridor. A pause while he opened the wicket and looked out. Then the drawing of bolts, the hollow snap of a lock. This was followed by voices: Challis's and another. Their voices were urgent. I had a sudden feeling of unease, and my breathing quickened. Glancing down the table at my employer, I saw his brow furrow with annoyance.

'What the deuce is going on out there?' he said.

The voices were stilled. Footsteps approached down the stone-flagged corridor, and Challis came over the threshold into the hall with a tall man in a long coat at his heels.

'Gentleman wants the doctor, sir,' said Challis, indicating his companion.

'Is it Mrs Proby?' asked Dr Prescott, rising. 'Has her time come? 'Tis a blessing I've managed to finish my dinner, at least.'

There was another man who remained in the background, beyond the archway. He still retained his tall hat on his head, though his companion had uncovered. With a sudden shock, I saw the glint of uniform brass buttons through the opening of the cape he wore.

'Not concerning any Mrs Proby, Doctor,' said he in the long coat. 'I am Sergeant Buller of the Cornish Constabulary. I call upon your assistance over a certain matter. Begging the pardon of you ladies and gentlemen for our intrusion.' He bowed slightly. He was a stern-faced man of about forty, with heavy side-whiskers.

'Matter?' It was Martin Revesby who spoke, rising to his feet. 'What is this matter, Sergeant?'

A pause before the reply, and then: 'There's been a death, sir. Calling upon the doctor, to request that he certify same, I was informed that Dr Prescott and lady were dining here.'

'Who has died?' asked the physician.

'A female person, Doctor. Not known to me – ' he indicated the uniformed officer behind him – 'nor to Constable Pannett of this village.'

'A stranger, then?' demanded Martin.

'That is so, sir.'

'And how and where did she die?'

'As to how, sir – that's for the doctor to determine, but 'tis my belief that she was manually strangled. As to where this was done, I cannot guess. But the unfortunate creature was found in the churchyard. Lying between two graves. The graves of two female persons who, as I am informed, suffered a like fate some twenty years ago.'

'No! Merciful heaven – no-o-o!' The anguished cry of the Reverend Mr Murcher.

To my own shocked mind came, all unbidden, some words that I had read only that morning.

Kill me, but you will not destroy me. Listen for me in the dark hours of the night and you will hear me.

And again . . .

For many, it will be the last thing they ever hear!

It began to rain about midnight: it was still raining – a steady, drenching downpour of the kind seldom experienced outside the West Country – when I rose and opened my shutters at seven-thirty next morning. The black rocks below glistened with wetness, and the flowerheads in the formal garden bowed under the steady stream. There was no one in sight. The sea, the clifftop, the garden – all empty of life.

Considering everything, I had slept soundly. So well, indeed, had I recovered from the events of the previous evening, that I was able to smile at the sight of the armchair which stood in place against my bedroom door, augmenting with its bulk and weight the benefits of lock and bolt. I had gone to bed in some terror. Taking all in all, I considered that that terror had been to some degree justified.

My thoughts returning to the arrival of the police, and the sergeant's shocking disclosure, I attempted to marry them with all that had gone before, but quickly became bogged down in doubt and confusion. I resolved, therefore, to sort out all these events – and my impressions and conclusions – on paper. And what better than to address my findings in the form of a letter to Uncle Gervase? Accordingly I sat down, still in my nightdress and peignoir, at a table by the window. There, with the sound of the rain sluicing down from the gutterings above, I wrote a complete account, with all my speculations tacked on the end – and felt better for it. I addressed and sealed the letter. Next, I turned to the folder containing Martin Revesby's previous day's work. I had not read more than half a dozen lines, before I realized that the poet's thoughts had taken a very different turn.

The first stanza, on the first sheet, continued the account of the two lovers' passion; and hinted, once more, at the terrible fate that lay in store for Tristan and his Iseult. The stanza – finished all but one line – had then been roughly scored through with a single slash of the pen.

What came after – three crowded pages of it – was as different from the doom-ladened saga of Tristan and Iseult as the crash of a mighty organ differs from the music of a flute, or as the light breeze of a summer's afternoon contrasts with a hurricane. Tristan and Iseult, in the hands of Martin Revesby, had been emotion of almost unbearable intensity. What followed was tender romance – as light and ephemeral as the thoughts between dreaming and waking.

It was a love poem, of the same seven-line structure as the other, and clearly intended to form part of the cycle of *The Saga of Love and Death.* It told of a lover's passion for a distant and unattainable she: a passion that was pure, tender, uncomplicated, and – seemingly – unrequited. If she – the unnamed she – was aware of her admirer's presence, she did not acknowledge it:

Her eyes for ever turned away, unknowing ...

Strangely, the lover's anguish was tempered with something else – a quiet ecstasy. Almost as if his love, new-found and unrequited, had come as a consolation for some profound unhappiness from which he had previously suffered:

The dead days fallen away, forgotten
In this newly-quickened love ...

And having said that, he referred no more to what was past; but rejoiced in what might yet be. I read through the poem with a growing sense of elation, and felt lost and left high and dry when I came to the end – the unresolved end, for the verses finished abruptly at the foot of the third page, and there was clearly more to come. With a contented sigh, I put the sheets back into the folder, to be dealt with later in the morning.

The long-case clock in the corner of the great hall chimed nine when I got downstairs. My place was laid at the table, and Challis crouched by the fireplace, placing dry pieces of kindling among the smouldering oak logs. He straightened up when he heard my approach.

'Good morning, ma'am.' He was still wearing the same neckcloth of the night before. It was soiled, and his chin bore a night's stubble.

'Good morning, Challis. Is Mr Revesby about?'

'Was up early, ma'am,' was the reply. 'Took a cup of coffee with him to the library and is now hard at work, I shouldn't wonder. Would you be wanting anything to eat, ma'am? There's devilled kidneys, kippers, black pudding . . .'

'A cup of coffee only, Challis, thank you.'

'Cup of coffee, ma'am,' he said resignedly.

There came a heavy tread from the direction of the kitchen quarters. Turning I saw a bowed figure shambling into the hall, stooped under the weight of a massive oak log some five feet in length or more, borne on a broad shoulder. One great arm, pelted with thick hair, was wrapped around the log, and a pair of small and incredibly bright eyes were peering at me over the rounded side of it.

'Get you out of here, Jabez!' cried Challis. 'You know better than to come into here at this late hour of the morning. Lay that log on the front of the hearth and begone!' He closed with the deaf-mute and shoved him roughly towards the fireplace, dragging at the log and hastening its descent. Having rid the other of his burden, he proceeded to bustle him back the way he had come. The man Jabez went in a docile enough manner, making no attempt to shield himself from the pushes and the slaps that the older man directed at him; but shuffling along, barefoot on the flagstones, and with great hands hanging limply by his flanks. All the time – alarmingly – those small, hooded eyes never left me, as I sat at table, looking on in mounting unease.

Having disposed of the intruder and shut the door into the kitchen quarters, Challis came back, full of apologies.

'Should never have happened, ma'am,' he said. 'Jabez knows well enough he's not allowed in this part of the house, but he's a cunning one is Jabez. And full of curiosity.'

'Indeed?' I said. If that terrifying creature's curiosity was extended towards me, I felt it a matter for some unease.

'He's quite harmless,' said Challis.

'Has he worked here long?' I asked.

'Since he was a lad,' was the reply. 'And that was a piece back.'

Sipping my coffee, I mused that – allowing for the difficulty of assessing the age of a creature who bore only a passing resemblance to a human being – Jabez looked to be in his late thirties, which could have made him what Challis described as a 'lad' in the fateful year of 1835. If so, a whole new field of disturbing speculations was opened up before me.

I decided I must unseal the letter to Uncle Gervase and add a brief postscript.

I finished making my three copies of the new poem by mid-morning, and, there being no other matters requiring my attention, I decided to take a short walk. The drenching rain had stopped, leaving an oppressive dankness in the air – even indoors, so that the stone walls of the staircase and passages leading to my room were moist to the touch. Outside, at least, there was a drying breeze that stirred the high treetops and ruffled the wavelets beyond the headland. I changed into my green wool, waterproofed bonnet, took up my umbrella, and went out.

Beyond the gates, I turned and looked back at Malmaynes, wondering anew at its bulk and starkness, its indefinable air of mystery. In doing so, I chanced to notice a slight movement in one of the upper windows: a second-floor window in that part of the building where I judged my employer's quarters to be. What I saw was a face, or so I believed; a face that was instantly removed when I looked in its direction, as if the watcher had not wished to be seen. Was it, I wondered, Mrs Challis, or her husband? Perhaps Martin Revesby himself – though that was unlikely. Or Jabez? I shuddered at the latter thought, and went on my way.

Deciding against the options of another walk down to the village or a long traipse inland, I set off down the road leading to the sea. After some fifty paces, it bent sharply and began a steep descent. All above, the horizon of sea and sky intermingled, grey against grey; below, a tangle of hawthorn thicket through which I should have to pass in order to gain the beach.

I delight in walking, maintaining that it provides both a healthsome exercise for the body and a useful stimulus for the mind. I am a confirmed daydreamer while walking; and had not gone far, on that occasion, before I was mulling over the events of the previous night – commencing with the arrival of the police . . .

The shock of the revelation about the discovery of the dead woman in the graveyard had reduced the Rector to such a state of collapse that Dr Prescott was obliged to delay his departure and revive him with charred paper held under the nostrils. Finally, when the physician left with the police, Martin Revesby accompanied them. It remained my task to say good night to the departing guests: to Lady Amanda and her fiancé; and to the Murchers, who took Mrs Prescott home in their dog-cart.

My strongest recollection of that particular incident was the moment of parting from Nicholas Pendennis. It may have been the shocking news that had sobered him and quietened his jealous anger; in any event, he took my hand very gently and gave me an earnest look.

'My sincere thanks, ma'am, for a splendid evening. And my apologies.'

I cast a swift, sidelong glance: his fiancée was being assisted into an ermine cape by Mrs Challis, and was out of earshot.

'There is no call for apology, Mr Pendennis,' I told him.

'I think there is, ma'am,' he replied. Lady Amanda having then called to him, I was left with something of an enigma.

What had he meant by his apology?

Quite clearly, in his more sober state, he had regretted his impulsive invitation for me to go riding out with him. This was a relief – or so I told myself. I had no wish to incur the resentment of his aristocratic intended – and there was no doubt in my mind that I should, for Lady Amanda flirting with her attractive host was one thing, but that her fiancé should hob-nob with her host's private secretary was another thing entirely.

So much for that: though I did not receive sufficient invitations from personable gentlemen to dismiss the matter entirely without regret.

Continuing with the events of the previous night, I remembered sitting alone at the long table, watching the

Challises clear away. Not a word passed between them, nor did they address any remark to me; but went silently about their tasks, with heads bowed and eyes averted. When finished, they both stole out of the great hall together, called a cheerless good night to me from the doorway, and closed the heavy oak upon themselves.

A long time had passed before I summoned up the courage to take up a four-branched candlestick from the table and make my way – slowly, with great stealth, and probing every dark corner with my anxious eyes – to my room, where I barred and bolted the door, adding the weight of my armchair for good measure. Then I went to bed, but never attempted sleep till, in a silence broken only by the hissing of the rain, my ears caught the sound of a carriage coming up the drive and halting outside the main door. Martin Revesby was back home. Then, and only then, did I close my eyes and drift away . . .

I came to the foot of the hill, and the sea was now entirely hidden from me by the tangled thicket of hawthorn, through which the roadway became a narrow path leading, I supposed, to the beach.

Three paces into the thicket, I had such a sudden and startling presentiment of peril that I quickened my pace, the sooner to be out of the hawthorn that arched overhead and closed me in, and reach the open beach. I went some way further before I realized that I was somewhere in the middle of a sizeable maze, with side-paths branching off in all directions. And then the main path – or what I had taken to be the main path – came to an abrupt end at an impenetrable tangle of undergrowth.

At that moment, someone coughed. Quite close at hand. Or it may have been – a brief, staccato *laugh*!

I turned and ran, back the way I had come. Taking the first turning that presented itself. Then the next. I ran till the breath sobbed in my throat and my sides ached; doubling down one path after another, with the certainty in my mind that I was a creature pursued, and that my hunter was close behind – perhaps within touching distance, so that I had only to turn my head and I should see him plain. I ran, cursing myself for being so unthinking as to go out alone and put myself in such a vulnerable circumstance, with a murderer at large in the vicinity. I kept running, even when the crook of my umbrella caught in a gnarled limb of hawthorn and I was deprived of the nearest thing to a weapon of defence that I possessed. I was still running, when the pathway took a final flourish, and I saw, at the end of a long tunnel of thicket, the bland grey sweep of the sea and the distant horizon.

Moments later I broke out into the open air, stumbled among the rocks on the beach and sat down – uncaring, from sheer exhaustion of body and nerves, whether I lived or died.

When I opened my eyes again, it was to see a pair of large boots standing close by me. Lifting my gaze, slowly and with mounting apprehension, I took in a great length of tweed overcoat, broad shoulders, a high stock, heavy side-whiskers.

'Good day to you, ma'am,' said Sergeant Buller of the Cornish Constabulary.

He must have observed my state, and made a shrewd guess as to the reason for it; but offered no comment about either. Instead, he courteously asked my permission to sit with me for a while, and took his place on a rock nearby. Nor did he speak again till he had taken up a flat stone and had tossed it seawards, and watched it skim over the wavelets and finally sink.

Then he said: 'You will have heard the latest news from Mr Revesby, ma'am?'

'I haven't seen Mr Revesby this morning,' I replied. 'I seldom see him before noon, and often not till evening.'

The police officer took off his tall hat and carefully laid it on the ground beside him, brim uppermost. 'Concerning the matter of last evening,' he said, 'the matter of the deceased female person.'

'Yes?'

'Dr Prescott was able to confirm the fact of her decease,'

he said. 'And my own opinion as regards the cause of same.'

'You mean, she was . . .'

'Manual strangulation, ma'am. This the doctor confirmed in my presence and that of Constable Pannett and Mr Revesby. Afterwards I spoke to Mr Revesby – touching on several matters.'

'Oh, yes,' I replied uneasily, conscious that, though he was not looking in my direction, but was turning a pebble over and over in his hand and gazing down at it, I was the object of his total attention.

'And we spoke of several persons,' he said. 'Including yourself, ma'am.'

'Mr Revesby spoke to you about me?' I asked, surprised.

'And of your interest in certain matters, ma'am.'

'Indeed?' I thought I knew what was coming.

'Matters, ma'am, that touch upon the subject of a long-forgotten murder case. You know the one to which I refer.'

'Saul Pendark,' I murmured.

'That is the name, ma'am. He whom the locals refer to as the Beast of Malmaynes – though not often, and then mostly behind closed doors and in the company of friends. From what I gathered in conversing with Mr Revesby, it seems you know quite a lot about the case – for someone who's only been in the district a matter of days, that is.'

I explained about Uncle Gervase, conscious all the time that I was being put on the defensive, and made to feel guilty for no very good reason – feelings that I resented. He listened with no discernible interest, and then nodded.

'Quite so, ma'am,' he said. 'Mr Revesby stated as much. Said you had excellent sources of information. Got a high opinion of you, ma'am, has Mr Revesby. "She's a wise head on those shoulders of hers, has my Miss Carew" – those were his very words to me.'

'Were they, indeed?' I said, smiling, despite myself.

'I may tell you, ma'am. And in the strictest confidence – ' here he looked about him, up and down the deserted beach and the tumbled rocks, back towards the silent hawthorn thicket – 'I may tell you that I have a need for as many wise heads as I can summon to my assistance on this present case.'

Puzzled, I said: 'Thank you for the compliment, Sergeant, but I can't see what possible assistance . . .'

He appeared almost not to have heard me, but continued, 'You may think, ma'am, that 'tis easy to get at the truth in such a small community as this. Not so. No one's for telling anything, least of all to me, a foreigner from Truro. And not to Constable Pannett, either: for all that he's lived among 'em for seven years, he's a foreigner also, though a Cornishman. Now I don't doubt for one minute but that you've formed certain opinions already, following upon the events of last night. And I don't doubt for one minute that *you'd* confide those opinions to me, if asked. Isn't that true, ma'am?'

I looked down at my hands. 'Well – yes, I suppose so,' I said tentatively. 'But . . .'

'Ah!' cried Sergeant Buller, with the air of a man revealing a profound truth, 'isn't that just what I was saying, ma'am? You will confide your opinions to me readily enough – but do you think any of the locals will do likewise? Not so.'

'It must make your task very difficult,' I said lamely.

He said: 'What are these opinions you've formed, Miss Carew?'

Though prepared for the question, I was shocked by the brusqueness of its delivery, and gave a start of alarm that he surely could not have missed. Again, I had the feeling of being put on the defensive; and again I resented it.

'Any speculations I may have formed are entirely without interest,' I said sharply. 'Because I have no knowledge of the present case upon which you are engaged.'

He picked up another pebble and tossed it into the shallows. 'As to knowledge,' he said, 'as to evidence, I can tell you that the murdered female was aged approximately thirty years, of good – I may say, handsome – appearance. Well and expensively dressed in the foreign manner. And I do not use the word in the narrow, local sense. The lady obtained her garments in Paris, as evidenced by the labels thereon. She was entirely unknown in these parts – this from the evidence of both the constable and the doctor. Some time yesterday – the doctor puts it at around the middle of the afternoon – some person took her life by strangulation and placed the body in the space between the graves of Ruth Rannis and Emily Jane Witham, both deceased.' He looked at me fixedly. 'Now, ma'am, what of your opinions?'

I said: 'I've nothing to go on, Sergeant. Nothing but a certain sense of unease, you understand . . .'

He nodded. 'Understood, ma'am. Please continue.'

I took a deep breath. 'But I have the feeling – I have had the feeling, and it struck me very forcibly last night, when you announced the news of the tragedy in the great hall – that the one they called the Beast of Malmaynes may not have died, after all. May still be – among us.'

'Ah!' He gave an exhalation, like one who has been waiting with bated breath. 'Now that is very interesting, ma'am. Very interesting indeed. Yet, as you say, that opinion is based only on – I think you said – a sense of unease. Nothing else? Nothing more tangible?'

Tangible? Strange sounds in the night. A strong sense of the dramatic (I had once wanted to be a playwright). I decided to say nothing about the sounds in the night . . .

'Nothing else,' I said. 'Just my intuition.'

'Just intuition,' he repeated. 'Well now, Miss Carew, I am grateful to you for confiding this to me. And I may say that I shall be grateful if, at any time in the future, you confide in me further – whether on matters of intuition, or on matters of hard fact.'

I got to my feet. 'Of course, I shall be only too happy to assist the law in any way I can, Sergeant. But I think it unlikely that hard facts will come my way, and you will speedily grow impatient with my intuition.'

He got up. 'We shall see, ma'am,' he said. 'We shall see.' Putting on his tall hat, he motioned me to precede him towards the path in the hawthorn thicket. 'I hope I may burden you with my company as far as the turn-off for the village.'

'It will be my pleasure, Sergeant,' I replied.

Along the path, we came upon my umbrella lying where it had fallen. Sergeant Buller picked it up, and looked surprised when I claimed it as mine.

'I dropped it in my headlong flight,' I explained, adding with a smile: 'I was so terrified when I heard you cough, or laugh, close at hand in the thicket, that I ran in panic. I thought – and you see what reliance can be placed upon my intuition – I thought that the Beast of Malmaynes was at hand.'

I felt the smile wither and die on my lips at the sight of his expression.

He said: 'Ma'am, I was never in the thicket. I was at the far end of the beach when you came out, and saw you from a distance.'

Chapter Four

After the incident of the hawthorn thicket, I resolved never to walk abroad alone again; but to confine myself to the greensward within sight of Malmaynes. Yet on the afternoon of that same day, I went on another excursion – and in entirely unexpected circumstances.

Martin Revesby appeared for luncheon. He seemed restless and ill at ease, and confided to me that the work had not gone well that morning – a confidence which prompted me to praise his new poem. He pulled a wry face at this, saying that the celebrated ancient Roman poet Horace who coined the tag 'He who has begun has half done' should have been made to eat his words. It was one thing, declared my employer, to take a stride into the dark with a new venture; quite another to lose one's way and fall on one's face. The lyrical love poem, it seemed, had lost its lightness and had become like an overcooked *soufflé* (his own words).

I responded by assuring him that things would be better on the morrow. The events of the previous night, I told him, were bearing heavily upon his mind. That, and the lateness of his return.

At that, he became sombre. Yes, it had been a grim ordeal, he told me. He had been present at Dr Prescott's examination of the murdered woman; and, though delicacy of feeling prevented him from elaborating to me, it had clearly affected a man of his refined sensibilities. I immediately changed the subject by reverting to his poetry, reminding him of the verses from my favourite *Reflections and Recollections* where he had earlier essayed – and with considerable success – the difficult and demanding genre of the lyrical love poem. My enthusiasm seemed to lighten his mood: he immediately plunged into a detailed explanation of his intentions regarding his current work. I am afraid that he once again quickly lost me in the complexities of his argument; but I was content to watch him, to delight in the unique privilege of being the intimate confidante of one of the greatest of our living poets – though painfully conscious of my own inadequacy totally to comprehend all that lay behind the processes of his artistic creation. I listened to Martin Revesby, breathlessly hanging upon his every obscure word and phrase, till the Challises had cleared the table about us and departed; till the mid-afternoon sun sent long shadows over the ancient flagstones of the great hall. Till the front-door bell rang.

'Who can that be?' asked the poet.

Challis went to answer it, and announced: 'Lady Amanda Pitt-Jermyn and Mr Pendennis, sir.'

Lady Amanda entered in a bonnet laden down with velvet pansies and many ribbons; in a crinoline so wide that she could scarcely get through the door. And Nicholas Pendennis walked at her heels – or as close to her heels as the scope of the crinoline allowed. He appeared to be in a better humour than on the previous evening; with the air of a man who had resigned himself to the inevitable. He smiled and nodded at me.

'Mr Revesby,' cried her ladyship. 'I am availing myself of your kind invitation to view the Malmaynes picture collection; but first I must ask you if you have any recent news on the dreadful murder of that poor creature down in the village. I declare that I never slept a wink last night, but sat up till dawn, with my maid reading aloud to me, to keep my mind from dwelling upon the awfulness of it all.' Lady Amanda, whose clear skin and bright eyes were mute evidence of a night of sound sleep, gave her hand for my employer to kiss as he rose and approached her.

'No fresh news, ma'am,' he said. 'The victim was a stranger to the district, and the constabulary have no idea as to the identity of her murderer.'

'Then he is still unknown – and still in our midst!' cried Lady Amanda in tones of alarm.

'Or already fled far from here,' replied the poet.

'Oh, I earnestly pray that you are right!' exclaimed Lady Amanda, with overtones of disappointment. 'I have no wish for more poor women to be done away with.' As she said this, her violet eyes lighted upon me, wistfully.

'So, then,' said Martin Revesby briskly. 'Let us to the picture collection. First, to the long gallery, which contains the best of the French eighteenth-century examples.'

Nicholas Pendennis coughed and shuffled his feet.

'I am afraid that my fiancé has no appreciation of pictures, Mr Revesby,' said her ladyship. 'They would be quite wasted on him. Nicholas, my dear, why do you not take Miss Carew, here, for a drive in the phaeton? I am sure she will find it agreeable.'

'Oh no, it's quite all right . . .' I began.

'By jove, yes!' cried Nicholas Pendennis, suddenly animated. 'What a capital idea! Fetch your bonnet and a warm shawl, Miss Carew, and we'll be off. Take as much time as you like over the pictures, m'dear. See you in an hour or so.' He pecked her porcelain cheek as it was presented to him. 'Your servant, Revesby.'

Five minutes later I was seated beside him in an extremely smart town phaeton drawn by two matched blacks with rolling eyes and a very great deal of foam about their bits. The way my driver plied his long whip, his tongue-clicking, the sharp cries of 'Giddap there, Castor: on with you, Pollux!' led me to suppose that I had put myself in the hands of one of those furious drivers about whom so much is angrily written in the readers' correspondence pages of *The Times* – nor was I mistaken.

Nicholas Pendennis drove his horses at a full gallop down the drive and through the gates. Without drawing rein, he took the phaeton round the corner and into the road leading to Truro. I declare that, but for the carriage's large wheels, we should have been over. I cast a glance upwards to his profile, which was set in a savage grin, the eyes narrowed and glittering. Noticing my attention, he cocked an eyebrow in my direction.

'Enjoying it, ma'am?' he demanded. 'Mighty exhilarating, what?'

'You are not taking a lady out for a drive in the country,' I told him calmly. 'What you are doing, in your own mind, is charging the Russian guns at Balaclava. And I expect you espy Mr Revesby up in front, among the enemy gunners.'

He laughed, and drew rein, to check the horses' headlong gallop into a smart trot.

''Pon my word, you are right, Miss Carew,' he admitted good-naturedly. 'I am given to releasing my feelings at the reins of a fast carriage, or astride a good thoroughbred. And, yes, I am mighty vexed with that fellow Revesby. Paintings indeed! Syrupy art bosh. I wonder that Amanda falls for the stuff.'

'She scarcely had it pressed upon her by Mr Revesby,' I replied tartly. 'As you must remember very well, at the dinner-party, it was Lady Amanda who introduced the subject *and* invited herself to come and see the pictures.'

He gave a boyish, sulky scowl. 'That's right enough,' he admitted. 'She's all over the fellow. Can't make it out; for, I promise you, Amanda was never one for things artistic. Used to care for nothing but horseflesh – till she set eyes on Revesby.'

'Perhaps,' I suggested, 'she really is beginning to take after her late father, who was such a devoted patron of the arts.'

He gave a contemptuous laugh. 'That's a good one! Patron of the arts – ha! The old earl – "old Nosey" they used to call him – had a very fine painted ceiling at Hundlesham, all nymphs and cherubs, that bears to this day the holes made by pistol balls when he and his cronies did a spot of target practice after a particularly vivid dinner. Patron of the arts – that's a good one! Amanda deserved to have a hairbrush taken to her for gulling Revesby so.'

'Hmm! I see,' was my comment.

'Do you now?' he asked, giving me a serious glance. 'Do you indeed see, Miss Carew? Then I should be greatly obliged if you would enlighten me on a couple of points about Revesby and my fiancée.'

I began not to like the turn of the conversation, and answered non-committally. For all his brash manner, Nicholas Pendennis was sensitive enough to discern that his question had strayed slightly over the bounds of the sort of propriety that should exist between a lady and gentleman who have but a slight acquaintance. In short, we simply did not know each other well enough for me to become the recipient of his confidences, nor to offer him enlightenment about his fiancée's motives for flirting with the master of Malmaynes – supposing, as seemed likely, that that was his intent.

We were away from the coast, in rolling countryside with drystone walls, stark little copses set on lonely hilltops, green pastures speckled with white dots of sheep. There was a rich, warm smell of a million herbs. The sun was out.

Presently, through a gap in a screen of poplars, I saw a white-fronted mansion set in a parkland. There was a noble line of columns along its façade, and a peacock was stalking slowly down the wide, balustraded steps from the front door, its tail spread, the hundred eyes staring.

'What a beautiful place!' I cried. 'Who lives there?'

'I do,' replied my driver unconcernedly. 'Tell you what – we'll go and have a spot of tea.'

'So you don't think Amanda has any serious intent towards Revesby?' demanded Nicholas Pendennis.

Over tea, in the civilized quiet of the spacious drawing-room, with its elegance, its air of wealth lightly borne, he and I had widened our acquaintance to that of the beginnings of a friendship. I had begun to like Nicholas Pendennis, furthermore. In small – yet important – things he showed the calibre of his mind: he was scrupulously civil to the serving-girl who brought our tea-tray, rising to his feet to assist her, and thanking her gravely; in his boyish fashion (which I found particularly engaging), it was obvious from his covert glances that he had set his fancy upon a certain cream pastry among the selection on the cake dish, but he pressed it upon me and himself took another and less exotic choice while I was still protesting. Over the second cup of China tea, I had consented to discuss Lady Amanda and her doings.

'I think she finds him attractive,' I said, after careful reflection. 'She could scarcely be blamed, for he is certainly that. But, if I may say so, Mr Pendennis . . .'

'Nick,' he prompted me. 'I would very much like you to call me Nick – which is what my family used to call me. I don't have any close family left,' he added gravely.

'Very well, Nick,' I assented. 'And, in return, I should like you to call me Charity – or Cherry, if you prefer it. Cherry is my family name.'

'Cherry it shall be,' he said. 'But please continue.'

'What I suggest is that Lady Amanda, who, as you say, was formerly only interested in horses but has now developed a sudden passion for the arts, has almost certainly done so on account of Mr Revesby. If I may say so without giving offence, Nick, it is the attraction of opposites. He is so totally unlike you.'

He pulled a rueful face. 'You mean – I'm just another rough-riding country squire, of the kind she's had around her all her life? That's true enough, Cherry. And her brother's cast in the same mould, and all the rest of his friends. We're all alike. You're quite right: it isn't to be wondered at that she's set her cap at Revesby, who's cultured, artistic, and – so they tell me – a genius of a poet. Is that correct?'

'Yes,' I told him. 'I don't set myself up to be a literary critic, but there are many of those who consider that he may well turn out to be among the great ones of this century. And, speaking personally, I couldn't but agree.'

He got to his feet and strode over to the window, crumbling a piece of cake and throwing it out on to the terrace, where the peacock was preening himself. The sound of many bees came very clearly on the still air.

'Then good luck to the fellow,' declared Nick. 'I don't bear him any grudge. 'Tisn't as if the fellow led her on. As you say, Amanda made all the running.'

'He could have offered her less encouragement,' I said in

a tone of voice which surprised me by its firmness. 'After all, she is an engaged person. All that talk about her looking for a Town house for him – "Thank you, my lady; you are very kind, my lady" – he had the opportunity, then, to tell her quite firmly that he was making his own arrangements.'

Nick looked glum. 'Mmm – so do you think that this infatuation is going to last? We were to be married in the spring.' He threw the last of crumbs and plunged his hands into the pockets of his hunting coat.

'No, I do not,' I replied confidently. 'I think it's no more than a passing caprice. There is not the slightest common ground between them. She has a fancy – or thinks she has a fancy – to launch Mr Revesby into Society and bathe in his reflected glory. He is flattered to be admired by a beautiful aristocrat. Tomorrow morning, Martin Revesby will be back at work, with not a thought in his head about Lady Amanda. And before very long, she will be back with her horses.'

'I hope so,' he said glumly.

'You must love her very much, Nick.'

He looked surprised. 'We've been more or less promised to each other since childhood,' he said. 'We're second cousins, and, because my mother and father were in India, I spent a great deal of time at Hundlesham during school holidays.'

'I see.' I thought I saw, very clearly.

The elegant French clock on the marble chimneypiece thinly tinkled the hour. 'Best get back to Amanda,' said Nick, without any enthusiasm. 'I must say, I've enjoyed chatting to you, Cherry.'

He gazed at me very earnestly – and a fraction too long. I looked away.

'And it's been a lovely tea,' I said briskly, rising.

We went back to Malmaynes at quite a slow trot, hardly exchanging a word, till we saw a young couple coming down the lane, on foot, towards us. As they drew in to the drystone wall to allow for our passing, the young man raised his cap to us, and the girl bobbed a curtsy. It was Alice Witham.

When we had gone well past, Nick said: 'I see young Edgar Portwell's walking out steady. He's one of my under-grooms.

A nice lad. I expect we shall have wedding bells there.'

I told him that I knew Alice and that she worked for us at Malmaynes – adding the gobbet of macabre information about her relationship to the unfortunate Emily Jane. It was news to Nick. We talked of the murders – old and new – till we reached the front door of Malmaynes, and it seemed to me that, with the turn in the conversation, the sun clouded over and the best of the afternoon was gone.

Lady Amanda and Martin Revesby must have seen, or been informed of, our approach: they were at the foot of the steps when Nick drew rein and handed me down.

'How was the picture-show?' he asked.

'A revelation!' cried Lady Amanda. 'Martin, you must let me come again, to learn to know them better, gradually, with great humility.'

'Of course, Amanda,' murmured Martin Revesby.

'Cherry and I went back to the Manor for a spot of tea,' said Nick.

'Indeed?' Her eyebrows went up at the sound of my pet name. The cold violet glance flickered over me from head to foot, reappraising me – and clearly arriving at the same conclusion as previously. I did not think it likely that I should be invited – soon or late – to enjoy the familiarity of dispensing with her title when addressing her.

By then, I had taken the running of Malmaynes firmly under my control (save in the matter of the formal garden: I could not bring myself to have any contact with Jabez, who continued to fill me with a strange dread). At about six-thirty it had become my habit to go along to the kitchen and inspect the progress of dinner, also to talk over the following day's menus with Mrs Challis, and to make suggestions about the régime of cleaning which I had instigated in the great house, where cobwebs hung in swags from many ceilings and the woodwork had never been waxed for centuries. Mrs Challis was taking the new régime with more grace than she had at first shown. Only in one particular did she continue to display stubbornness: after the two new daily kitchen maids and

Alice Witham, there had been no more help brought in. I was determined to bring the staff up to the number I had indicated to the housekeeper; and had decided to give her another week in which to carry out my wishes – after which I would take matters into my own hands and bring servants from Truro, if necessary.

This thought was passing through my mind as I walked down the passage towards the kitchen. When I reached the head of the steps leading to the basement, I heard the sound of voices raised in anger. They came from the kitchen. One was Mrs Challis's voice. And someone crying.

'Idle good-for-nothing!' cried the housekeeper. 'Sliding off when you think no one's looking. Shameless baggage!'

'I didn't mean no harm. There wasn't anything to be done in the kitchen, and I'd finished all me cleaning.' I recognized the voice of young Alice Witham, and quickened my pace.

'Sliding off to meet your fancy-boy! No-good hussy, like the rest of your family!'

'You've no call to speak thus to the lass!' Another voice.

As I entered the kitchen, the new kitchen maid Janey Pinner – she who had helped at table during the dinner-party – was rounding on Mrs Challis in defence of Alice, who stood in tears before the housekeeper. This brought Mrs Challis's fury down upon her head.

'Keep your tongue in your head, or you'll be out of here – and no wages!' cried the housekeeper. It was at this moment that she saw me. Not so Janey Pinner, whose back was turned to the door.

And Janey Pinner said: 'I'll speak my mind, no matter what, Edith Challis. You've no cause to say such things to the young lass, nor speak so slightingly of her family – *seeing as how it was your own son who murdered her father's sister all them years ago!*'

My own sharp intake of breath sounded startlingly loud in the silence that followed. Janey Pinner heard it and turned. Her hand went to her mouth, and her eyes grew round with alarm. Mrs Challis continued to stare at me, and I thought that she aged twenty years in an instant. Alice began to sob quietly.

I found my voice. 'Dry your eyes and find something to do in the scullery, Alice,' I said. 'And you, Janey, go with her.'

'Yes'm.' Janey Pinner curtsied, and, taking the younger girl by the arm, she bundled her hastily out of the door, closing it behind them. I was alone with the housekeeper.

Slowly, by easy stages – looking first at the floor, then at her feet, then her hands – I brought my gaze, again, to that tragic face. The pale, deep-set eyes met mine challengingly, almost with defiance. There was a certain dignity about the woman, even in her moment of torment.

'Is it true?' I asked her.

'It's true, right enough.'

'You are – were – Mrs Edith Pendark?'

A bitter smile twisted her thin lips. 'I wasn't a Mrs by reason of a parson saying words over me – not till I wed Challis.'

I took a pace towards her, anxious to bridge the gulf of age, of class, of hideous experience, that yawned between us.

'I'm very sorry, Mrs Challis,' I said. 'It must be awful for you. Please sit down.'

She obeyed meekly enough: sat down on a straight-backed chair at the kitchen table. She continued to stare at me, watchful, dry-eyed.

'They tormented him,' she said. 'He was a good lad to me, none better. Those women – shameless hussies – they tormented the life out of him, forever whispering about him, calling things after him. I know their sort.'

I took my place opposite her, in another chair.

'But he – your son – wasn't well, was he, Mrs Challis?' I asked gently. 'You had to send for the Rector, didn't you?'

She was no longer looking at me, but was staring into the distance, a far-off expression in her eyes – as if she was attempting to see down the years and find fresh answers, new explanations.

'He was like two people, my Saul,' she said. 'One time he'd be as right as a trivet; next, there'd be these black moods for no reason. Then he'd maybe break something. Hurt some animal. Once, he struck me. The night I sent for Mr Murcher, he lay upon his bed and screamed that demons were tearing at his insides. Mr Murcher said words over him – but it didn't do any good. Nothing did any good – not for any while.'

A long silence, broken only by her heavy breathing. I nerved myself to put the question that was screaming in my mind to get out . . .

'Mrs Challis,' I said, 'will you tell me, please – is your son, is Saul, really dead?'

The pale eyes came round to meet mine, suddenly surprised.

'Why, yes,' she said. 'Why do you ask?'

'I – I just thought . . .' the words died in me.

'Oh yes, he's gone, has my Saul,' she said. 'Him who I loved so dear, and him as loved me when the black moods weren't upon him; him as treated his mother with pride and proper respect when the demons weren't in him – that Saul, he perished down there among the rocks. Don't you think any other for one instant, miss.'

Two days went past. Uneventful days, save that Martin Revesby – as I had promised him – quickly regained his muse. The lyrical love poem blossomed anew, with the stanzas gliding from his pen in glorious profusion. Mindful of Lady Amanda, I searched each and every line for clues about the unnamed she for whom the lover rejoiced, since it seemed to me – considering the suddenness with which the poet had turned from the tragedy of Tristan and Iseult to the new theme – that it might have been inspired by a personal experience. I have to say that, even allowing for the pardonable exaggerations of a man in love, I saw nothing there that even remotely called to mind the ice-cold beauty of Lady Amanda. And one line clinched the matter:

Pansy-brown eyes. Modest, chaste . . .

– for, of course, her ladyship's eyes were violet. For some reason – presumably out of consideration for Nick Pendennis, I told myself – I was greatly relieved to read that line.

It must have been four days after the murder of the unknown woman – she was buried on the third day, and the tolling of her funeral bell reached me in my room at Malmaynes and laid a heavy burden of depression on my mind – that I received a swift reply to the letter that I had written to Uncle Gervase the morning after the tragedy. I had been awaiting it with some impatience, and had with considerable difficulty restrained myself from sending him the startling new piece of information about the housekeeper of Malmaynes till I had heard his reactions to my earlier news and views. It was a fine morning: I took the letter and read it in a sheltered part of the greensward before the mansion, sitting on a tussock of close-cropped grass by the drystone wall.

Rose Cottage,
Poltewan.
Sept. 27th, 1856

My dear Cherry,

What an astounding coincidence that yr arrival at Malmaynes should be heralded by yet another murder. And the connection with the Pendark killings seems, on the face of it, to be somewhat more than a coincidence.

I take your point about the monstrous creature, the gardener Jabez; though your view of the possibility that he might be the supposedly 'dead' Saul Pendark tends to sound a little high-flown. Extreme repulsiveness of appearance, my dear Cherry, does not – despite the abundant evidence to the contrary provided by the appearance of the English judiciary – always denote malevolence of character!

Your point about the late philanthropic Mr Henry Tremaine, on the other hand, strikes me as being extremely shrewd and sets my legal nose a-sniffing the air. It is indeed odd that Mr Tremaine could find the money to send his

Rector's lady to Baden-Baden (a dreary place if there ever was one!) yet so soon after his death, the parish church of St Gawes presents the dilapidated appearance you describe. Did Mr Tremaine's philanthropy dry up in the intervening years? And if so – why? I should like to be enlightened on this point.

I took tea with the handsome widow. There was another gentleman guest present: a Capt. Arbuthnot, Royal Navy (Retired). I have a fancy that Madame cannot make up her mind at which of the two of us to set her cap; and, though it is only of academic interest, I await her decision with an amused curiosity.

Pray send me any news, however slight.

Fondest wishes, as ever, my dear Cherry.

Yr aff.
Uncle G –

Returning to the house, I went to my room and penned a hasty reply to Uncle Gervase, bringing him up to date with the newest developments, including the astonishing revelation that Mrs Challis had mothered the Beast of Malmaynes. Sealing the letter, I took it down to be posted. The first person I encountered was Janey Pinner, who was sweeping the flagstones of the great hall. She gave a start at my appearance. We had not met face to face since the incident in the kitchen, and I had gained the impression that the woman had been deliberately avoiding me. I glanced towards the double doors leading to the kitchen quarters: they were closed. The two of us were alone. I decided to seize the opportunity of questioning her.

I laid my letter on the table. 'When you go home this evening, Janey,' I said casually, 'I should be obliged if you would post this in the village, please.'

'Yes'm.' She went on sweeping.

'Janey,' I said, 'it was kind of you to take Alice's part against Mrs Challis the other day. Well-meaning – but indiscreet!'

The sweeping brush paused in its movement. Without meeting my glance, the woman replied, 'As you say, ma'am.'

'Is it widely known in the village – about Mrs Challis?'

'Yes'm.'

'Is there great resentment towards her on that account?'

She shrugged. 'Not specially, ma'am.'

I said: 'Not even on the part of Alice's family?'

She gave a short laugh. 'Catch Ned Witham caring about anything so long as he can find the price of a mug o' cider. And he's all Alice's got now.' Her face wrinkled with disgust. ''Tis to be hoped that Edgar Portwell will wed the poor lass and take her away from that drunken sot afore he does her harm.'

'You mean Edgar Portwell who's under-groom at the Manor?' I said. 'Yes, I've seen them together. Mr Pendennis thinks very highly of him. He'd make Alice a good husband, you think?'

She put aside her broom and looked at me at last. 'Ma'am, 'twould be the best thing out for the lass. And there's nothing that stands in their way but a place to live. And Mr Pendennis, he do have a cottage on the Manor farm that's empty by reason of Bert Petherick dying last month.' She stared appealingly at me.

'I will have a word with Mr Pendennis about that cottage next time we meet,' I said.

She clasped her hands together, her eyes sparkled. 'Oh, ma'am, if you only could!' she cried. 'For I tell you that Alice is the dearest child as ever drew breath, for all that she's been reared under the shadow of that Ned Witham.'

'I can't promise anything, Janey,' I told her. 'But I will certainly do my best with Mr Pendennis. I know that he is well-disposed towards the young couple.' Then I added something which had sprung, all unbidden, to my mind: 'Tell me – Ned Witham's sister, Emily, she who was murdered – was she a bad lot like her brother?'

Janey's mouth turned down at the corners. 'Not to speak ill of the dead, ma'am, but I were always led to believe that

Emily were no better than she ought to have been – if you get my meaning.'

'And the other murdered woman – Ruth Rannis – what of her?'

'The Rannises left the district afterwards,' she replied. 'I were only a little one at the time, you understand, ma'am. But I have heard tell that Ruth Rannis, she were the same sort as Emily Witham. No good.'

('*Those women – shameless hussies – they tormented the life out of him . . .*' I seemed to hear Mrs Challis's angry, anguished cry.)

I took a deep breath, and said: 'Janey, do *you* believe that Saul Pendark's dead and buried?'

Stark terror blazed in her eyes, and I had the thought that she was going to turn and run from me. A fit of ague seemed to take a grip of her body, her hands shook, her nether lip began to tremble. Seeing the grave effect my question had had upon the woman, I took her gently by the elbow and guided her to one of the chairs that stood at the table and eased her, unresisting, upon it.

Presently she found her voice. 'How – how can you even think of such a thing, ma'am? That he be still – *alive*!'

'Clearly, you don't think so,' I said. 'But what of the people down in the village generally? The older people – the people, say, who were grown adults twenty years ago when it happened – do *they* think that he's dead and gone for ever? And, if so, how do they account for the new murder, and the victim found between the graves of the other two?'

'Why, ma'am,' she said in an awed voice, 'they do all believe in the Legend of the Beast!'

'The Legend of the Beast!' I repeated, and I felt my skin prickle. 'Do you mean . . .?'

'Folk do say, ma'am, that Saul Pendark cried out, afore they sentenced him to be hanged, that he would come back in the dark hours of the night.'

' "*You will hear me*," ' I whispered, remembering. ' "*And for many, it will be the last thing they ever hear!*" '

She nodded vigorously. 'His very words, ma'am – just as they've been handed down.'

'And the people in the village believe that what – what Saul Pendark threatened has already happened?'

'Many times, ma'am!'

'*Many* times?'

'In all those years, ma'am, there's places in St Gawes and hereabouts where no one, man or woman, will venture after dark. Nor in daylight, if they be alone. And there's many who claim to have heard him – the Beast of Malmaynes. My old grandma, she said she'd heard him one night of a full moon – down in the hawthorn thicket above the beach.'

'The hawthorn thicket!' I cried. 'And what – *what* did she hear?'

Janey furrowed her brow in an effort of recollection. 'I do seem to recall,' she said, 'how Grandma spoke of what she heard. A laugh it was . . .'

'A laugh!'

'Low and menacing like, my gran did say. With an evil note to it. Such as you would expect, ma'am, from a crazed person. And, again, she did say 'twere like the cough of a wild beast.'

It was some time before I could bring myself to continue the interrogation. And then I asked, as calmly as I was able: 'But *you* don't believe all that, Janey – *you* don't accept the Legend of the Beast?'

She shook her head. 'Not me, ma'am. Why, it stands to sense there's no such thing as folk returning from the dead. But there's many as do believe. And in all those years, every unaccountable thing that's ever taken place has been laid at the door of the Beast. I mind that, when Lizzie Spender were set upon one night, folk said it were the Beast. There were many who came forward and said they'd heard his laugh in the churchyard that night. Others claimed to have seen him, all bathed in a green light. I can tell you, ma am, that there was red faces a-plenty in St Gawes when it turned out to be one of the village lads who had frightened Lizzie for a wager.'

'And the recent murder, Janey?' I asked. 'How do the villagers account for that? Do they attribute it to the Beast?'

She nodded vigorously. 'That they do, ma'am!'

'And what about you, Janey?'

She said: 'I reckon, ma'am, as how that foreign lady happened past and was done to death by a travelling tinker, maybe one who gave her a lift in his wagon and then killed her for her purse.'

'You take a very sensible and matter-of-fact view,' I told her. 'Yet I am puzzled – for, when I asked you if you thought Saul Pendark might still be alive, you were filled with alarm. Now, why was that, Janey?'

She looked me straight in the eye, her face free of any guile. 'Tales o' folk returning from the dead butter no parsnips with me, ma'am, for I know better. Nor do I believe there's anything but chance and superstition that's kept the legend alive all these years. But the thought that Saul Pendark never died . . . that he still walks this earth . . .'

'That terrifies you?'

'If I thought,' she said, 'if I thought that creature, that devil in human guise, were still among us, ma'am, I tell you that I would pack my traps and leave St Gawes this very day. Nor stop fleeing, till I had put four score and more miles behind me. And that's the truth of it, ma'am.'

A sudden flurry of rain rattled, like fingertips, against the big windows behind us. We both turned in alarm. The sky had blackened while we had been conversing, and the morning's fair promise had vanished in the sullen clouds.

Janey stood up, taking her broom in hand.

'I'd best be getting on,' she said. 'I'll post your letter on my way home, ma'am. And you'll not forget to mention that matter to Mr Pendennis, please.'

'The very next time we meet,' I promised. And I crossed the hall in the direction of the staircase. Half-way there, I remembered something that Uncle Gervase had requested.

Turning, I said: 'Janey, was not the late Mr Tremaine a great benefactor to the village? Didn't he give money to the poor, help the church, and such things?'

She sniffed sharply. 'That he did not, ma'am! Mr Tremaine, he never so much as handed out a few pence at Christmas, nor spared a few shillings to help bury a pauper. Help the church, indeed! Why, ma'am, you should see the state o' the place. There's not a dry pew after a shower of rain.'

'So he wasn't thought of very highly in the village?' I asked.

She shrugged. 'Mr Tremaine, he took no heed o' the village, and the village took no heed of him. The only folk I ever heard with a good word to say for Mr Tremaine (save for the Rector – and it's part of his calling, as you might say, to speak well of all) are the Challises.'

'They thought a lot of their late master?'

'Never stop speaking of his generosity, ma'am; and harking back to the good days when he was alive. Before – ' here she glanced cautiously towards the double doors leading to the kitchen quarters ' – before Mr Revesby took over.'

'You mean, they resent the coming of Mr Revesby?'

Another glance towards the doors, and she nodded.

I crossed over and picked up my letter. 'I'll bring this down later, Janey,' I told her. 'I've just remembered that I must add a postscript.'

Martin Revesby did not appear for luncheon – a fact that caused me an unexpectedly sharp pang of disappointment. He sent word by one of the maids that he would, nevertheless, like to see me. Accordingly, I took his meal tray of cold cuts into the library, together with his previous day's writings which I had transcribed that morning.

The poet was in his usual straight-backed chair at the table. He threw down his pen as I entered, and greeted me affably.

'Hello, Miss Carew. I have the greatest pleasure in informing you that the work goes exceedingly well today, so well, indeed, that I cannot bring myself to stop – even for the inestimable pleasure of your company at table.'

'I'm so glad, Mr Revesby,' I told him.

'If you could spare a few moments, I wonder – would you care to hear what I have written this morning?'

Would I not! I thrilled at the prospect. To be able to cherish the memory all my life that I had been present at Martin Revesby's first reading of a portion of what would certainly be one of his major works. A privileged audience of one!

I intimated that nothing would delight me more. Accordingly, he poured me a glass of Madeira and one for himself, then, after making sure that I was comfortably settled in a chair at the other side of the rent table, he began his reading.

His delivery – in his deep and well-modulated voice, the voice of an actor, or a preacher of the better sort – was arresting in the extreme; so that the slightest interruption, the fall of a pin, the scratching of a mouse in the wainscotting, would have been an intolerable intrusion upon the senses. He sat with his profile turned towards me: that regular, noble profile, high-browed, patrician. As he declaimed, he made occasional gestures with his free hand, to point up a word or a telling phrase. And after every stanza or so, he took a sip of his wine.

The lyrical love poem by now had progressed to speculations on the poet's part about a future life that he and the object of his love might pass together at some future time. He told of a possible marriage, and of an idyllic honeymoon spent on some far-off shore overlooking a wine-dark sea; in a villa of white marble, all overhung with hibiscus, bougainvillaea and columbine, where exquisite statuary of antiquity gestured amid whispering cypresses and the plash of fountains. He spoke of his love's qualities, and added a few more touches to the tantalizingly vague portrait of her appearance that was slowly being built up in my mind.

She was certainly no one of my acquaintance, and emphatically not Lady Amanda. And yet, strangely, there was an indefinable aura of familiarity about the lady. I supposed that this was accounted for by the genius of the poet, in his ability to touch upon those elements of womankind which are common to all.

All too soon, the reading was finished. He laid the sheets of manuscript aside, took a draught of his wine, and gazed at me quizzically.

'Well, now, Miss Carew,' he said. 'Am I mistaken, or have I not, by a determined exercising of the culinary arts, revived that unsuccessful *soufflé* of the other day? In short, do my poor verses touch any response in you?'

'It's beautiful, beautiful!' I told him earnestly. 'You mustn't change a single line, nor a word.'

He spread his hands, smiling. 'What need have I of the London critics when I have you, dear Miss Carew? And now, be off with you, please, and let me continue, while the muse is still whispering in my ear.'

'First your cold beef and ham,' I admonished him. 'For even the most impatient of muses will wait while the inner man is satisfied.'

'You are something of a tyrant, Miss Carew,' he said with mock severity. 'But a benign tyrant for all that. I will see you at dinner, ma'am. Till then, *adieu*.'

He was stabbing at a slice of beef with his fork while already taking up his pen with his right hand and frowning in concentration over his manuscript by the time I shut the library door on him and went for my own luncheon.

On the previous evening, during my daily consultation with Mrs Challis, the housekeeper had spoken of her intention of going to Truro with her husband the next day, on what was their monthly shopping expedition for the establishment.

While sipping my after-luncheon coffee, I heard the hired dog-cart leave the kitchen entrance and sweep round the front of the mansion, to fade away down the drive. On an impulse, I was on my feet and rushing to the great door, where, through the barred wicket, I surreptitiously espied the Challises seated side by side in the front of the conveyance: she in a huge bonnet with a kerchief of waterproof American cloth draped over the top and tied under the chin; he in an over-large hat that bobbed back and forth on his ears with every turn of the wheels. I watched till they were out of sight, expressing the quiet hope that both were carrying umbrellas, for the sky was by then so blackened that it was hardly feasible that they could possibly make Truro and back without running through a thunderstorm. And, when they were out of sight, I experienced a curious sense of – *freedom.*

For the first time since I had set foot in Malmaynes, I was free of Mrs Challis's sly, disapproving eyes, and from the ambiguous presence of her spouse. Moreover, the day's régime of cleaning having been largely completed, and the daily staff – as I knew – by then taking their main meal of the day in the kitchen, and my employer lost to the world in the library, I was – for the first time ever – free to come and go where I pleased in the great mansion, without the scrutiny of prying eyes. Suddenly I felt like a child who has been given the unexpected run of a large and tangled orchard, all crammed with the prospect of heaven knows what delights.

I do not know, to this day, what prompted me to make a determined search of Malmaynes. I only recall that, having made the decision, I did it in a hurry – as if sensing that the unique freedom of movement was something finite, having a certain proximate end.

It was – I glanced towards the long-case clock in the corner – three in the afternoon. And even as I looked, a flash of distant lightning over the inland hills was quickly followed by a rumbling peal of thunder, and the rain started almost immediately after.

I set off, to search Malmaynes. For what reason I had no idea then – as I have no idea now. But it was a prompting more intense than mere curiosity.

The main part of the old mansion, containing the great hall on the ground floor, and also my own quarters on the third, was built squarely on to the sea, with the windows of the hall facing seawards, to the south. At the westward end was attached a smaller wing which projected towards the sea, forming a rough L-shape. It was there, bounded by the two wings and the cliff edge, that the formal garden lay. The lesser wing contained the kitchen quarters and the servants' bedrooms; and the walled kitchen garden, where I had first seen the sinister Jabez, was at its western end.

I began my search by ascending the main staircase from the great hall and investigating the rooms on the floor above, being determined, swiftly yet methodically, to devour the contents of Malmaynes as a hungry caterpillar will devour a succulent lettuce leaf.

The rooms above the hall were all spacious and grand: almost like State apartments, such as are found in the great ducal seats for the accommodation of visiting Royalty. They ran one into another, with connecting doors, which, all being open, formed a continuous corridor along the window wall. Alternately furnished as sitting-rooms and bedrooms, they provided self-contained suites, and were done out in the taste of the previous century, with carved and gilded panelling, suave silks and satins, yielding carpets of Oriental make. There were many portraits of ladies and gentlemen in the costumes of bygone days. None carried titles, but many of them had the same cast of features – which I took to be that of the Tremaines and perhaps the Revesbys. I detected, in some of them, the high-browed and patrician look of the present master of Malmaynes.

My swift passage along that floor took but a few minutes. Nothing there of interest, I told myself. All very grand. And all very bland. The cheerful pastel shades of the hangings, the brightness of the gilt-work – it all seemed at odds with my impression of Malmaynes, which was of a tall and brooding stone hulk of a ship stranded on its lonely clifftop. Closing the door upon the last apartment, I took to the staircase again and continued my ascent.

The floor above was as different from the preceding one as night from day. Here was Malmaynes indeed. No gilded panelling masked the uncompromising roughness of the granite walls; only limewash darkened with age and swagged with cobwebs. Nor were the apartments set out in the straight and formal manner of those on the floor below; there was a cramped corridor which twisted and turned in a crazy and haphazard manner, ill lit by the narrow slits of windows, with mysterious pools of shadow through which I hurried with unease. Some of the rooms were mere cupboards, jutting out from the main wall and formed by panels of blackened oak, such as one sees aboard ship. I opened the door of one of these. It contained a cot bed and a washstand with hand-basin and water jug – nothing else. A cry rose to my throat as I saw a movement on the bed. A spider as large as a five-shilling piece scurried across the dusty coverlet and disappeared under the pillow.

It was at that moment I heard a door close.

The sound came from the middling distance, back the way I had come, in the direction of the main staircase. It had not been the action of the wind (that had been the first, consoling thought which leapt to my mind). No abrupt slam. The door – wherever it was – had been slowly and deliberately closed by a living hand. And without any attempt at masking the sound. As if the person had – wanted to be heard. Had wanted me to know of his, or her, presence on that floor – or so it seemed to my uneasy mind.

Holding my breath and willing my pounding heart to quieten itself, I took the two silent steps to the door of the tiny room and looked out into the corridor, back the way I had come. There was no one in sight. Ten paces from where I stood, the corridor turned a corner, presenting a blank wall. I strained my ears for any sound, seeking to determine whether the other person had, on quitting one of the rooms and ostentatiously shutting the door, proceeded towards the staircase in the other direction or was coming towards me. I had an impulse – immediately quenched – to call out in a bright and strident tone, to ask who was there.

No one *should* have been there – for were not all the servants at their meal in the kitchen?

Fully a minute went by. I decided to count up to another sixty, and then retrace my steps to the staircase, perhaps encountering my mystery companion. The prospect was not inviting – but what alternative was there? For all I knew, the other direction would bring me to nothing but a blank wall, and place me further away from the staircase.

I began to count silently in my head, all the time looking

and listening, my eyes fixed on the edge of the wall ten paces distant, my ears pricked for the slightest sound.

At twenty-five, my heart lurched, as I heard the sound of a floorboard creaking under the weight of a foot. It came, quite distinctly, from somewhere round the bend in the corridor. Quite close at hand.

I knew, then, in which direction the unknown one was moving. It was towards me!

My eyes, strained with staring unwinkingly at one spot, began to glaze and water. I longed to blink, to rub them with my fingers, but dared not. It seemed vital to me – almost as if my very life depended upon it – to see the unknown one immediately he, or she, came round the corner; for surely the manner of the stranger's coming would immediately indicate that person's intention towards me. A sauntering walk, a smile – these might denote friendly designs. In my baffled, trapped terror, I assumed a rictus grin – a travesty of my best smile – to greet the newcomer.

The grin froze on my lips; and all my hopes of life, of safety, of survival, died like a snuffed candle – as a hand crept slowly round the corner of the wall!

Crept – the fingers walking delicately along the dusty stonework, like spider's feet. At waist level. Then pausing. Still. Nothing but a hand and the curve of a bare wrist.

Somewhere in my shocked frame, my instinct for survival found the will and energy to move my paralysed limbs. Turning on my heels, dragging my horrified gaze from what I might see behind me, I fled down the narrow corridor – away from my tormentor. Nor did I dare to scream, for I sensed that the sound would serve no purpose but to increase my own terror. I rounded the next corner, and another – and all the time I shrank from the anticipated grasp upon my shoulder, the touch of extended fingertips against the small of my back. My only thought: to keep moving, to retain some distance, however small, between myself and that hand.

One more turn in the corridor – then came the thought of how it could well end: at a blank wall somewhere not far ahead, where I should be obliged to turn and face my pursuer and see him plain for what he was. To suffer whatever he intended for me.

Sobbing for breath, crying aloud in my mind for deliverance, I came at length to the end of the corridor. Blessedly, there was a narrow staircase by the far wall – but it only went upwards, up into a dark hole in the ceiling. No matter: this was the deliverance I had prayed for. Setting my foot upon the stairs, I mounted them without pause, or without looking back.

I had anticipated that the staircase would bring me immediately to the floor above; but such was not the case. The steps continued upwards, turning at every floor, till the steep slope of the dark ceiling above showed me that I must be directly under the roof, and there the staircase ended. All round me was darkness, pierced by fitful gleams of light from narrow slits in the walls. I heard the drumming of heavy rain on the slates above my head. No other sound. I stole a glance down the staircase well: no sign of my pursuer. Slower now, and with caution, holding my hands out before me, I set off, keeping one elbow close to the wall. In this manner I must have traversed almost the entire length of the main block of the mansion on the attic floor. I was aware of passing dark doors and rickety wooden steps leading to heaven knows what dark holes and corners high in the roof void. Cobwebs as substantial as fishing-nets brushed my face, showering my head and shoulders with a fine, choking dust. I nearly screamed when something brushed against my feet: it was a rat, I saw it dart away, in and out of the shadows.

Presently, at the far end of the attic floor, I saw the balustrade of another staircase, and I descended it at a run, counting the storeys as I went. When I reached the ground floor, I found myself in familiar surroundings: I was in the passage above the kitchen, and the steps continued down into the basement. From where I stood, I could hear the hum of conversation below.

The women sitting round the big kitchen table looked up in surprise as I opened the door and went in: Janey and Alice, the other new kitchen maid, the two long-established daily women; five pairs of eyes, round with amazement; five mouths paused in the act of eating; hands frozen in mid-gesture.

'Mercy me, ma'am!' cried Janey Pinner. 'Where have you been, to get yourself all covered in dust and cobwebs like that? And you look so pale, ma'am – as if you've seen a ghost. Sit you down, do, and let me get you a cup of tea.'

'Thank you, no,' I said. 'I – I'm perfectly all right.' I crossed over to the window wall, towards the sink. On the draining-board stood the plain wooden tray with stained pewter plate and spoon, a pewter mug with lees of beer at the bottom.

Carefully controlling my voice, to keep out the note of hysteria that threatened to take control, I murmured, 'Where is Jabez today?'

'Haven't seen him all afternoon, ma'am,' came Janey's reply. 'Has any o' you lasses seen aught of Jabez?'

The question brought a chorus of casual denials. No one had seen him since midday.

I looked out of the window, into the walled kitchen garden, where the rain drummed down upon the neat lines of startlingly green cabbages and plucked at the swaying tendrils of the climbing bean plants.

No sign of the hideous gardener of Malmaynes; only a spade left standing on the edge of a newly dug-over patch of earth.

Chapter Five

I never spoke to anyone of that disturbing encounter. There were only two people to whom it would have been feasible to mention the matter: Martin Revesby and my new friend Nick Pendennis. The former I dismissed almost without a thought; it seemed out of the question to burden a poet – an artist in the throes of producing his master work – with a tale of my being frightened by some unknown person while engaged upon an impertinent search of his own house. And by the time I next saw Nick, I had quite convinced myself that it was Jabez whom I had encountered, wandering about the forbidden rooms in the aimless, mischievous way of the half-witted; taking advantage, no doubt, of the Challises' absence.

Nick rode in through the gates two days after: tall as a scarlet dragoon in the saddle. He uncapped to me and bowed low, grinning. We had some small talk of this and that, and I asked him how Lady Amanda was. He pulled a long lip at that: told me she had gone to London by railway train. And one of the things she intended doing, he said, was to look for a suitable Town house for Mr Revesby, somewhere in Knightsbridge, Belgravia or Mayfair – from which, with her aid, he would be launched into Society.

In the hope of comforting him, I expressed surprise that her caprice had lasted so long – and added that I was sure it could not possibly flourish for much longer on such barren soil. Mention of houses reminded me of the small commission I had undertaken to perform on behalf of young Alice Witham and her swain; and I asked him about the vacant cottage of which Janey had spoken. Nick was instantly all enthusiasm. Yes, they could have it with pleasure, he said. Let them by all means get wed, and he would provide them with Mill Cottage rent free – and lend his own town phaeton for a wedding-carriage to bring the bride to church and to bear her off with her groom. That settled, he came to what had been the reason for his calling at Malmaynes: would I care to accompany him on a drive to Truro the following day?

My first impulse was politely to decline the invitation, since I could see nothing but trouble in store if I allowed our light friendship to develop into something more substantial. That Nick Pendennis was attractive, and that I found him attractive, I made not the slightest attempt to conceal from myself, being the sort of person who can look a fact squarely in the face. By the same token, I was aware that he was not entirely indifferent to my own scant charms: I had not forgotten that moment in the drawing-room at the Manor when his eyes had held mine for a brief moment longer than prudence permitted. And he was a man already spoken for – albeit by a baggage who treated him like a gauche schoolboy in company and made no secret of her infatuation for Mr Revesby.

So my first thought was to say no – till I saw the cloud of disappointment gather in his open, handsome face as he sensed the beginnings of my refusal. So I thought: what harm in an excursion to Truro? We were living in the mid-nineteenth century, citizens of an enlightened age. What harm could possibly come, and what indiscretion be construed, from two friends going for a drive to the big city? And in an open phaeton.

So I said that I would accompany him with pleasure, for did I not want to visit a dressmaker and order myself a gown for dinner, and another for formal, day occasions?

Over dinner that night, I had the opportunity of praising Martin Revesby on his newest verses, which seemed to please him; though in a preoccupied sort of way – as if the subject of his poetry was not the most pressing thing on his mind. He seemed abstracted: ate little, and sat crumbling pieces of bread, tapping the side of his wine glass with a fingernail; nervous, intense. And, from time to time, he threw sharp glances at Mrs Challis, who, with her husband and Janey, was serving us at table.

At the end of the meal, when the servants had cleared away, leaving us to our coffee and shutting the doors to the kitchen quarters behind them, he became instantly animated; cast a swift glance over his shoulder to ensure himself that the doors were indeed shut.

'Miss Carew,' he declared, in tones of barely-suppressed excitement, 'I have news for you – about *her*!' And he pointed in the direction of the kitchen quarters.

'About Mrs Challis?' I asked.

'Yes, yes!' he cried. 'Who else? What I have to tell you – what I have learned today – will astonish you. Are you ready for it? Steel your nerve, Miss Carew. If you feel the need, by all means help yourself to the brandy decanter.'

'I thank you, sir,' I replied, 'but I think I shall survive without it.'

'As you please, Miss Carew. Now then, here it is –' he fixed me with a steady glance of his fine eyes – 'what would you say if I told you that our Mrs Challis was less than frank with me on that occasion – you will recall it – when I questioned her quite closely about him whom legend persists in giving the sobriquet of the Beast of Malmaynes? What would you say if I told you – and I am telling you now, Miss Carew – that Mrs Challis's admission, reluctantly given, that she knew that fellow Saul Pendark, knew him well, was a monumental understatement to say the least?'

'He was her son,' I said.

The effect upon my employer was to cause his brow to furrow with sudden anger and his mouth to harden. For the first time, I saw that Martin Revesby, poet and visionary, had at least one very human failing that he shared with the rest of us mere mortals: he did not much care to be second at a secret.

'You already know?' he demanded.

'I found out several days ago,' I admitted.

'And you did not think to tell me?'

'You've been so busy, so absorbed in your work – in the creation of *The Saga of Love and Death* – that almost anything seemed an intolerable intrusion to impose upon you.'

'Even the fact that my housekeeper – the woman who serves my guests and me at table – is the mother of a convicted killer?' The furrows on his brow deepened and darkened.

'Mr Revesby,' I pleaded. 'That was more than twenty years ago. Even in the village – and you know what folks are like in a remote Cornish village – they don't bear any resentment towards Mrs Challis on that score. I have spoken to her and believe me, Mr Revesby, the woman bears her tragedy with a great dignity. I don't much like her, I have to admit it; but I respect her for the frankness, and indeed the honesty, with which she spoke to me after her secret had been revealed.'

He nodded slowly, understandingly. The furrows faded from his brow. I felt a wave of relief.

'Those are good sentiments, Miss Carew,' he said, 'and they do you honour. I appreciate your reasons for withholding the information from me. On the matter of the woman herself, I am in two minds, and I think I shall leave it to you to decide. If, now or at any future time, you think that the Challises should be sent packing, I give you complete *carte blanche* to effect it.'

'I don't think – I hope – it won't be necessary, Mr Revesby,' I told him. 'Not for the reason we've been speaking of, at any rate. And she is really co-operating quite well in my reorganization of the household. No, I'm sure it won't be necessary to dispense with her services.'

'So be it, Miss Carew,' said my employer, rising. 'I will say good night. I am going to do a little more work before retiring.'

'Good night, Mr Revesby.'

He paused half-way across the great hall, turned and regarded me.

'You have done very well here, Miss Carew,' he said. 'You have given – you continue to give – the greatest satisfaction.'

I faltered my thanks, painfully aware that I had coloured up like a schoolgirl – though for what reason I could not for the life of me imagine, because I possess quite sufficient poise and assurance to enable me to accept compliments.

Next morning, dressed in my green serge for the drive to Truro, I was down early. Young Alice Witham had just finished laying the breakfast table in the hall and was singing happily at her work when I entered. I had immediately given her the good news about the cottage, and she and her Edgar had been to see the Rector the previous evening to arrange for the banns to be read, the wedding being fixed for Saturday a month hence.

Martin Revesby joined me for breakfast, but made no allusion to what had passed between us the previous evening. He had had some letters delivered in the post, and sat reading them in an absorbed manner throughout the meal; at the end of which he asked me to write a short note to his bank in Truro, instructing them to arrange the sale of certain bonds held in his name. I told him that I should be going to Truro that very morning and would deliver the letter by hand, to which he nodded agreement.

At nine-thirty o'clock I finished the letter and he signed it. Nick was due to collect me at ten, and I was taking up some needlework in a small sitting-room adjoining the hall when Janey tapped on the door and came in.

'Sergeant Buller to see you, ma'am.'

'Good morning to you, Miss Carew, ma'am.' The policeman loomed into the room, dwarfing us both in his absurdly long coat. 'May I have a few words with you?'

I nodded, dismissing Janey, who looked as if she would have preferred to stay and listen.

'Sit down, Sergeant,' I told him. 'I'm glad you called. Indeed, I was only thinking yesterday that I should have to seek you out. You see, I have something to tell you.'

The ghost of a smile flitted across his unaccommodating

countenance, and died for want of practice. 'Would this be a matter of intuition or a matter of hard fact, ma'am?'

'A matter of fact – concerning the mother of Saul Pendark.'

'Mrs Challis,' he said flatly.

'You already know!' I felt the same slight pang of disappointment that Martin Revesby must have experienced the previous night when I had usurped his news.

'I knew from the very start, ma'am. I spoke with Mrs Challis, just as I spoke with almost everyone in the parish, yourself included. No sooner did I touch upon the subject of Saul Pendark than she admitted their relationship without any prompting.'

'I see.'

He must have noticed the touch of sharpness in my voice, for he again attempted a smile. 'Ma'am, I think you are vexed with me,' he said. 'I think you're vexed because I didn't confide in you earlier on this matter – seeing as how you confided in me.'

'You are at liberty to do as you please, Sergeant,' I replied. 'You are the law.'

'I did not tell you, ma'am,' he said, 'because I wished to make a small test.'

'And what was this test?' I asked.

'I wished to see how long it would take, ma'am, before the news reached your ears about Mrs Challis – and by what means.'

It was then I told him of the incident in the kitchen, when I had been witness to Janey's denunciation of the housekeeper. I also mentioned that Martin Revesby had only found out the previous day.

'Mr Revesby had it from me,' said Sergeant Buller. 'I called here to see him yesterday afternoon.'

The clock on the chimneypiece chimed the quarter-hour. I put aside my needlework.

'Was there something you particularly wished to speak to me about, Sergeant?' I asked. 'I am due out at ten.'

'Yes, ma'am,' he said. 'And it will take but a moment.

What I have to say to you might be regarded as a warning.'

'A warning?'

'Warning might be a trifle strong, perhaps. Shall we say – a caution?'

'You wish to caution me about what?' I felt a prickle of unease.

'We spoke last time, ma'am, of your intuition. Prompted by your intuition, you said, you have come to a certain conclusion about Saul Pendark.'

'That he may still be alive – yes.'

'You still have that feeling, ma'am?'

I thought of my conversation with Mrs Challis, and seemed to hear again her broken, tragic voice: *'He perished down there among the rocks. Don't you think any other for one instant . . .'*

'I have inclined away from that opinion now, Sergeant,' I told him.

He nodded. Clasped his large, bony hands together and cracked the knuckles loudly. 'I'm glad to hear it, ma'am, for to think of Saul Pendark as still being alive might lead a person to several wrong conclusions. Now, Pendark was eighteen when he stood trial – which would make him something in the region of forty were he still alive. If I took it into my head – as once you did – that it was he who murdered the unknown lady in the churchyard, I would be confining my search to a man of forty. Now, what conclusion do you draw from that, ma'am?'

I saw it very clearly. 'If the murderer is not Saul Pendark,' I cried, 'it might explain why he put her body between the graves of the women who were murdered all those years ago. He did it in order to start the suspicion that Saul Pendark is still alive.'

'Yes, ma'am – yes?' Sergeant Buller fairly beamed with pleasure at me, as if I were his promising pupil. 'And what further conclusion do you draw?'

'That the murderer is either discernibly younger than forty, or he is older – and as such could not possibly come under suspicion of being Saul Pendark.'

'Or,' said the sergeant, 'the murderer is a woman. Which brings me to the caution I had in mind to pass on to you. I think, ma'am, that the one I seek is among us, in this parish of St Gawes. Add to that, I think that he – or she – is probably as unlike Saul Pendark as could be.

'And the caution that I would offer you, ma'am, is this: *Be on your guard! Trust no one, man or woman!*'

Well enough for Sergeant Buller to offer caution; but mistrustfulness is not in my nature. For instance, it was clearly out of the question to suspect Nick Pendennis of being any other than the person whom he presented to the world at large: healthy, uncomplicated, not overburdened with imagination, and quite incapable of deceit. I stole several covert glances at him while we drove to Truro that morning, and liked what I saw.

He was in a cheerful mood. He had had a letter that morning, he told me, from his fiancée. Lady Amanda was lost in the social whirl surrounding her brother, Lord Pitt-Jermyn, and had scarcely found any opportunity to search for a suitable property for Mr Revesby. And she would not be returning to Cornwall much before Christmas.

'The longer she's away in London, the more chance she has of ridding her mind of Revesby's influence,' he informed me. 'And putting all that art bosh behind her. I shall discourage her from coming down here for Christmas, and suggest that she proceeds straight to Suffolk. That means she will not set eyes on Revesby again till after the pheasant-shooting season's over. The infatuation will have fizzled out by then, for Amanda's really quite a sensible gel at heart.'

'I'm quite sure you're right,' I smiled. 'But don't you miss her terribly?'

He shrugged. 'I suppose so,' he said. 'Mark you, we never seem to have much to say to one another, Amanda and I. I suppose it comes from having seen so much of each other since childhood. One tends to have said almost everything there is to be said. And that several times over.'

I shook my head in wonderment at their strange and carefully unemotional betrothal.

And so we came to Truro, which was a sea of mud after the recent rains, and crowded with countryfolk in for market; with tinkers and other travelling folk, a brass band, barefoot children running wild, dogs everywhere. The circulation of the traffic was so slow in the narrow streets that Nick drove the phaeton into an inn yard and handed it over to an ostler. From then on we went on foot: first to the bank to deliver Martin Revesby's letter, thence to the emporium of Mrs Gillis, dressmaker, of Tregolis Road, who had suited me admirably on several occasions in the past. Nick was quite content to lounge in an easy chair while I went through the pattern books with Mrs Gillis.

My principal concern was for a moderately formal gown to wear at dinner, for it seemed to me that my employer must be heartily tired of the sight of my white muslin, occasionally alternated by the green wool. I was greatly attracted to a simple design with a not-too-wide, single-tiered skirt and a suitably modest neckline, with sleeves to the elbow. Mrs Gillis said she could make it up in a light oyster-coloured velvet with a taffeta lining for £3.7s.6d., which was a little more than I had bargained for, but still within my purse. The day dress was a more difficult choice, but I finally settled for one with a dolman jacket over it, which I thought would be very suitable for Alice Witham's wedding, particularly made up in pale blue, with lace at collar and cuffs. Mrs Gillis promised faithfully to have it ready within the month, though I have no doubt that her price – £2.15s.0d. – was enhanced on that account. She ushered me into a changing room to take my measurements, and we were out of the shop with the whole transaction completed within an hour. I am not one to take an age when it comes to making up my mind over clothes.

'After that interminable time, you must be famished,' said Nick. 'It's now one o'clock, and I am taking you for luncheon.'

Truro was well-served with inns and chop-houses; and it was in my escort's mind to eat at the establishment where we had left our transport; accordingly, we set off to walk back there, past the main part of the market. The crowds had increased while we had been in the dressmaker's; and to the shouts of the vendors and the auctioneers was now added the raucous lowing of a whole herd of cattle which were being driven into pens that had been set up in the market square. The din was indescribable, likewise the diversity of odours: in addition to the smells of the animals and humans, we were assailed by a conglomeration of hot meat pie and pasty smells, black puddings, potato cakes; baked oysters, whelks, winkles, smoked mackerel; the scents of caramel and vanilla from the sweetmeat stalls; everywhere the reek of beer and cider. Most folk seemed to be eating as they strolled. And the brass band played continuously.

When I recall the horror of what immediately followed, there comes to my mind, and to my senses, the sights and smells of that crowd; and I am back again in Truro market on that overcast September midday.

It began with a shout: urgent, louder than the rest – stilling all other sounds. And in the silence that followed:

'Bull loose! Watch yourselves, he's a bad 'un!'

The press of people in front of me melted like dry leaves before a gust of wind. I clutched at Nick's arm, irresolute of how to move, and to where – as I perceived the massive creature standing not ten paces from us.

It was a great white bull: one that I immediately recognized as of the Dewaine herd, which had achieved a great fame – and something of a notoriety – in Cornwall of the fifties. Huge and magnificently built, with a cruel spread of horn like Highland cattle; bred from mixed English and French stock for beef, they were possessed of a strain of fighting fury. The terrifying specimen before us stood goring at a heap of tangled rags that lay before it, presenting us with its hindquarters and its angry whiplash of a tail.

Something screamed in terror and agony – and I saw that the bundle of rags was a man!

Nick thrust me behind him. 'Get away from here, Cherry!' he said. 'Take cover behind one of the pens.' And he started towards the bull.

'Nick, come back!' I cried.

The great animal may have heard me. In any event, it raised its horned head from its grisly task. The wretched victim seized his chance of life: rolled over and over, and squirmed beneath the lower bars of a nearby pen – where he was immediately gathered up by members of the crowd who were hiding there.

I seized hold of Nick's hand, and we both turned to run for safety. The crisis was over. We had not far to go. And the bull was not even looking in our direction.

Then, like the slow figures in a solemn dance, the players in the scene moved into tragedy . . .

Round the side of a building at the opposite end of the square from where we stood, and out of a narrow lane that led down a hill, emerged two small figures: a girl of some five or six years, hand in hand with a younger boy, a mere toddler. They were chattering animatedly to each other, and both had toffee apples on sticks. With no thought for anything but the enjoyment of their goodies and of each other's company, they came directly into the square, looking neither right nor left, nor ahead; deaf to the shouts of warning that were hurled at them from behind the pens, heedless of their peril.

Ten or fifteen paces from them stood the great white bull. They were walking straight towards it. And it had seen them on the instant.

I made no attempt to check Nick as he stepped forward, whipping off his coat; I only breathed a prayer for his safe deliverance.

'Ho, there!' he shouted. And he flourished the coat.

Slowly the animal turned its massive head and regarded the man who stood behind it, shaking out the folds of the coat and uttering sharp, encouraging cries. A long, contemptuous glance; then, with an angry snort, it transferred its gaze to the children!

They had by this time seen the bull. The girl, realizing their peril, was pulling at her brother's hand; but the little lad was entranced by the bull and was pointing his finger at it and gabbling with excitement, struggling against his sister's hold, eager to approach the animal.

Somewhere a woman screamed. A horrified silence followed, as, after raking at the cobblestones with a fore-hoof and emitting a deep-chested roar, the great white bull moved forward towards the helpless children.

Nick darted after it, a challenging shout on his lips, flailing with his coat. He came abreast of the huge animal just as it broke into a trot, a trot that changed its gait within two strides to a canter, and would be a gallop at the next pace. Closing with the high shoulder and neck, he swung his coat and looped it over the sharp tip of a spreading horn.

The bull's furious bellow echoed across the square. It broke its stride – awkwardly – slowing the dreadful onrush and half-turning to its blind side, where the coat hung, pierced through and through by the cruel point. And, still turning, it saw the man standing before it.

Nick never had a chance of escape. His own swift dash had taken the best of his energy, and there was nowhere for him to run, nor even time to turn. He had no opportunity to do other than take one step back, before the bull was upon him, head lowered, raking at its victim with one horn, catching bone and sinew and yielding flesh, gathering up the writhing figure like a broken marionette, tossing it on high, right over its back, to fall on the cobblestones and lie very still.

The very violence of the bull's first assault was Nick's salvation. Half-blinded by the coat, the animal lost its bearings and looked about it for the tossed victim; a brief respite that allowed two men to dart out from behind the pens and gallantly gather up the insensible Nick. They had scarcely regained safety with the limp form swaying between them before the bull came to a slithering halt against the barrier and stood there, snorting, tossing its head and lashing its tail.

I pushed through the crowds behind the pens, forced my way to his side. His rescuers were standing over him. One of them was comforting the two children whom Nick had saved.

I took him to be their father, and indeed this turned out to be so.

'Someone's gone for the doctor,' they told me. 'By God, that was the bravest thing I ever beheld.'

Nick lay with his head pillowed on someone's coat, his eyes closed, face as pale as death. His shirt and waistcoat were ripped to shreds about the left shoulder and chest, and soaked with blood from neck to waist. A thick dribble of carmine was issuing among the ruts between the cobblestones on which he lay: snaking in and out, meeting up and parting, spreading wide.

Fearful that he would bleed to death before help could arrive, I made a thick wad of my serge jacket and pressed it hard against where I judged his wound to be. He stirred and gave a low moan of pain. Behind me, a woman was crying heartbrokenly.

After an agonizing length of time, during which it seemed to me that poor Nick was dying beneath my hands, I heard cries of 'Stand back, there. Make way for the surgeon,' and a short, stout young man in a dusty tall hat bustled into view, laid a bulging bag on the ground and fell on his knees beside me.

'Gored by a bull, they say?' he muttered. 'Oh, my! Dear me! I don't like his colour at all. Are you the gentleman's lady-wife, ma'am?'

'No, Doctor,' I replied. 'Is he – fearfully hurt?'

'Well, now, let's see,' replied the other cheerfully. And he took from his bag a pair of long scissors and cut through the sodden waistcoat and shirt. There was a concerted intake of breath from those surrounding us, and the ring of faces drew closer.

'Tch, tch!' said the surgeon. 'Very nasty lacerations of the *pectoralis major, deltoideus* and *sternocleidomastoideus*, together with, I perceive, a compound fracture of the *clavicula*. However, it appears that the chest wall has not been pierced, and that the wound – though alarming in appearance – may properly be described as superficial. Heaven preserve me from a superficiality of such a sort! Are you the fainting kind, ma'am – or are you able to give me some assistance as I sew him up and set the bone?'

I assured him of my strong nerves, but found them to be sorely tried when the cheerful surgeon drew together the ragged edges of the long slash with stitches of silk thread, whistling through his teeth all the while. I dabbed away the seeping blood and handed him the scissors, thread, splints, and other instruments at his direction. Over the entire wound, he then laid a piece of damp lint and covered it in oiled silk.

'Well, now,' he said, when he had done, 'if our friend does not suffer any inflammation or mortification of his wound, if he does not develop a fever, or, worse, a locked jaw – he should be as right as a trivet in a month or so. Who is he, ma'am, and where is he from?'

'Mr Pendennis of St Gawes Manor,' I told him.

'Mr Pendennis, eh?' cried the surgeon. 'I thought I recognized the cut of his jib. Well, I shall not be kept waiting for payment if Mr Pendennis of St Gawes Manor is involved.'

'What's to be done now, Doctor?' I asked.

'Get him back to his bed, ma'am,' replied the other. 'And send for my good colleague Dr Prescott of St Gawes. He will prescribe the onward treatment. Do you have a carriage, ma'am?'

At my directions, a couple of willing youths were dispatched to bring the phaeton from the inn. By the time it arrived with the ostler at the reins, Nick had recovered consciousness and was smiling weakly up at me. The surgeon was of the opinion that he had not suffered any considerable concussion of the brain. This was confirmed by all around who had witnessed the dreadful scene: Nick had been somersaulted right over the bull's back, and had landed feet-first.

'Soon be home, Nick,' I murmured. And he squeezed my hand.

As they laid him gently in the phaeton and covered him with blankets from the inn, the crowd was already dispersing about its business and pleasures. The cries of the meat pie and black pudding vendors and the shouts of the auctioneers began anew. The sweet smell of caramel and vanilla drifted afresh across the square. And the band struck up a lively sea-shanty.

Alone in his pen, the big white Dewaine bull stood as meekly as any lamb; ruminating, perhaps, upon its brief moment of terrible glory.

I drove the phaeton back to the Manor, keeping Nick's spirited blacks well in check and sparing the whip. Nick dozed all the way – being, I suppose, in a state of some shock after his frightful experience. I was grateful to see the white façade of the Manor appear through the poplars; and as we approached up the curve of the drive, Nick's butler and housekeeper came out on to the porch.

Briefly, I told the horrified couple what had occurred. A hurdle was brought, covered with an eiderdown, and two strong footmen bore their master up the wide stairs to his bedroom and laid him on his great four-poster.

Dr Prescott, being immediately summoned, was swift to arrive on a little grey cob, red-faced and puffing with the effort of his ride. He promptly cleared the bedroom of the gaping servants, nodded for me to remain, and addressed himself to the patient: taking Nick's pulse, turning up his eyelids and feeling his brow.

'No call to disturb the wound again today,' he said. 'I am happily familiar with the excellent handiwork of my colleague Dr Arthur, who learned his surgery in the hard school of the Royal Navy, on the China Station. He is to be kept very quiet, ma'am. On low diet: gruel, arrowroot and such. I shall purge him with five grains each of calomel and antimonial powder and let him sleep till morning, when I will call again. May I beg that you will also be here then, ma'am? Between ourselves – ' he lowered his voice, glancing at the still figure in the bed – 'there's not a servant in this establishment with the wit to follow a simple instruction. I should be mightily grateful if you would act as occasional nurse.'

'Of course, Doctor,' I assured him. 'Mr Revesby will wish me to render every possible assistance. What time shall you be here?'

We made an arrangement for the following morning. The housekeeper was sent for and instructed as to the patient's diet. Two housemaids were to sit with him, turn and turn about, through the night, and a horse was to be kept saddled and ready, for a groom to summon the doctor if the patient showed any signs of fever.

Nick was asleep when I took my leave of him. I passed my hand over his brow, smoothing back the tousled hair.

Brave, I thought. How brave and splendid he is. And how wasted on such as Lady Amanda.

News had reached Malmaynes, by way of folk returning from Truro market, of Nick Pendennis's gallant action. Martin Revesby had left word for me to go to him in the library as soon as I returned. This I did, and gave the poet a full account of all that had happened. As I had anticipated, he gave his full support to my acting as Dr Prescott's nurse. The work could wait, he told me. And anyhow – here he ruefully tapped a couple of sheets all covered with erasures and crossings-out – the poem had got itself bogged down yet again. But he was planning to work on through the evening – and even into the night should his muse chance to begin whispering in his ear again, so he would not be present for dinner.

I bade him a good evening and took my leave. On the way through the great hall, I found a letter lying on a salver upon the table. It had come in the afternoon post, and was from Uncle Gervase. I went up to my room and read it behind the locked door.

Rose Cottage,
Poltewan.
Sept. 30th, 1856

My dear Cherry,

A swift reply to your latest. Your news that the Malmaynes housekeeper was mother to Pendark sent me back to Joe Shearer for more information about the said lady. Considering the passing of time since he last saw her (and bearing in mind, also, his fast approaching dotage), my old friend retains a surprisingly clear recollection of the former 'Mrs' Pendark – a circumstance that he attributes to the woman's truly astonishing presence. He will never forget, he tells me, the way she acted towards her son. 'Like a she-leopard towards her wayward cub' – those were Shearer's words. Adding: 'Full of a strange savagery, as if she herself would have clawed him down for his transgressions. Yet, even while rending him asunder, loving him still.'

Her assurance to you that Saul Pendark died must be taken as sincere. This brings me to the conclusion that the murderer of the unknown lady who was wont to purchase her raiment in Paris (and from what dressmaker, might one ask?) left the body where he did for no other reason than to make everyone suppose that the Beast of Malmaynes was resurrected.

I like the sound of your police sergeant. He demonstrates good sense in enlisting your aid (and, incidentally, mine!)

Pray write again immediately, bringing me up to date on the latest developments. And, my dear Cherry, I beg you to be on your guard. If not the resurrected Saul Pendark, THE MURDERER COULD BE ANYONE IN ST GAWES! Take care, my dear.

My fondest regards, as ever,

Yr aff.
Uncle G –

PS. By reason of the fact that the handsome widow has sent me a gift of excellent pears from her orchard – *and has not extended the same favour to Arbuthnot* – I take it that I am clearly in the lead of the gallant Captain for her favours. I shall have to watch my step!

Another warning! Strange – and deeply disturbing – that

both Uncle Gervase and Sergeant Buller should have lit upon the same point about the murderer being any one of the people in the parish – and enjoining me to be cautious.

There and then I wrote a letter to my uncle, telling him all that had happened during the previous few days, including the terrible event of the afternoon in Truro. What I did *not* mention (as I had similarly not mentioned my other private terrors, such as the mad laughter in the night and the unnerving experience in the hawthorn thicket above the beach) was my secret search of Malmaynes, and the appearance of the sinister hand that had sent me fleeing in mindless panic through the fastnesses of the old dark mansion. What point, I thought, in unnecessarily concerning the dear old fellow with my overheated imaginings? For I had by then firmly decided in my own mind, and to my complete satisfaction, that the odd and frightening phenomena I had experienced were the work of Jabez the gardener. The deaf-mute, I was convinced, had conceived a mischievous desire to terrify me. I clearly remembered the morning in the great hall when he had come in bearing the log of wood, and had fixed me with those searching, inhuman eyes. But I had dismissed the idea of Jabez being in any way connected with the recent murder, or Saul Pendark.

And all that led me to the conclusion that Jabez must go.

A grotesque but curiously touching incident prevented me next morning from following up my resolve to have the deaf-mute dismissed from Malmaynes. When I got down to breakfast, Challis was in attendance. He came rushing out of the door to the kitchen quarters, pulling out my chair, settling me in, unfolding my napkin and laying it across my lap. As he did so, I caught the whiff of spirits on his breath.

'Mr Revesby will not be breakfasting, ma'am,' he informed me. 'He was working till the small hours.' Then he clicked his tongue in annoyance.

'What's the matter, Challis?' I asked him.

There was a large red apple lying on my side-plate. Its smooth skin had the heightened polish that transcends the efforts of mere nature and betrays the employment of a cloth and much elbow grease. With an irascible snort, the butler took it up.

'It's that Jabez, ma'am,' he said. 'Been in and out of the kitchen all the morning, he has, jabbering away in his strange lingo and showing us the apples he's picked that he's so proud of. Brought that in here and laid it at your place while my back was turned, I don't doubt. I'll take it, ma'am. You'll not want to touch that apple – not after Jabez has been polishing it on his sleeve.'

On an impulse, I said: 'No, wait, Challis. I wouldn't wish to hurt the poor creature's feelings. I'll keep the apple.'

He grunted. 'From all I've ever seen, ma'am, there's no feelings in the brute. He's no more than a dog or a dancing bear who'll sit up and do a few tricks for a bite to eat.'

There was a prim rebuke on my lips for the butler's callous attitude, but it was never delivered. Glancing past Challis, I saw a pair of bright eyes watching me from the door into the kitchen quarters; a domed head half-hidden.

Challis followed my glance. 'Be off with you, Jabez!' he cried. 'You know you're not allowed in this part of the house. Get you gone before I take a whip to you.'

'Leave him be,' I snapped. And I beckoned to the figure hiding behind the door. 'Come here, Jabez. Here.'

'Don't encourage the brute, ma'am,' admonished Challis. 'Or afore you know it, he'll be taking liberties. There's a cunning in him.'

'Will you be quiet, Challis!' I demanded. And I beckoned again.

Slowly, Jabez revealed himself, edging round the door and coming into the hall, great arms dangling to his knees, advancing with a shuffling step, horny-soled feet rasping on the flagstones.

He halted a few paces from the table and stood facing me with head on one side, lower lip slack, the strange eyes unwaveringly upon me.

'Thank you for the beautiful apple,' I said brightly, picking it up. 'Did you grow it yourself?'

'He don't understand you, ma'am,' muttered Challis. 'Deaf he is, you see.'

I ignored the butler and went on, 'I shan't eat it just now, Jabez, but will take it up to my room and enjoy it later.'

'You'll need to give it a good wash first, ma'am,' grunted Challis.

'So thank you very much, Jabez,' I said, with a nod and a smile. 'That will be all. You may go now.'

He made no move to go; instead a change came over his hideous countenance. His lips worked, and his tongue protruded. After a mighty effort, he produced from the depths of his great chest a gabbling sound, a hoarse grunting. One of his hands came up and pointed to his open mouth. He repeated the gesture several times.

'I think, ma'am,' said Challis, with a touch of malice, 'that he wants to see you eat the apple here and now.'

I had no option. The hideous apparition would not go away; but continued to address me in his unearthly language, growing ever more frantic the longer I hesitated, and stabbing his finger towards his mouth; till finally I overcame my scruples and – after giving the apple a swift and surreptitious wipe with my napkin – took a bite. It was delicious.

Instantly a seraphic smile spread over the deaf-mute's countenance, transforming it, by contrast, into a thing of real humanity, so that the ill-assembled features were almost pleasing to look upon. And he gave a sigh of pure pleasure.

'Ah, now you have a friend for life, ma'am,' said Challis sarcastically. 'And you're welcome to him, indeed you are.'

One more glance at me, and Jabez gave an awkward, bobbing bow and shuffled off the way he had come. He paused at the door. The little eyes swept back to me briefly. Then he was gone.

I was not unpleased with the incident. If I had indeed established a tenuous bond of friendship with Jabez, he might cease trying to terrify me. In any event, it was now quite out of the question to get rid of him.

I questioned Challis about the deaf-mute's origins, and

his reply confirmed me in my view and increased my reluctant compassion.

'He were a tinker's child,' said Challis. 'While yet a lad, though already as strong as any man, his father displayed Jabez in a sideshow at Truro fair for a ha'penny a look, and for that you could throw rotten fruit at the monster. The old master, Mr Tremaine, did take pity on him; bought him from his people for five sovereigns and rode back to Malmaynes with the young brute sitting before him.'

I wondered at this tale: thinking what an enigma the late Mr Henry Tremaine had seemed to be, tight-fisted and generous all at the same time.

I walked to the Manor, and was overtaken in the driveway there by Dr Prescott on his little grey cob. We entered the patient's bedroom together.

Nick was awake and looking better than he had been the previous afternoon. He made no bones when Dr Prescott uncovered and examined his wound; but lay uncomplainingly, smiling at me as the physician probed at the edges of the sewn gash for signs of heat and inflammation. There were no such unhealthy symptoms, so Dr Prescott deemed that the only treatment which was necessary was the application of a warm poppy fomentation in place of the lint. He instructed me in the manner of preparing the fomentation and applying it to the wound; then, declaring himself satisfied with the patient's progress, he took his leave till the following day at the same hour. I was left alone with Nick.

'Would you like me to read to you?' I asked him.

'I'm not much of a one for books,' he said. 'Not the scholarly sort. A rough country squire.'

'A very brave and gallant country squire,' I corrected him.

He gave a shrug, and winced when it caused his wound to pain him. But he would make no comment on his courageous action of the previous day; and clearly regarded it as a commonplace that a man should conduct himself without thought for his own safety, even to the point of putting his own life in jeopardy for the sake of others. I marvelled at his code of behaviour and was full of curiosity to know more about the kind of upbringing which had produced this modest and quite remarkable young man.

He was a good talker and, not being over-tired, was happy to tell his life story, after a little prompting. It started out to be a bland account of a boy born with a whole canteen of silver spoons in his mouth – but soon became something very much more.

His father, Colin Pendennis, had been a Director of the East India Company, a man of tremendous importance in the Indian sub-continent, wielding the sort of power over teeming millions of natives that is usually reserved for kings and emperors. And yet this man, this great nabob, had counted the world well lost for true love, when he met a lovely and modest girl, the daughter of a humble clerk in the service of the Company. It was an immediate and mutual coming together of two people who were destined for each other, despite the disparity of their social positions, their backgrounds, education, upbringing.

Upon declaring his intention of marrying the girl of his choice, Nick's father was threatened with dismissal from the Company, with social ostracism, with being deprived of membership of his exclusive club. Back home in England, his own father exerted intolerable pressures, threatened disinheritance, refusing ever to receive his proposed bride or any offspring of the marriage. His own mother set the seal upon the rigid rulings of their caste by supporting her husband. It would have taken a profound and overwhelming love indeed to have stood firm against such assaults.

It was, happily, just such a love.

The young nabob, the uncrowned emperor, married the girl of his choice – and was, as had been promised, deprived of his empire, blackballed from his club, cut dead by the small and tightly-knit society that ruled India. On their honeymoon journey to England, the bride and groom were not received at St Gawes Manor, nor at the family's Town mansion in Mayfair. Only once did the disgraced son see his mother: she passed him in her carriage in Upper Brook Street – and looked the other way.

Nick told this dreadful tale without any malice; and his voice took on a note of pride when he told how the couple had returned to India to carve out a new life for themselves. Colin Pendennis, for whom the suave hand of nepotism had formerly smoothed all paths, who had never needed to struggle, whose family name and riches had always opened every door, went out and sought employment. Starting as an overseer in a tea plantation (a post scarcely better than the sort usually reserved for natives), he worked his way to the position of manager, where his acumen and enterprise commended him to his seniors. While still a young man, he was promoted to the control of all the tea plantations in northern India. Eventually there was nothing for it but to make him a Director – once more – of the East India Company; for, by a supreme irony, it was, of course, the Company who held the monopoly of all the tea production of the sub-continent!

So it was that Colin Pendennis, raised to the position of uncrowned emperor by virtue of his family connections; then struck down for betraying the code of his caste; was brought again to the same high state by his own efforts. Moreover, his wife was at his side throughout it all; and by virtue of her character, gradually overcame the prejudices against her.

It was upon the birth of their son, their only child Nicholas, that Colin Pendennis's father relented at last. Nick was a baby when he first sailed to England to be shown to his grandparents. He later returned to attend boarding-school, staying with the Pendennises and his titled relations the Pitt-Jermyns during the short vacations.

At this point in his story, Nick's voice took on overtones of sadness, as when a melody changes from a major to a minor key. Attributing it to tiredness, I begged him to close his eyes and sleep for a while. He could tell me the rest of his tale the next day, I suggested.

He shook his head. Having come thus far, he said, there was nothing for it but to go on to the bitter end.

In a voice scarcely above a whisper he told me how, as a

schoolboy of fifteen, in England, he was summoned to the headmaster's study. Thinking he had been found out in some minor misdemeanour, he resigned himself to a reprimand – or, at worst, a caning. What matter? It was nearly the end of term, and his mother and father would be taking him down to Cornwall for the long vacation. There was the whole of the glorious summer ahead, to go riding out across the moor beyond St Gawes, to take his sailboat round the headland and fish for mackerel. His parents were already on their way from India; were due to dock in Southampton within the month . . .

There was to be no reprimand, no caning. The headmaster, after gently inviting him to sit down (in itself a sign that the interview was of an unusual sort), began what was clearly a carefully rehearsed delivery that was intended to prepare the hearer for some disturbing news. The schoolmaster's good intentions were entirely wasted; not all his verbal skills could shield the boy from one particle of the hurt in store. In the end, the man fell silent with mingled pity and embarrassment, while the boy fought to live up to the code of his age and class and not be seen to cry.

His mother and father were dead. Drowned at sea. Caught in the maw of a hurricane off the African coast, the East Indiaman had been driven, dismasted and rudderless, upon a rocky outcrop. All but one boat was smashed to matchwood, and that boat offered the only chance of life for a tragically small number of the souls aboard the doomed transport, which was rapidly being broken upon the rocks. The ship's captain ordained that all the children and half the women – all the boat would hold – were to be rowed in the direction of the distant shore. Mrs Pendennis was among those chosen for that one chance of life. She declined the opportunity; preferring to remain with her husband and share his fate. Another woman took her place. And the boat reached a safe haven.

Quietly, Nick told how one of the survivors – she had been his mother's lady's maid – had seen them for the last time : the nabob and the poor clerk's daughter for whom he had defied the world standing on the poop deck of the dying ship, hand in hand, smiling into each other's eyes.

When he had finished, Nick's eyelids fluttered. Moments later, they were shut, and his breathing took on the regular rhythm of sleep. I smoothed his pillow and settled his eiderdown more comfortably. Then, after closing the shutters of the window, I left him and walked home to Malmaynes.

There followed nearly a week when I spent every morning at the Manor, arriving with the doctor, assisting him to dress Nick's wound, and afterwards sitting with the patient for an hour or two. In exchange for hearing his life story, I offered my own – which was a dull, sad tale in all conscience.

He appeared to have had no further communication from his fiancée: nor had it seemed necessary to him to write and tell her about his injury. If he did so, he said, she would only think it was worse than it was, and come rushing down to Cornwall, expecting to find him at death's door, and being furious to find that she had curtailed her stay in London unnecessarily. As ever, I marvelled at the oddness of their dispassionate betrothal.

Another betrothal was proceeding with a great deal more zest. Alice Witham and her Edgar were busy painting and refurbishing the cottage in which they were going to start their married life. Nick had generously given orders for the place to be furnished from top to bottom with items from the estate storehouse. He had also promised to provide his beloved phaeton for the wedding coach, and was giving them a present of a canteen of cutlery. Nor was Martin Revesby so absorbed in his work as to be insensible to the approaching nuptials. Over dinner one evening he asked me what I thought would be a suitable present for the bride – did I think that it would be in order for him to provide her with a wedding dress? I voted it a splendid gesture, and suggested that Mrs Gillis of Truro would make it beautifully. The following afternoon, Alice and I went in the village hackney coach to Truro, where at Mrs Gillis's emporium the delighted girl chose from the pattern book a dream dress in organdie and a chaplet of pink roses – she who had never worn shoes on her feet till coming to work at Malmaynes.

Alice lived with her father at a cottage on the Truro road, above the village; accordingly, since she had finished work for the day, she alighted from the carriage at her home. Her father – the notorious drunkard Ned Witham – came to the cottage door when he heard our arrival. A fine sight he looked, with his unkempt appearance and rheumy eyes. Small wonder, I thought, that Janey Pinner had been so eager to help get Alice married and out of his clutches.

When I arrived back at Malmaynes, there was a message for me from Dr Prescott. Nick had taken the fever, and would I join him at once at the patient's bedside?

Chapter Six

'I have bled his veins of six ounces,' said Dr Prescott, 'and the leeches will take away the morbid blood from around the wound.'

The patient was half-conscious and muttering in a delirium. His wound – now uncovered to our gaze – was surrounded by a wide area of inflammation that stretched from neck to breast. Circling the edge of the ragged line of stitches were twelve leeches, all attached to the tight, reddened skin.

'He was quite well this morning,' I said. 'Though he did seem to tire rather quickly.'

'He complained to the housekeeper when she brought him his midday gruel,' said the doctor. 'Happily, though a woman of limited intelligence, she sent a groom to fetch me immediately. I decided to summon Lady Amanda from London. She really should be at his side.'

'Is he in very grave danger?' I whispered.

The doctor pursed his lips. 'The morbid state of fever is undoubtedly a peril,' he said. 'And likely to remain so, for its very cause must always remain an unsolved mystery to medical science. I have administered a mixture of powdered nitre, carbonate of potash, a little antimonial wine and sweet spirits of nitre, which is the sovereign remedy for fevers of this kind – those which are brought about by the mortification of the tissues.'

We sat, one each side of the great bed, watching poor Nick in his crisis. I had prepared, at Dr Prescott's instructions, a warm poppy fomentation, to apply to the wound as soon as the diligent leeches, having gorged themselves, dropped off. From time to time I crossed over to the table by the window and re-lit the spirit stove under the pan containing the fomentation, to bring it again to the required heat.

Outside, it was nearly dusk. The world was winding down. Beyond the curve of the drive and the elegant, formal garden, I espied a line of women gleaning in a scythed cornfield; stooping forward, step by step, the last of the sun's rays casting their long shadows in front of them. Were they aware, as they laboured, that the young squire was battling for his life? And, if so, did they care? I thought they did, for I had observed the devotion with which Nick's servants and estate workers regarded him. In a sense, the women were giving testimony of that devotion by accepting, with diligence and humility, their perquisite of the gleanings, the ears of corn left behind by the reapers – the squire's gift to them.

Presently Dr Prescott said: 'The leeches have done their work, and I really think that the patient is past the worst of the crisis. We will now apply the poppy fomentation and cover up the wound.'

This we did. And I was greatly relieved to observe that indeed the deathly hue had gone from Nick's cheeks and that his breathing was less laboured, his feeble mutterings quietened.

At about eight o'clock Dr Prescott said that he felt safe to depart. I told him that I would stay the night at the Manor, and would he be so kind as to leave a message at Malmaynes to this effect on his way past, to which he gladly agreed.

When the doctor had gone, Nick's housekeeper brought me a bowl of excellent soup and a new-baked roll, which I devoured with much enjoyment. I then settled down in a comfortable armchair to keep vigil over my friend.

Alas for the vigil. I must have dozed off, for the chimes of midnight coming from a clock somewhere in the mansion brought me to with a start. Glancing across at Nick, I saw that he was not only fully conscious, but also smiling weakly at me.

'Hello, Cherry,' he murmured. 'Have I been a lot of trouble to you?'

'You've been very ill,' I told him. 'But, thanks to Dr Prescott's skill and the healing hand of Mother Nature, you are past the worst. Is there anything I can get for you?'

'Thank you, no. But you could talk to me, if you please.'

'Of course. What would you like me to talk about?'

'Anything you choose.'

'I'll try to think of something. Let me first make you quite comfortable.' And I crossed over to the bed; smoothed the coverlet and plumped the pillows. He looked down at my hands as I performed these small tasks, and then he laid his own on mine: they felt hot and feverish. He looked at me. What I saw in his eyes made me instantly withdraw my hands and clutch at the first stray thought that leapt to my mind.

'Do you know that, with the Stenographic Sound System, I can take down your words as quickly as you speak them?' I asked him.

'Cherry,' he began earnestly. 'There's something . . .'

'It has revolutionized journalism,' I went on. 'As you may well imagine, newspaper correspondents are now able to take down speeches verbatim, and do not have to rely upon their memories to supply a garbled version of what they have heard. And in the law courts . . .'

'Cherry, please listen to me.'

'In the law courts,' I said, 'it's now possible to have a true record of every item of evidence given orally. My Uncle Gervase, however, who is sometimes very cynical about his profession, says that there is not a judge yet born who possesses the intelligence and application to learn the Stenographic Sound Hand; so the judiciary will continue to write down the evidence in longhand for evermore.'

'Cherry, I think I am in love with you.'

I exhaled very slowly and looked down at my fingers, being surprised to see how steady they were; not a trace of a tremor.

I said: 'In the field of business and commerce, the full

potentials of the Stenographic Sound Hand have scarcely been explored . . .'

'The notion came to me quite suddenly,' he said. 'The third time we met. The day you came to tea here.'

'The clock had just struck five,' I said, without looking up. 'And you had remarked that it was time you returned to Lady Amanda.'

'By jove, you are absolutely right, Cherry!' he cried. 'That was the very moment that it first dawned on me. However did you guess?'

I smiled down at my fingers. 'You are a very transparent person, Nick. And I mean that kindly. Entirely without guile. I shall miss your company – and your friendship – very much.'

'Cherry! You can't mean . . .'

'You must realize, Nick,' I said gently, 'that after what you've just said, it's quite out of the question for us ever to meet again alone, while in company we shall revert to the formal politenesses of normal social contact. And you don't have to ask me why this has to be so.'

'You think me a cad, don't you? To make a declaration like that, when I'm engaged to another.'

'I think – I think it shouldn't have been said,' I replied. 'But I am willing to attribute your indiscretion to the fact that you are still rather feverish.'

'So I am forgiven?'

'Yes, you are forgiven. But the thing has been said, and cannot be unsaid.'

'So – in your own phrase – we must return to formal politeness? Our friendship is at an end?'

'Nick,' I said, 'you know that it must be so.'

'And we are never to be alone together again?'

'How can it be possible?' I cried.

'Who's going to nurse me till I'm well?' he demanded. And when I made a helpless gesture: 'Not my housekeeper Mrs Plant. Not any one of those ham-fisted wenches from below stairs. You can't condemn me to that. Friendship, though flown out of the window, leaves behind it some commitments, some responsibilities. Do you not agree?' He settled back in his pillows with a smug grin. I could have thrown something at him.

'Nicholas Pendennis!' I cried. 'You are meanly taking advantage of my sympathies. You are using your condition to serve your own ends. This is blackmail!'

'Guilty!' he declared smugly. 'I stand self-accused, self-denounced, self-convicted. And now I should like to have my punishment, which will be very pleasant. Talk to me. Tell me more about the Stenographic Sound Hand.'

The danger was past – for the time being. Behind the badinage, Nick knew very well that he had gone too far and had broken the delicate threads of platonic friendship which we had woven between us; but, by the way he had deftly smoothed over the subject with light talk, he had displayed a delicacy of tact and understanding that many, myself included, would scarcely have given him credit for possessing.

But I did not intend that my patient should get away with his punishment too lightly . . .

Reaching for my reticule, I said: 'I think I have adequately covered most aspects of the Stenographic Sound Hand in its practical uses. However, by a happy chance, I have with me my favourite book, which I will now proceed to read aloud to you till you go to sleep. Then, since it is clear that you are now out of danger, I will instruct Mrs Plant to have an occasional eye kept on you throughout the night, and will ask your coachman to drive me back to Malmaynes.

'The book is a collection of poems by Martin Revesby. It is entitled: *Reflections and Recollections*.'

Nick gave a groan, and shrank further down in bed.

Two days passed uneventfully. I continued to attend the patient in Dr Prescott's company every morning: assisting with the dressing of the wound and relaying to the housekeeper the doctor's instructions as to diet; but, disregarding the silent appeal in Nick's eyes, I departed with the physician.

On the third day, the sky fell in.

I had been to the Manor as usual. Nick was so far on

the way to recovery as to be able to get up and sit in an armchair in his bedroom, and Dr Prescott attributed the remarkable progress to the patient's excellent constitution and also to the fact of the fever, which, he explained, had brought out the mortification of the tissues and dispelled the evil humours from the blood.

It was towards three in the afternoon, and I was in the small sitting-room, transcribing Martin Revesby's work of the previous day. The love poem, which had suffered another check in its creation earlier in the week, was back in full flow; and was clearly mounting to a climax. The poet, it seemed, was steeling himself to declare his passion – but there was some impediment. It was this impediment – this barrier that stood between the lover and the declaration of his feelings – that most puzzled and intrigued me. Many times I mulled it over in my mind. Was there, perhaps, a great disparity in their ages – was she merely a girl and he a man well past his prime? Or was she so far exalted above him in the social scale that he – a beggar, perhaps, or a slave – was only able to gaze upon her, hopelessly, from afar? Maybe, I thought, he suffered some terrible physical affliction, such as blindness. On the other hand, it could be the object of his passions who suffered this condition. Whatever the impediment to the fulfilment of his desires, it was sufficient to reduce his images of the idyllic honeymoon they might one day spend to mere daydreams. I often wished that I dared to question the poet on this point; but it seemed an intolerable intrusion into the mind of the creative artist. Besides, the poem was clearly approaching its end – and I was certain that all would be made known in the final stanzas.

At three o'clock, I laid aside my work, as Challis entered the sitting-room.

'Lady Amanda Pitt-Jermyn and another lady, ma'am,' he announced.

I suffered a shock of wayward guilt, which I instantly quenched. What cause had I to feel guilty on account of Lady Amanda's susceptible fiancé? But my guilt was swiftly replaced by unease when I saw her ladyship's face: she looked furious.

'Good afternoon, Lady Amanda,' I said, agreeably enough, rising to greet her. 'Would you like some tea?'

'Thank you, no,' she replied coldly.

'Please sit down,' I said.

This she did; then, reluctantly, as if it hurt her to conform with the simple rules of civilized behaviour on this occasion, she indicated her companion: a plain lady of indeterminate age, dressed in dowdy brown. 'This is my cousin, the Honourable Miss Pitt-Jermyn, who has been chaperoning me in London.'

'How do you do, Miss Pitt-Jermyn,' I said.

'How do you do, Miss Carew,' replied the other, after a nervous glance in her cousin's direction. 'It is – er – quite mild for the time of the year, don't you think?'

'Very mild indeed,' I replied.

'Quite close, in fact. I declare I was all of a glow, on our way here from the Manor.'

'Indeed?' I said.

'We are not here, Cecilia,' snapped Lady Amanda, 'to discuss the weather.'

She glared hard at me as she said this. The gage had been thrown down. Useless for me to pretend any longer that I thought the visit to be of a sociable nature.

'Then what, may I ask, are you here about?' I asked mildly.

Her head went up, as if she was not used to being so boldly addressed by one of the lower orders. The violet eyes were as cold as chips of bottle glass.

'We are here,' she said icily, 'to discuss – certain *improprieties*.'

I think I did not show any sign of unease. 'Indeed?' I replied. 'Please go on.'

Lady Amanda fussily arranged the folds of an elaborate and richly-embroidered silk shawl that she wore about her shapely shoulders. This she did with all the air of a peahen preening herself. The dowdy cousin watched her with wistful envy.

'Summoned by electric telegraph by my fiancé's physician, Dr – I cannot recall his name – the vulgar person who was placed on my right when I dined here . . .' Her ladyship broke off.

'Dr Prescott,' I supplied.

'Summoned by this Dr Prescott, I hastened here, by express train, accompanied by my cousin as chaperon, and took up residence in the dower house in the Manor grounds – as is my habit.' Here she stared at me pointedly. 'I am very particular about the proprieties,' she added.

'It does you credit, Lady Amanda,' I murmured.

She acknowledged my small compliment with a slight inclination of her head, and resumed her tale: 'Upon visiting my fiancé in his sick room, accompanied by my cousin, I found that far from being at death's door – as represented by Dr Whatever-his-name in his electric telegraph message – Mr Pendennis was up and about.'

'With respect, Lady Amanda,' I corrected her, 'that is a slight exaggeration. When I saw your fiancé this morning, he had with some difficulty been assisted to a nearby armchair.'

Her head went up. Staring at me down her aristocratic nose, she reiterated: 'I found Mr Pendennis up and about. By that I mean his condition did not tally with that which had been represented to me by electric telegraph. For which I dropped everything and rushed down here by express train.'

'Dr Prescott summoned you some time during the afternoon,' I explained. 'By eight o'clock that same evening, your fiancé had passed through a very grave crisis and was beginning to mend. There was no assurance, however, that the fever would not recur. I don't suppose Dr Prescott – and certainly not I – thought it wise to cancel the summons to you.'

'I thought – and indeed I said as much to you, Amanda dear – that Nicky looked very poorly,' said the poor cousin.

Lady Amanda ignored her. 'I dropped everything and rushed down here,' she repeated, 'to find . . .'

'The process of dropping everything and rushing down

here by express train took you three whole days!' I snapped. 'During that time, your fiancé happily survived the danger of a recurring fever and is now well on the way to complete recovery. I would have thought that that was a matter for some rejoicing!'

Our eyes met and locked. Lips pursed and finely-chiselled nostrils quivering, she was breathing heavily. I, also, was breathing heavily. The air was charged with menace. The preliminary skirmishing was done; battle was about to be joined.

'And what of those three days when Mr Pendennis was – as you say – surviving the fever and becoming well on the way to complete recovery?' she demanded.

'I don't know what you mean,' I said, with less than the complete truth: her meaning was written all over her face.

'I think you know very well, miss,' she sneered.

I said: 'Lady Amanda, you spoke earlier of improprieties. Am I to suppose that you are implying improprieties between myself and your fiancé?'

'Can you deny it?' she said flatly.

I took a deep breath. 'Dr Prescott himself asked me to act as his nursing assistant,' I said. 'And I agreed without hesitation.'

'You were also present in my fiancé's room on other occasions,' she said. 'When the doctor was not present. One evening, you were there till gone midnight! Is that propriety?'

I said: 'But that was the night that Nick . . .'

'*Mr Pendennis,* if you please!' she cried. 'You will not refer to him informally in my presence. I have, from the first, found your assumption of an intimacy with my fiancé most offensive!'

Stung to hurt indignation, I cried: 'There has been a platonic friendship between your fiancé and me – nothing else!'

She pointed an accusing, gloved finger at me. A diamond bracelet on her wrist glittered in the shifting light from the leaded windows.

'In the course of this friendship – this *platonic* friendship,' she sneered, 'do you allege that nothing has been said or done by either party, that could be construed as *unsuitable conduct* between a betrothed man and a person of the opposite sex?'

I hesitated.

'Unsuitable conduct'? How far was it 'unsuitable' for Nick to have made a declaration of love for me . . .?

'Well?' demanded Lady Amanda.

'Have you questioned your fiancé on this matter?' I asked.

Her violet eyes widened with a glare of savage triumph. 'So!' she cried. 'You are being evasive with me. I suppose you fear that Mr Pendennis may have told all, and revealed you for what you are!'

I leapt to my feet, all control gone. 'How *dare* you?' I cried. 'How dare you sit there, accusing me of impropriety, of an assumption of intimacy, as you put it, when you, yourself, have made poor Nick's life a sheer misery with your own blatant impropriety? You and your shameless oglings, your humbugging lies about your late father the patron of the arts and all the rest of the shabby subterfuges you got up to, as part of your absurd and undignified schoolgirl infatuation with a man who, by artistic sensibility, by intellectual stature – as by every other yardstick save that of so-called aristocratic breeding and the possession of a hollow title – dwarfs you into insignificance!'

'Du-dear me!' exclaimed the Honourable Miss Pitt-Jermyn, mouth agape.

Lady Amanda rose, palely, slowly and sedately – like boiling milk.

'How dare you?' she cried. 'How *dare* you call me "undignified"?'

I was not to be put down. Righteous indignation had rid me of any notions about the deference that should be paid to personages of noble blood.

'Mr Revesby would laugh at you,' I taunted, 'if he but heard of the painted ceiling in your ancestral home, which your art-loving parent and his friends riddled with pistol balls!'

We faced each other, arms akimbo, both. I have seen fish-wives on Poltewan quay facing up to each other so – and generally about some man.

'In more enlightened days, I would have had you horse-whipped!' she shouted.

'Mr Alfred Tennyson indeed,' I jeered. 'And Mr Charles Dickens! A fine literary hostess they would find *you*! With what high-flown literary tittle-tattle would you beguile them, I wonder? With the advantages and disadvantages of a martingale and a snaffle bit, and the price of horseflesh at Newmarket this year?'

'You are insolent!' she screeched, in a most unladylike manner. 'Insolent!'

'What do you know of Gainsboroughs and Reynoldses?' I demanded. 'Or of anything but a mindless devotion to horses, French millinery, Town houses in Mayfair and Knights-bridge, pheasant-shooting in Suffolk, salmon-fishing in Scot-land, and all the mindless, idle, time-wasting obsessions of your breed? What hope do you think you have with a man like Martin Revesby?'

At that she became very calm, and eyed me with a cold assurance that caused my fury to evaporate, leaving me un-sure of myself.

'I knew it,' she declared complacently. 'I knew, right from the first, that you had set your cap at Martin!'

'What did you say?' I cried, aghast.

'I think,' said the Honourable Miss Pitt-Jermyn, 'that we should leave now, Amanda dear. It is beginning to look like rain.'

I stared, dumbstruck, at Lady Amanda. Her mouth was set in a prim line, and her whole expression was that of someone who has been completely vindicated, whose views have been put to the test and found to be correct. She took up her umbrella.

'I know your cheap sort, miss,' she said. 'Servants with a thin veneer of gentility. Women desperate to escape poverty and spinsterhood. Some of you describe yourselves as "act-resses" – low creatures of the common music halls who prey upon gentlemen who should know better. I have a cousin who was trapped by such a creature. Do you remember, Cecilia?'

'Cousin Arthur,' supplied the Honourable Miss Pitt-Jermyn. 'The family hurried him away to Australia with his new bride. I recall she drank stout at the wedding reception. And it rained all that day.'

I continued to stare at Lady Amanda; incapable of any coherent thought.

She said: 'Even if you had not declared your feelings just now in such a shameless and blatant manner, I would have known. It was obvious during the dinner-party. Everyone must have noticed, and commented. The way you contrived to give the impression of – how would *you* put it? – a bond of artistic sensibility and intellectual stature that existed between you. But I was not gulled; I saw in you, miss, a poverty-stricken spinster on the make. An upper servant with an eye to the main chance. Well, miss, having set your cap at your master, and having – presumably – failed in that enterprise, you looked elsewhere. There, also, I assure you, you have failed. The platonic friendship – so called – between yourself and Mr Pendennis is at an end. I bid you good day. Come, Cecilia.'

Numbly I watched her sweep towards the door.

The Honourable Miss Pitt-Jermyn treated me to a nervous smile, and a nod. 'Such a pleasure to make your acquaintance, Miss Carew,' she said. 'A pity we have to rush away. The inclement weather, you know . . .'

'Cecilia!' snapped Lady Amanda from the door.

'Coming, Amanda dear.'

Was it true . . .?

Up in my room, locked against the world, I stared at my reflection in the mirror, searching my face; seeking it as a mirror of my inward self.

Lady Amanda's empty and hackneyed phrases – 'set your cap at your master, a poverty-stricken spinster on the make' – were of the kind that I had never thought to hear applied to myself, being alien, cheap, shoddy – qualities that I could not attach to the person I had known all my life; the self behind the face in the mirror; Charity Carew, spinster of the parish of Poltewan.

And yet, and yet . . .

Was there not some truth in what she had said? Was it not true that I had hero-worshipped the poet Martin Revesby from the very first when, after buying his first slim volume of verse at the bookshop in St Errol, I had fallen in love with the images that his lines conjured up in my imagination? Had I not sought his acquaintance by writing to him like any lovesick schoolgirl who worships an actor, a singer, a famous hero? And, having received a courteous reply, had I not persisted in the correspondence, closing my mind to the implications of his tardy responses, to the letters that had been dutifully penned by his secretary? And the offer of employment as his secretary: had I not accepted it without a second thought, because it was the thing I most wanted to do in the whole world?

'Set your cap at your master' – on reflection, the alien phrase began to sound uncomfortably like the truth.

I am a candid person, I tell myself. Able to face up squarely to unpalatable facts about myself: as, for instance, that my mouth is too big, my hair unmanageable, that I do not suffer fools gladly, and – contradicting my name – am a mite uncharitable. I have to say, however, that I shied like a nervous palfrey from the prospect of examining myself on the charge of being 'a poverty-stricken spinster on the make'.

I was poor, having no fortune of my own, nor any prospect of inheritance. Uncle Gervase was my only relation, and he, poor dear, had almost literally drunk away his slender patrimony. All that would be left on his demise – and, presumably, left to me – would be Rose Cottage, Poltewan. Mortgage included.

Being poor, then, was I looking for a husband to support me? I looked my reflection straight in the eye and answered that question aloud – 'Yes!' In so far as I am a normal, healthy woman, with none of your new-fangled notions about wanting to stand on equal footing with men (for I am shrewd enough to know that, as soon as we bring ourselves down to equality, *they* will speedily make us their inferiors!) I held then, as I have always held, that a woman's destiny is to be the prop and comfort of a good man, to bear his children, to make his home.

No, I did not want to eke out my life, and grow old and alone, as a practitioner of the Stenographic Sound Hand. I wanted to love and to be loved. And to wed the man of my choice. And if that made me 'a poverty-stricken spinster on the make', then Lady Amanda was a better judge than I had thought.

But – Martin Revesby? Had I already – and certainly unknowingly – chosen him? Was I in love with him?

I recalled three occasions. The first, our first meeting, in the library. He had been everything I had imagined: handsome, distinguished-looking, brilliant in speech and modest in manner.

A second occasion: the evening of the formal dinner-party, when, while waiting the arrival of the guests, we had toasted the success of *The Saga of Love and Death*, and our eyes had met over the rims of our glasses. I had been greatly affected by the incident – more so than I had chosen to accept at the time, or immediately afterwards. In the light of my self-examination, it took on a new significance.

The third occasion which I remembered with a startling vividness was that on which Martin Revesby had summoned me to hear his first reading of the newly-written verses of the love poem: the verses concerning the lover's marriage to the unknown lady, and of their idyllic honeymoon. The verses had transported me into a mental state that could only be described as ecstatic. Had it been the power of the artistry? Or, in light of what I was now considering, had it been because – all unknowingly – I saw myself playing the role of the secret lady, with Martin Revesby the lover?

Throughout the late afternoon, I meditated upon my feelings and searched my inner self. At the end of it, I remembered Uncle Gervase telling me of a contrivance by which, under Scottish law, an accused person can be dismissed from a case with a cloud of guilt still hanging over him, by the verdict of 'Not Proven'.

As to the matter of whether the accused Charity Carew was a poverty-stricken spinster on the make, I had in candour to deliver the verdict, 'Guilty'. On the charge of setting her cap at her master: similarly, 'Guilty'. But whether the accused was in love with Martin Revesby: only the verdict 'Not Proven' could truly be said to fit the evidence.

That night, as usual, I dined with Martin (significantly, it was from that very day that I began to call him in my own mind by his given name). Watching him in the candlelight – that intelligent, mobile face, those eloquent hands, his manner of stopping in mid-sentence during some elaborate artistic dissertation to make a disarmingly commonplace observation, his total charm of manner – all those things brought me to the conclusion that the Scots' verdict would have to be amended in my case, to: 'Not Proven – but Likely'.

As for Lady Amanda, it was my guess that our painful interview would go a long way towards ridding her of her infatuation for Martin!

The next three weeks passed quickly and without alarm. The murder seemed almost forgotten: leastways, no one at Malmaynes, nor such of the local tradesmen with whom I came into contact, any longer referred to it. As for Sergeant Buller, he seemed to have vanished from the face of the earth; gossip had it that, having failed to make any headway with his enquiries, he had been recalled to Truro in disgrace, and that the hunt for the unknown woman's killer had shifted to another part of the duchy.

All the local talk was of Nick Pendennis's brave action in Truro market. There was mention of a petition being got up to send to the Queen, requesting that he be rewarded by some form of decoration. I never saw any such petition, and would certainly have added my own name if I had. Further gossip relating to the inmates of St Gawes Manor had it that Lady Amanda and her plain spinster cousin were to be seen out in a victoria daily with Nick; he with his left arm in a sling and his face still rather pale. I never saw them, and would have been greatly embarrassed to have done so.

Alice Witham's wedding being set for the first day of November, I went with her to Truro on the Tuesday of that week to collect her wedding gown and my own blue day dress. We drove there through a violent rainstorm, but the skies were patchworked blue by the time the village hackney coach rattled through the market place; and I shuddered to see again the fateful spot where Nick had tackled the Dewaine bull.

Alice looked enchanting in her gown. In the short time she had been working at Malmaynes, thanks to regular nourishment, she had filled out amazingly; no longer the starveling waif I had espied at the other side of the drystone wall, but a very picture of newly-blossomed womanhood. Mrs Gillis, who was proud of her handiwork and delighted to have it so well displayed, declared that she had never seen a bride looking lovelier, and promised that the sun would certainly shine upon her on Saturday. Alice, overcome by the wonder of it all, cried a little upon my shoulder and said she owed everything to me – a sentiment of which I was quite unable to rid her.

After the bridal gown, came the anticlimax of my own costume: the pale blue day dress with the dolman jacket which I was to wear at the wedding. Anticlimax it may have been, in a relative way of speaking; but when I looked at myself in the pier glass, I had to admit that I had never looked better. And I had the wayward thought that, surely, I had read somewhere that women in love grow in attractiveness. I put the thought firmly out of my mind.

The sun shone on our return to St Gawes, with the two big dress boxes on the seat before us, Alice chattering all the way about how she and her Edgar had done up the cottage so that it was like new. And Mr Pendennis had ordered his groom Dickon to bring the phaeton at a quarter to eleven, she told me, to pick up her father and herself. Mr Pendennis would have driven them to church himself, she added, but for his injury.

At the mention of Alice's father, and remembering that he would be giving her away, I resolved to have a tactful word with Witham *père* in the hope of concentrating his mind upon his responsibilities in the forthcoming nuptials. Accordingly, when we reached her home, I used the pretext of helping her with the dress box to enter the cottage and confront Ned Witham.

He was somewhat the worse for drink, but quite amiable with it, rising from his chair by the fire and swaying back and forth with a grin on his flushed face.

'Good day to you, ma'am,' he said, touching his forelock with a knuckle. ''Tis a fine thing you have done for my little lass, and I am glad of this opportunity to thank you.'

'You are very kind, Mr Witham,' I said smoothly. And to the girl: 'Alice, I should advise you to take your gown upstairs and hang it up immediately.'

'Yes'm,' said the girl. And, with a dubious glance at her father and another at me, she mounted the narrow steps to the upper floor of the cottage.

'Yes, ma'am,' said Witham. ''Tis a crying shame that her mother, my dear lady wife, is not alive to see her little one wed off, that it is.' And he dabbed a rheumy eye.

'But you will be there, Mr Witham,' I said brightly. 'And you will have to do duty for both. And be a credit to Alice, as she has brought credit to you.'

His face took on a slyness. 'Say no more, ma'am,' he said. 'Say no more. I am a sinner, ma'am. Weakness of spirit has led me away from righteousness. But there'll be none o' that on the day o' my little girl's wedding, that I promise you, ma'am. Not a drop shall touch my lips, as God is my judge. Not a drop, ma'am.'

'I am glad to hear it,' I said tartly.

'Not only weakness of spirit has led me away from righteousness, ma'am,' he said. And one rheumy eye was regarding me searchingly, the other being closed. 'It were twenty-one year ago, come next May twenty-third, that my dear sister Emily were foully done to death by – ' he jerked his head towards the direction of the village – 'him as we don't speak of by name. That deed, it laid a great weight o' misery on my spirit, ma'am. Such a sister she was – as fine and fair a lass as ever walked this earth – that I have never got over it, ma'am.'

'It was very tragic,' I said, feeling the inadequacy of the comment.

'Should have been strangled at birth, ma'am!' he cried. 'He were a monster. And that woman as bore him – that Edith Pendark – she knew it better than any. Did his own mother not lock him up in the time o' the full moon, when he became like a wild animal? Edith Pendark knew the evil that was in the brute. Yet she hid it from the world. Would have everybody think that he were but a little soft in the head.'

'It was a terrible business,' I said.

'I rejoice to hear you say that, ma'am,' he said. 'For it shows that you have a generous heart. Ah, you should have known our Emily, ma'am. The finest lass who ever walked this earth. A saint, ma'am. A saint from heaven.'

'Very sad,' I murmured sympathetically. 'And now, Mr Witham, I really must be going . . .'

'Her grave,' he said. 'Emily's grave, ma'am. Now, me not being in work at the moment, I have little enough to keep a roof over my head and Alice's. None to spare for flowers for Emily's grave. And I fell to thinking only this afternoon – ' the searching eye flickered towards my reticule – 'how 't would be most fitting to have our Emily's grave decked with a few flowers on the day o' the wedding. And me not being of the gardening sort, I'd have to buy 'em in the village . . .'

I took out my purse and extracted a shilling, giving it into his eagerly extended hand.

'For flowers,' I said, knowing with a complete certainty that it would be spent on drink.

When I arrived back at Malmaynes, the sight of a letter from Uncle Gervase brought back to my mind the curiously disturbing detail I had heard from Ned Witham – how Pendark's mother had had to lock up her insane son during the period of full moon, a fact that I must remember to pass on to Uncle.

His letter was very brief, and contained only passing reference to the murders. To my amusement, he seemed to have taken up a lively interest in the campaign of the handsome widow Mrs Parnes; and – despite his earlier protestations – appeared to have developed an eagerness for his own success in the campaign.

How else to explain his postscript? '. . . my triumph over the gift of pears was short-lived. Today I hear that Madame has presented Arbuthnot with a bottle of her home-made parsnip wine. And it was not sent, but delivered by her own fair hand! A palpable hit for the Royal Navy!'

The Saturday of the wedding dawned with a clear sky that was too good to last. By nine, it had started to rain, and I began to fear that Mrs Gillis's promise of a sun to shine upon the happy bride was doomed to be an empty one. However, by the time I had breakfasted and made myself ready for the village hackney coach which was to call for me at half past ten (the bride and her father being due at the church at eleven), the sky was cloudy and blue in roughly equal proportions: anything could happen before eleven.

Martin had joined me for breakfast. Naturally, he was not attending the wedding; indeed, that morning was destined to be a notable occasion in the composing of the poem cycle: he had every hope of completing the final stanzas of the love lyric. His only problem, he told me, was to light upon a theme – an image – to bring the poem to a conclusion. Unable to be of the slightest assistance, I could only give him my heartfelt assurance that his muse would be bound to whisper a timely theme into his ear before the day was past. We parted company at the library door, and I went upstairs to change for the wedding – my heart lightened by having spent half an hour in the company of the man who played such an enigmatic role in my life.

Since Lady Amanda's denunciation, and my own self-examination, I had progressed no further in settling the matter of my feelings for Martin. But the new awareness of the possibility that I might be in love with him had heightened my sensibilities: to be in his company had become a heady and zestful experience, a time for covert glances when his eyes were averted from me, of speculation about his feelings for me, a growing awareness of my dependence upon him. And I only had to re-read the new poem to be almost convinced that I had, indeed, given my heart to its author.

Half past ten found me ready for departure to the church. The village coachman was right on time, and handed me into the vehicle, which he had polished and refurbished for the occasion. Janey Pinner and the other women travelled with me, having been given time off to witness the nuptials of their fellow-servant. It need scarcely be added that neither Mrs Challis nor her spouse were attending.

My companions, all in their Sunday best, with new ribbons and flowers in their bonnets, chattered gaily all the way to the church, through the gates of Malmaynes, down the winding lanes and past the silent cottages (all their inhabitants being gathered in the church or outside, waiting for the arrival of the bride). They spoke about village weddings gone by: of brides drawn to church on hay-carts and taken off with their new grooms by the same conveyance; of dancing and merrymaking far into the night; and strange rituals dating back to pagan times, such as the hanging of mistletoe over the newly-weds' porch, even the daubing of lambs' blood on the lintel – done for reasons that had long been forgotten.

And we came at last to St Gawes church; to the lychgate, with barefoot children perched up on high on its slated roof, the better to see the bride when she passed through; and the womenfolk gathered for the first sight of Alice's fine wedding gown from Truro that had already become part of the folklore of the village, along with the hanging of the mistletoe and the daubing of the lambs' blood. A sudden peal of bells from the high steeple set rooks in flight from the surrounding ring of high trees, set them circling the graveyard, great wings flapping clumsily, harshly cawing.

Everyone stood aside to let me pass. There was much doffing of caps, touching of forelocks, bobbed curtsies – for was I not the representative of the local gentry, come to bestow the gentry's blessing upon the village nuptials? There were shy, winning smiles all around; and a little girl was pushed forward by her mother to present me with a posy of flowers that must have cost much time and effort the night before. I thanked the child and kissed her. Everyone looked very pleased.

Down the path to the church porch. Past the graves of the two murdered women. I noted that, in token of my contribution, half a dozen dog daisies were stuck forlornly in a jam jar before Emily Witham's headstone.

The Reverend Mr Josiah Murcher was in the porch, cassocked and surpliced. He nodded to me and murmured something in a low voice that I did not catch. His short-sighted eyes behind the pebble lenses swam over me vaguely. It occurred to me that he looked very ill.

They had mopped up the puddles of water from the aisle, but the ancient pillars were still streaked with mould. Not even the scrubbed, carbolic smell of the gathered congregation could mask the odour of decaying woodwork; but the font was piled high with the flowers and foliage of hedgerow and cottage garden, likewise the altar, and every speck of brassware had been polished till it shone like burnished gold.

A hundred pairs of eyes marked my progress down the aisle to where a verger in a rusty black cassock was gesturing to me and indicating a vacant seat in the front row of pews. I took my place. Moments later, a hand slid towards me, laying a prayer book opened at the page relating to the Marriage Service. I glanced round – and into the face of Sergeant Buller.

'Thank you,' I murmured, surprised.

He nodded, heavy face devoid of any expression.

A spinsterish-looking lady in a black bonnet, whom I took to be a Miss Pertwee, the village schoolteacher, was picking out a hesitant tune upon a small harmonium beyond the pulpit. The groom and his best man loomed largely before me: two bucolic lads in shiny navy blue suits and a lot of white neckcloth, each with a huge white dahlia and attendant fernery in his buttonhole, hair slicked down with macassar oil, great red hands hanging awkwardly, boots shined to mirror finish. I smiled at Edgar Portwell, and he bowed to me, blushing the colour of port wine.

A distant rumble of thunder sent a murmur running through the congregation. Through the windows on the northern side, the sky inland grew black. Dark shadows spread across the floor of the nave. Miss Pertwee's short-sighted eyes went closer to her music, and the notes faltered. Then the rain began.

Groom and best man muttered to each other, glancing anxiously towards the windows at the streaming world outside. It occurred to me to wonder if someone had had the forethought to provide an umbrella to protect Alice on her way from the lychgate. She would have a dry ride in the phaeton, which was fitted with a hood for raising in inclement weather. Alas, though, for the promise of sun to shine upon the happy bride.

Miss Pertwee came to the end of her music, and, after an anxious look towards the porch, she turned over the sheets and started again from the beginning. The thrumming of the rain on the roof above was joined in counterpoint by a steady drip, drip on the flagstones of the aisle nearby. I gave an involuntary shudder and buttoned my dolman to the neck.

Sergeant Buller stirred at my side. Glancing, I saw him take out a large brass timepiece and stare down at it. He looked round and met my eye.

'Gone ten minutes after eleven,' he murmured.

'They're probably waiting for the rain to give over before they set off,' I suggested.

He nodded, put back the watch in his waistcoat pocket. A concerted buzz of comment from the congregation seemed to end on a note of mutual reassurance: they, it seemed, had all come to the same conclusion as I.

Miss Pertwee, lost in the intricacies of a difficult passage, allowed it to straggle away into silence, turned over the page and started another tune. The best man whispered something in the ear of the groom that made him smile and nod. An atmosphere of relaxation, of patient waiting, settled over us. People began to talk quietly among themselves.

'How are you keeping, ma'am?' murmured Sergeant Buller.

'Well enough, thank you,' I replied. 'I trust you also are well. I heard that you had left us for good.'

'Not for good, ma'am,' came the reply. 'Oh no. There's still much to be done here. But I've had to go away for a while.'

'Ah yes.' I nodded. He had given me the distinct impression that I was being given the opportunity to ask a leading question. Something prompted me to try him a little further.

'Yes,' he said. 'My enquiries on this case have taken me quite far afield.'

'All over Cornwall?' I ventured.

'Ah, further, ma'am. Much further.'

'To London, perhaps?'

'Further than London, ma'am. Abroad. To foreign parts.'

'Indeed?' I said, impressed. 'To where, pray?'

'To Paris, ma'am.'

'Ah!' I exclaimed dutifully.

The stern glance was bent towards me, and the eyes were searching; nevertheless I seemed to detect an air of indulgence in his manner, as of a schoolmaster who is giving a lesson to his prize pupil.

'Now, ma'am. Why do you suppose I have been to Paris?' he asked.

I had the reply for that. 'To enquire into the identity of the woman who was murdered here, perhaps?' I answered. 'You told me her clothes were all bought in Paris. Presumably you hoped to be able to trace her by means of the dressmakers' labels.'

He attempted one of his rare smiles, but it never materialized beyond the beginnings of a rictus grin. 'By heaven, ma'am,' he said, 'Mr Revesby was right when he said you had a wise head on your shoulders. He was indeed.'

'It did not require any particular mental agility to come to that conclusion,' I said, carefully making no mention of the fact that I had been prompted in the matter by a remark that Uncle Gervase had made in one of his letters. 'And was your visit successful, pray?'

'In the strictest confidence, I may tell you that it was not totally without success, ma'am,' he replied enigmatically.

'I see,' I replied. He had turned his head away from me. At this tantalizing juncture, it seemed, the teacher had finished his lesson for the day.

I do not know for sure, since memory is a fickle thing that selects inconsequential details and quite obliterates some essentials, but I think it was very shortly after that I became aware – and it is probable that everyone present in that dank, overcrowded little church became aware – of a strange atmosphere that had, all unsuspected and unnoticed, settled among us.

An atmosphere of *unease* . . .

It manifested itself at first in a most intense silence – as when people strain their ears far beyond the limits of hearing for the vestige of a distant sound. The woman sitting behind me had a hoarse way of breathing. In that special silence, all around her became aware of it. She became aware of it: so she held her breath, the better to hear.

The sound of Sergeant Buller groping in his waistcoat pocket to bring out his timepiece sounded intolerably loud. So did the snick of the brass cover, as he opened it to disclose its face.

He held it before me so that I should see the time: half past eleven, gone.

The rain was still coming down, but not with the same pelting violence; it had settled into a steady downpour that looked to be set in for the rest of the day – typical Cornish rain. The groom and best man, after a muttered consultation, set off down the aisle towards the porch, where the

Rector was still waiting. They walked swiftly, hobnailed boots clattering loudly on the flagstones. I heard their mumbled voices and the deep bray of the clergyman.

Somewhere at the other side of the nave from me, a woman began to sob quietly.

'Pardon me, ma'am.' Taking up his tall hat from the floor, Sergeant Buller carefully edged his way in front of me, bobbed a bow towards the altar, and walked swiftly to join the other men in the porch. This brought a hubbub of excited comment – instantly quenched – from the congregation.

The verger also went down to the porch. From this vantage point he was able to whisper information to those in the back rows: small gobbets of news that were passed forward, mouth by mouth, to us in the front pews.

'Edgar says he'll give her another five minutes, then he be off to fetch her.'

'The best man have gone down to wait by the lychgate.'

'Edgar have gone to join he there.'

'Rector he ain't looking any too pleased.'

And then: *'She be coming!'*

We all heard it in the sudden silence that followed the cry: the distant clip-clop of two horses trotting in unison and the rumble of iron tyres on cobblestones.

A sigh of relief rose from the congregation as the horses' hooves came ever closer. There was a shrill neigh. The trotting ceased abruptly – as if the driver had reined-in with considerable suddenness. Another loud and frightened neigh: someone was having trouble with the horses; one could almost see them rearing up, those two mettlesome blacks, eyes wild, mouths a-lather.

Silence . . .

And then, from out in the rain, somewhere at the end of the path through the churchyard, past the graves of the murdered women and beyond the lychgate there came a cry the like of which I had never before heard and would give a piece of my life never to hear again: the primitive cry of a man in anguish; torn from the breast and howled to the treetops; full-throated, continuing; breaking, dying away in a keening wail.

I was far behind in the rush for the porch: they had little concern, then, about my place there as a representative of the gentry. I was roughly elbowed aside in the press through the doors. I saw the Reverend Murcher's domed head as he was carried along ahead of me down the rainswept path towards the lychgate, where the women in the forefront, who had passed through the gate, were already screaming.

I saw Nick Pendennis's treasured phaeton and pair. There was no sign of the driver, but the best man had the two blacks both in hand, standing at their heads, trying to soothe them. Between the shoulders of the two men ahead of me I caught a glimpse of Edgar Portwell the groom. He seemed to be kneeling on the ground. His face wore an expression of uncomprehending horror and disbelief. The figures closed about him, shutting him from my view.

Two of the men were half-pulling, half-dragging Alice's father from the phaeton. His head was lolling and his eyes shut, though he cursed them for their rough handling.

'Is he dead?' cried someone from behind me.

'Dead drunk, more like!' was the contemptuous response.

The tall bulk of Sergeant Buller loomed up before me. His hand was on my arm, trying to lead me away.

'What's happened?' I cried.

'Nothing you can do, ma'am,' he said. 'Come away, now. Best for you to come away.'

I broke from his grip and pushed past him; pushed past two others, nor cared when they reviled me for it. And what I saw will remain forever imprinted upon my mind.

Edgar Portwell was kneeling in the wet beside a slight figure lying in the gutter. The bedraggled crinoline of a white wedding gown was already soaked and soiled. One limp arm lay outstretched. The face, head and shoulders were – mercifully – covered by someone's coat.

Sergeant Buller took my arm again, and he led me away, unresisting.

'How?' I pleaded with him. 'How could it have . . .?'

'Someone found the means to do it,' he said. 'Somewhere betwixt her home and here, someone – some fiend – found the means to strangle the lass on her wedding morn!'

The last I saw of Edgar, he was impotently beating the wet cobblestones with his big, bunched fists and crying like a babe.

Chapter Seven

I did not return immediately to Malmaynes. Janey Pinner, who had been greatly attached to poor Alice, having regarded the motherless girl more in the light of a younger sister than a friend, was so stricken by the tragedy that I helped one of the other women to take her home. There I was drawn into the protracted ritual that follows a death or a funeral. Janey's elderly mother put a black kettle on the cottage fire and a large earthenware pot of tea was the outcome. Wet sat around a scrubbed table and talked in hushed, awed tones of the horror that had come among us; while from time to time the male members of the family rushed in with news from the outside.

It was late in the afternoon before I won free of the Pinner family and went back to Malmaynes in the village hackney coach. Martin was waiting for me at the porch when I alighted. I saw the figures of Mrs Challis and her husband in the shadows behind him. From their faces, I knew that they had heard of what had happened.

'Is it true?' demanded Martin. His face was shocked. Pale. 'One of the men from the village has just left the news at the kitchen door with Challis. But, surely, such a thing couldn't have happened. Not in broad daylight!'

'It's true enough,' I told him. 'Alice Witham is dead – strangled, like her aunt before her.'

I preceded him into the hall. There was a stack of six-foot logs blazing and crackling in the great fireplace, and I was instinctively drawn to its comforting warmth. I stretched out my hands towards the flames and closed my eyes. When I opened them again, Martin was giving me a brimming glass.

'Madeira,' he said. 'No arguments. Sip it down slowly. Don't speak any more of what's happened.'

'But I *must* speak of it!' I cried. 'Though I've gone through it a score of times in my mind, and aloud to the people down in the village, I have to tell you.' I searched his face, pale and brooding in the firelight and the shadow. 'Perhaps you, and only you, with your poet's insight, will be able to find some order, some reason, behind it all: be able to explain to me how anyone, however malignant and insane, could do such a thing. Could take a young girl in all her loveliness on her wedding morning and . . .'

'Sip your wine,' he said soothingly. 'Sip, and then tell me what happened. If I can offer any enlightenment, I shall. If not, I will share your burden of horror and bewilderment.'

I obeyed him. Over the rim of the wine glass, I could see the Challises lurking at the other side of the hall, well within earshot. I resented them, as intruders. And when I spoke to Martin again I kept my voice low.

Striving to control myself, deliberately sounding as matter-of-fact as I could, I said: 'Mr Pendennis's groom Dickon is the only one who knows anything of what happened, and that's little enough. It came about this way: Dickon rose early and prepared the phaeton and pair, which he then drove to the Withams' cottage on the Truro road, arriving there at a quarter to eleven as arranged. At about that same time, I was taking my seat in the church . . .' I felt my voice falter.

He nodded. 'Quite so. Please go on.'

'Alice was ready, but weeping. Her father was already the worse for drink, but nevertheless insisting on accompanying her to the church to give her away. Dickon comforted the girl as well as he was able, telling her that the drive in the fresh air would have her father as right as a trivet by the time they arrived at the church porch. Somewhat heartened, she assisted Dickon to help her father into the phaeton, and they set off. They had reached the top of the lane leading down into the village when there was a rumble of thunder and the sky began to darken.'

'I heard the thunder,' said Martin. 'And, shortly after, I had to light a whole battery of candles in the library.'

'The rain followed soon after,' I said. 'Dickon, who had hoped to deliver the bride to the church, in all her glory, in the open carriage for all to see . . .' My voice faltered again.

He laid a hand on my arm. 'Tomorrow,' he said gently. 'Unburden yourself tomorrow, when you have recovered from the worst of the shock.'

'I must finish telling you now,' I said. 'Please listen to me. I won't weaken again.'

He nodded. 'Please continue.'

I went on. 'The carriage was open, you see, but, with the rain coming down quite heavily, and like to get worse, Dickon pulled to a halt and got down in order to raise the hood. It was, he said, a little stiff.'

'Pardon my interrupting,' he said. 'But whereabouts in the lane did this take place?'

'I didn't have it from Dickon's own lips,' I explained, 'but I'm told he said he stopped the phaeton about half-way down the lane to the village, on a bend . . .' I stiffened with a sudden resentment, to hear a mutter of hurried conversation at the other side of the hall. The Challises had overheard and were making their own comments to each other.

Martin Revesby turned. 'Will you please be silent!' he called to them angrily. 'And if you cannot be silent, will you kindly go to your own quarters?'

The couple did not reply, but stayed where they were.

I said: 'Ned Witham was of no assistance to Dickon, having fallen into a drunken sleep; but Alice put aside her wedding bouquet and gave what aid she could. Dickon, it seems, was standing at the side of the phaeton, facing Alice, who remained in the carriage, and they were both struggling to raise the hood, while the rain continued to come down . . .'

He knew that the climax was coming. 'Yes?' he said. 'And?'

I had come to that part of the account which by reason of its terrible implications I most feared to tell – but tell it I must. So I continued:

'Dickon said that, Alice's face being directly before him, he instantly saw her change in expression when she saw someone approaching from behind his – Dickon's – back. Her eyes lit up, he said. She smiled, and remarked: "*Well, I shan't get too wet after all. Here's someone who'll help us, Dickon.*"'

'She said – that?' whispered Martin. 'Are you telling me that she saw . . .?'

'The face of her murderer!' I replied. 'And that is all anyone knows of it: next instant, Dickon was struck over the head from behind and knew nothing more till much later, when, having been found unconscious where he fell, he was carried down to the village and tended in the cottage of Police Constable Pannett.'

Martin's face, dramatically lit by the leaping flames, was a mask of compassion. 'And the tragic bride-to-be?' he asked.

I said: 'Half an hour later, or a little more, the bride-to-be was borne down to the village, through the streaming rain, in her bridal carriage, with the drunken sot of a father lolling beside her. Her bridegroom-to-be and his best man were waiting – anxious and distraught – under the shelter of the lych-gate. They saw the phaeton coming towards them, the horses with the reins flying free, uncontrolled. The best man, himself a skilled groom, leapt forward and, seizing a bridle, brought them to a halt.

'And then they found . . . they found . . .'

The wine glass fell from my trembling fingers and tinkled to fragments on the black granite hearth. Blinded by tears, I reached out for support and met the waiting arms of Martin Revesby. He pulled me close to him, pressed my face against his shoulder, stroked my hair.

I retired early to my room, hopeful of finding oblivion in sleep, but gravely doubting if my teeming mind would ever relax sufficiently to allow me that consolation. Martin had been wonderful: strengthening and reassuring me as best he was able; but, as I had known, even he could provide no easy answers to the terrible mysteries of life and death. On bidding me good night, he had pressed some sheets of verse into my hand: the end of the lyric love poem. Some good, at least, had come out of that dreadful day. Perhaps, I told myself as I made ready for bed, perhaps this is the answer: all life is like a piece of woven cloth, the warp and the weft made up of good and evil, of cruelty and loveliness. There is poetry, there is murder.

I resolved to let the verses be the last thing to occupy my mind before snuffing my candle. Accordingly, I settled back against my pillow and began to read, eager to know the outcome of the tender love story that had beguiled me through the weeks in which I had been transcribing the stanzas, and hopeful to learn that the lover had been able to overcome whatever mysterious impediment prevented him from declaring himself to the object of his passions.

I had not read more than two verses before it was apparent that Martin had quickly discovered his theme for the closing of the poem, and it was a theme in the minor key, a bittersweet ending and not the one for which I had hoped: the departure of the loved one upon a journey that might take her away from him for ever. I read on with growing concern, as he described that departure: the arrival of the coach which was to bear her away; her appearance as she descended the steps to the waiting conveyance; the very clothes she wore . . .

Minutes later, heart pounding, I was out of bed and relighting all the candles in the room. That done, I hastened to the tin box on my bureau and took out my brown paper folder with *Mr Martin Revesby, his work* written upon it, and separated the thirty or so sheets devoted to the lyrical love poem. These I laid on one side, while I took me a blank sheet of paper, on top of which I penned, in hurried capitals: THE EVIDENCE.

It was eight o'clock, give or take a quarter of an hour, when I commenced my careful task. It was past midnight, and the full moon shone like day through the cracks of the shutters, by the time I had filled my sheet of paper.

Putting down the pen, I regarded what I had written. A sudden and astounding revelation had been tested beyond all shadow of doubt. The evidence was all before me, and the dates and times confirmed by the calendar, also by the diary that I have scrupulously kept all my adult life.

The mystery lady of the poem, the unattainable she, was – *myself*!

The final clue was the description of my pale blue, lace-trimmed dress with the dolman jacket – the costume I had worn that morning on my departure for the church; that and the details of my leaving. The earlier evidence was scattered throughout the whole of the long poem – *and I had never noticed it*!

As to appearance, the eyes of the lady in the poem were described, variously, as 'brown', 'pansy-brown', 'softly melting brown': I have brown eyes. My chestnut hair was spoken of, no less than seven times, as having reddish lights in it. My nose – my retroussée nose – inspired the poet to tell of 'a tip-tilted elegance of witchery'. He drew a veil of discretion over my too-large mouth.

But it was the conjunction of dates, of times and places, of the very clothes I wore on various occasions, that fixed the truth of it. From my diary, I learned that I had worn my green wool on the day of the dinner-party when I had gathered flowers and foliage down on the greensward (where I had first met poor Alice Witham). The following day (the date noted by me on the corner of my copy manuscript), there were lines that ran:

My love with her nosegays of celandine and rue,
Lady Greensleeves . . .

In no less than five other instances was I able to cross-check, between poem and diary, some reference to my comings and goings and the garments I had worn, whether it was raining at the time, or fine. Taken singly, none of these instances stood out in an obvious manner – which was why

I had never had the slightest suspicion that it was I who was being written about. Nor was any single instance conclusive; it was only the sum total of the evidence which proved beyond all doubt . . . what?

That I was loved by one of the greatest of living poets!

There was no longer any question of sleep. The long night that stretched before me needed to be crammed with activity. I must cry my news from the rooftops. I wrote to Uncle Gervase. First I penned a sober and straightforward account of the tragic event of the day, omitting nothing and embellishing nothing – and this in the hope that his undoubtedly keen mind and what he called his 'legal nose' would seize upon some clue to the identity of the murderer. That done, I took a separate sheet and unburdened the secrets of my doubting heart – as I might have done to my own mother, had she lived. I told him of my attraction towards Martin Revesby and how I had not been able to make up my mind as to the depth and durability of that feeling: whether it was love for the man or hero-worship for the poet. I closed by telling him how my confusion was now all the greater for discovering that (unless the poem was a complete work of the imagination, in which I had been introduced merely as a lay figure – and that seemed scarcely likely) Martin was in love with me. How had that affected my own feelings with regard to him? I confessed that I scarcely knew. And I begged my uncle's advice as to what to do.

I had finished the letter and was about to seal it, when, glancing up, I caught the reflection of the shuttered window in the pier glass. Clear-edged, the almost full moon was etched in the crack of the shutters and moving slowly past.

A chill ran through me, as I seemed to hear the slurred voice of Ned Witham: '*Did his own mother not lock him up in the time of the full moon, when he became like a wild animal?*'

An hour or so of uneasy sleep served me badly for the trials of the following day – and they were to be many.

I decided that it was out of the question to pretend to Martin Revesby that I was any longer unaware of the poem's true meaning. Indeed, after re-reading the final stanzas a hundred times, I came to the utter conviction that the references to my pale blue dress and my departure in the coach were so free of any poetic circumlocution, so unequivocal, that he must have intended that I should at last recognize the unknown lady as myself. Accordingly, when I descended to the great hall at about eight o'clock, I took with me the folder containing the entire poem.

But – how to frame the words? How, I asked myself, could any woman say to a man: 'Mr Revesby, I have at last realized that you have glorified and idealized me in what must surely become acknowledged as one of the most beautiful poems in the English language. Am I to infer from this that you are in love with me?' I shrank from the very thought of it.

Better, I decided, to make no sweeping statement, but, if Martin was present at breakfast, to introduce the topic of the poem, to discuss it in detail – and to let the truth emerge between us.

As it happened, the emergence came about in an infinitely more dramatic manner.

I heard voices echoing in the great hall by the time I reached the landing above. Mrs Challis's and a man's voice that I thought I recognized.

Sergeant Buller's tall figure was silhouetted against the long windows looking out over the sea and the headland. He turned to face me when I reached the foot of the staircase.

'Good morning to you, ma'am. I hope you have much recovered from the terrible shock you experienced yesterday. A bad business, ma'am. A bad business indeed.'

I murmured something or other, and glanced to see that Mrs Challis was standing near the fireplace. Her hair was still in the single plait she must have worn in bed, and her ruined features stood out like a death mask from the dark panelling.

'The sergeant has called to question us all, ma'am,' she whispered, 'and I have sent Challis to summon Mr Revesby, who has not yet risen.'

'Not Miss Carew,' corrected the officer. 'I have no questions to put to Miss Carew. Though 'tis always pleasant to pass the time of day with you, ma'am,' he added with a touch of awkward gallantry. Then, addressing the other woman again: 'That'll be all, Mrs Challis. You may go now, thank you.'

The housekeeper shuffled out of the hall and closed the doors to the kitchen quarters behind her – all without so much as a backward glance.

I motioned Sergeant Buller to take a seat at the refectory table and sat opposite him, placing the folder containing the poem at my elbow.

I said: 'What questions are these that you're asking?'

His head went on one side and he eyed me quizzically. I realized that we were back in the role of teacher and favourite pupil.

'Now, ma'am,' he replied, 'what questions should I put to, say, Mr Revesby, to the Challises, to the fellow Jabez, that I would not be putting to you – nor to nigh on a hundred other folk in this village?'

'We – those of us in the church – were all under your eyes at the time Alice Witham was killed,' I said. 'The remainder, Mr Revesby and the others, will be asked what they were doing at that time.'

'Quite so, ma'am,' he replied. 'They will be asked to establish what we call an alibi.'

'That will not pose any great difficulty – not so far as the people in Malmaynes are concerned,' I said.

The large hands were clasped together, and he cracked the knuckles loudly. 'You will recall a recent conversation we had, ma'am. We arrived at a certain conclusion on that occasion, and the conclusion was this: that the person I am seeking could be anyone, man or woman, in the parish of St Gawes.'

'You think that the murderer of the unknown woman and poor Alice Witham's killer are one and the same?' I asked.

He spread his big hands. 'Can there really be any doubt, ma'am?'

I said: 'I suppose not. But, surely, as far as the people who remained behind in Malmaynes are concerned . . .'

A notebook appeared in his hand, and with it a pair of steel-rimmed spectacles, which he placed on the end of his nose, further adding to his schoolmasterly appearance.

'The man Challis,' he said, referring to the notebook, 'and his wife and the deaf-mute Jabez were all three together in the kitchen of this house between a quarter to eleven and eleven-fifteen o' the clock. This fact they all attest, the one supporting all the others, all three – including the deaf-mute Jabez, who ain't so soft in the head that he can't point to the hands of the kitchen clock and give an alibi for himself and the Challises by means of sign language and his infernal jabbering. So much for them: none of that three could have been in that lane at the time of the murder. Impossible. Quite impossible.' He looked at me over the top of his ridiculous spectacles. 'Not unless all three of 'em are lying.'

'And Mr Revesby, of course, was working in the library all morning,' I said. 'Almost certainly didn't stop for luncheon, and was working most of the afternoon.'

The sergeant slowly took off his spectacles and put them carefully back into a steel case, which he snapped shut noisily.

'Be that so, ma'am?' he asked mildly, reverting to the Cornish turn of phrase. 'Be that so, indeed?'

Stung to sudden irritation, I said: 'Oh, come, Sergeant. You can scarcely doubt what I am telling you!'

There was sorrow in those watchful eyes, sorrow for the promising pupil who had shown herself to be less promising than her teacher had thought. 'But surely, ma'am,' he said, 'you were not here to give alibi for Mr Revesby – as the other three were able to do for each other in the kitchen.'

'No, but . . .'

'And I must further tell you, ma'am – and this in view of the confidence there exists between us – that, if Mr Revesby does not offer the support of any other party, or parties, to attest to him being in the library of this house at the time of the murder, he will remain on my list of suspects, ma'am. Now, what do you think of that?' He sat back in the chair and regarded me, head on one side.

'Do you have many such suspects, Sergeant?' I demanded coldly.

'That I have, ma'am,' he replied. 'That I have.'

Inspiration had come flooding into my mind even as he had been speaking of the need of support for Martin Revesby's alibi. With it came a sudden nervousness, a breathlessness, and an inability to control a tremor of my nether lip as I said: 'I am able to offer you proof that Mr Revesby must have been working all morning and most of the afternoon.' And I opened the folder at my elbow, disclosing the pile of manuscript.

'What's that, ma'am?' he asked, puzzled.

'Poetry, Sergeant,' I replied. 'And the last four sheets, containing some hundred and twenty lines, were penned yesterday. And, as I have said, Mr Revesby could scarcely have found time for a mouthful to eat, let alone go out and commit a murder.'

'Poetry,' replied my companion lugubriously, 'may as likely be written on one day as another.'

'This particular piece was written yesterday,' I said with a conviction that I knew. 'As I am able to prove to you. Read this.' And I passed the sheets over to him.

Out came the spectacles again. He read quickly, eyes scanning the lines, lips occasionally mouthing the words. At the end of it, he laid the sheets aside and looked at me over the top of his lenses.

'Well, ma'am?' was his comment.

'You are a trained observer,' I said tartly. 'What did you observe in those lines.'

'I read a description of a costume which, if I am not mistaken, is the one you wore at the church yesterday, ma'am.'

'Excellent observation,' I said. 'And *that,* Sergeant, is your proof.'

'A costume is as likely to be worn on one day as another,' he said.

'Not the costume in question,' I declared triumphantly. '*That* costume never saw the light of day till I first wore it out yesterday morning at exactly half past ten – at which time, Mr Revesby must have observed me from the library window.'

My statement was greeted with silence. He regarded me for a few moments, then picked up the sheets again and scanned them through, one by one. Presently, he gave a sigh and laid them down again.

'I am not one for poetry and the like, ma'am,' he said. 'But the sentiments contained in these verses strike me as being very fine sentiments. Very fine indeed.'

'Your critical judgement does you justice, Sergeant,' I told him. 'And I ask you to consider this: in the middle of writing such verses, of expressing such sentiments, would a man find the heart – even supposing he had the time available – to break off and go out to strangle an innocent young girl on her wedding morn?'

'That he would not, ma'am!' replied Sergeant Buller without an instant's hesitation. 'No, indeed. 'Twould be out of the question. 'Twould not be in the nature of a human being.'

'Thank you, Sergeant. And thank you, Miss Carew.'

Martin Revesby's words – delivered in his deep, sonorous voice from near the foot of the staircase – made me turn my head with a start. My heart gave a lurch, as I wondered how long he had been standing there, and how much of our conversation he had overheard.

Falteringly, I said: 'The sergeant and I were discussing ...'

'You were discussing my alibi for yesterday morning, and an extremely commendable task you were making of it.' He came towards us, a bland smile on his lips. Neatly dressed in a dove-grey frock-coat and pantaloons, with his cheeks smooth of stubble, the master of Malmaynes had obviously not hurried himself unduly over rising and getting ready.

Sergeant Buller lumbered awkwardly to his feet. 'As a pure formality, sir,' he said, 'if you would indeed confirm that you were engaged upon this employment at the date and time in question.' He tapped the sheets of verse.

'"Engaged upon this employment."' The poet smiled with pure pleasure. 'A capital way of putting it, Sergeant! Yes, I was so engaged, from shortly before the time of Miss Carew's departure until about an hour before her return in the late afternoon.' As he spoke the last words, a shadow of compassion flitted across his expressive countenance and he looked towards me.

'Well then, sir, I will trouble you no further,' said the police officer, taking up his tall hat from where he had laid it beside his chair. 'I bid you a good day, ma'am. And you, sir. Pray don't bother to see me out – I know the way.'

He lumbered towards the archway leading out of the great hall. Arriving there, he slowed irresolutely, as if struggling with something in his mind. Then, stopping and turning to face us, he said:

'If it be not, as one might say, a presumption, sir and ma'am, I should like to take this opportunity of wishing well to all concerned. Indeed, while not desiring to overstep the bounds of propriety, I should like to express the wish that all will turn out in a manner as shall ensure the lifelong happiness of all concerned.'

Sergeant Buller had done better than merely to observe the detail of the pale blue lace-trimmed dress with the dolman jacket; he had grasped the burden of the poet's inner meaning.

We possessed no conveyance at Malmaynes, nor any coachman, so it was the village hackney coach, as ever, that had to be pressed into service to take us to Truro the following Monday.

In Truro, we sought out the principal jeweller's emporium the city boasted, and there, from innumerable trays of rings, I selected a diamond solitaire surrounded by a hoop of tiny garnets (my birth stone). We then retired to a nearby inn (not the same inn where Nick Pendennis and I had left his phaeton on a memorable occasion), where, in a private dining-room, we had a celebration luncheon and toasted our mutual future in the finest champagne the cellar could offer.

'Is it customary for poets to be so oblique in their courting?' I asked him. 'I declare that, but for the item of the pale blue dress and dolman, I would have gone on for ever transcribing the verses and trying to puzzle out the identity of the lady in question.'

'You are a goose,' he said. 'A darling goose. I was always led to believe that women knew instinctively about these things. The verses – well – they simply had to be written. Once I had become aware of my feelings, the turgid goings-on of poor Tristan and Iseult became of secondary importance. The lyrical love poem sprang instantly to mind.'

'I puzzled over the identity of the lady,' I said. 'But, even more, I think, I puzzled over the impediment . . .'

'The impediment!' He laughed shortly and drained his glass. 'Well, that's no longer a secret, is it, my dear?'

'Your age – oh, Martin!' I shook my head in bewilderment. 'The thought certainly crossed my mind that a disparity of ages might be the cause. But, in your case – why, to me you seem scarcely older than I. And in many ways younger – as men very often seem to women.'

'I am gratified to hear you say it, Cherry,' he declared. 'Though there are many who will murmur behind our backs that I have taken a young wife.'

I replied: 'Martin, there are many uncharitable folk who will say I married you for your money and your fame.'

'Little enough fame, as yet,' he said ruefully.

'There will be fame in plenty,' I promised him.

His hands reached across the table and took hold of mine. Our eyes met. It occurred to me, for the first time, that our brief courtship had been notably lacking in the sort of endearments that are encountered in the pages of the popular novels. On his formal declaration of his feelings towards me, immediately after the police sergeant's departure, Martin had taken my unresisting hand. On my acceptance of his proposal of marriage, which had immediately followed, chaste kisses had been exchanged. That was the sum of the demonstrations rendered one to the other, and I found it entirely proper and right – though in my imaginings I had always pictured exchanges of a more protracted and emotional nature between affianced persons.

As I saw it, ours was a coming together of two minds, of two completely attuned personalities. And yet, even as I told myself that this was the way of it, some maggot of perversity in my brain kept nagging at me that something was missing . . .

'What are you thinking, my dear?' he asked me.

I sought for a convincing fib, and found one. 'I am recalling that your conduct with Lady Amanda left quite a lot to be desired,' I said with mock severity.

He made a *moue*. 'I was flattered by her attentions and by her assumption of patronage,' he admitted. 'Ask me why, and I shall have to admit the truth of it: under the austere mask of the dedicated artist, I am also a tremendous snob.'

'There is something of a snob in the best of us,' I countered lightly.

'In my case,' he said, 'the snobbism is very highly developed. My upbringing, my early experiences of life – all these contributed to this end: I am simply incapable of resisting flattery from the daughter of an earl!'

He was smiling, there was a twinkle in his eye; but I detected something behind the façade of levity: a kind of sadness, like a background note played curiously off-key.

'Tell me about your upbringing and your early experiences, Martin,' I asked him.

The view from the window of the private dining-room looked out across the slated rooftops of Truro to the wide river estuary beyond, with the brown sails of the fishing-boats and white gulls wheeling in the steely sunlight of the dying year. Martin's thoughtful gaze was directed towards all that for so long that I thought he had misheard my question; till, by a slight glazing of his eye, I saw that he was near to tears, and my heart melted within me. I reached out and squeezed his hand.

'Don't speak of it if the subject hurts you, Martin,' I whispered.

He shrugged and smiled wryly. 'It hurts me little enough now,' he said. 'The cause of my early misfortunes – as with so many unfortunates – was partly due to a lack of family finances. That would have been bad enough, had not my dear mother, who made some claim to aristocratic lineage and was a walking encyclopædia on the genealogy of the nobility and landed gentry of the realm, conceived the notion from the very hour of my birth that her son should – as she put it – take his true place in the world. The Revesbys, you see, unlike our kinsmen the Tremaines, have been engaged in the lowly pursuit of trade for as long as anyone can remember; and my poor father was a particularly poor tradesman at that: a small-town grocer, so inept that it was said of him in Liskeard that Cyrus Revesby bought dear when goods were scarce and sold cheap when they were plentiful – and rejoiced that his shop was always full of customers.

'When I was seven, the bailiffs turned us out into the street, and there, but for the grudging charity of my mother's family, we would have starved. By the same grudging charity, I was provided with a schooling; and, when it became apparent that I had some ability as a scholar, family influence smoothed my admittance to Oxford, but without the means to keep body and soul together. Have you any notion, my dear Cherry, what it feels like – for a sensitive youth – to be detected in the act of wearing, at a Commemoration Ball, a pair of dancing pumps whose soles are patched with brown paper; or, at a party given by the President of his College to be caught slipping sandwiches into his pocket against a hungry morrow?'

'Poor Martin,' I murmured, so affected by his droll manner of telling the tragical comedy of his former poverty that I was somewhere betwixt laughter and tears.

He spread his hands. 'And there you have it, my dear,' he said. And now, by a swift change of mood, he was the complete droll. 'Given such humiliations, and influenced by my mother's reiterated assurances that – notwithstanding Mr Tennyson's naïve belief to the contrary – kind hearts count less than coronets and simple faith pales in comparison with Norman blood, is it to be wondered at that I positively dote on such things as titles and honours? To a person of my sensibilities, there is something very *reassuring* in being smiled upon by the daughter of an earl. It almost – but not quite – shuts out the recollection of the look on the President's wife's face when she saw me pocket the cucumber sandwich.'

I smiled. 'I think you are gulling me, Martin Revesby,' I declared. And then, more seriously: 'But I'm glad you've confided in me about your early hardships. It explains a lot.'

'What does it explain?' he asked. 'Apart from my fascination for Lady Amanda?'

I considered for a few moments. 'Your tremendous industry, for a start,' I said. 'Scarcely a day has passed since I came to Malmaynes when you haven't written. That suggests a tremendous discipline, a powerful driving force. Add to that, you really do hunger for fame, for honours. That decoration the Belgians gave you – you are very proud of it, for all that you speak of it with some disparagement.' I regarded him with head on one side, this man to whom I had that day promised myself – and liked what I saw. 'I really think, Martin, that the role of poet laureate, with a knighthood added, would suit you admirably.'

'Indeed it would,' said Martin. 'We must put the idea to Lady Amanda, to get her brother to whisper in the Queen's ear that I should succeed Tennyson.'

We both laughed.

I was to be a December bride. Martin would brook no delay, and I was of the same heart. Accordingly, we asked the Rector to publish the banns, and the wedding was set for Friday the 5th, at eleven o'clock.

Did I, at that time, see any conjunction between my own forthcoming nuptials and those of poor, tragic Alice Witham? I have searched my mind an uncounted number of times, but can recall no such impression. It is curious, however, that – without any deliberation – I avoided going to Mrs Gillis for my bridal gown, but went instead to a Miss Faversham of Penryn, the quality of whose work was completely unknown to me. In any event, within days of our engagement, there began a series of terrifying events in the parish of St Gawes that tended to push Alice's murder into the past: a reign of terror that forever afterwards was known as 'The Time of the Beast'.

It was the village milkman, calling before dawn, who brought news to the kitchen door of Malmaynes that a girl had been attacked the previous evening while walking alone through the village street. Her assailant had attempted to take her by the throat, but she had evaded his grasp and, having the good fortune to be fleet of foot, had run to the nearest cottage door and hammered for admission. The cottager, opening up to find himself enveloped in the arms of a hysterical girl, had glimpsed a dark figure flitting away into the distant shadows. Nothing more.

But – a shocking footnote to the account – later that night, many in the village had heard the sound of demoniacal laughter coming from the churchyard!

The second incident followed hard on the heels of the first. The morning after, Sergeant Buller called upon us to say that we need not expect Janey Pinner to arrive for work that day. It seemed that Janey, who slept on the ground floor of her parents' cottage, was awakened shortly after midnight by the sound of tapping on the window-pane. Thinking it to be her younger brother, who was something of a ne'er-do-well and given to staying out till the small hours, she opened up the window to admit him – and was instantly met by a pair of hands that leapt to her throat! As on the previous occasion, it was the intended victim's quickness and agility that saved her: Janey threw herself backwards, meanwhile slamming the window hard against the wrists of her attacker. She heard a bellow of pain. The deadly grip flew from her throat. When her family came, sleepy-eyed and alarmed, from their beds to see what was amiss, they were in time to hear the sound of running footfalls receding up the lane.

The sergeant's reason for bringing the news to Malmaynes (apart from his special pleasure, I am sure, in imparting the same to his 'favourite pupil') was to ask Martin if he would agree to enlist in a vigilance force, to augment the slender protection afforded by Police Constable Pannett and the sergeant himself. Naturally, Martin readily agreed, and that same night, armed with a stout blackthorn walking-stick, he set off on patrol with Challis. I had the distinct impression that the latter would have preferred the safety and comfort of his quarters; but he was urged into the enterprise by none other than his wife, who told him that only by such means would we all be able to rest easy without fear of being murdered in our beds. If I had any doubts remaining that Saul Pendark still lived, and that his continued existence was known to the woman who had borne him, they were entirely abandoned at that moment.

That night, I locked and bolted my bedroom door, as ever, adding the weight of the armchair and a leather trunk against it. It was quiet in the old dark mansion; not so much as the rustle of a dead leaf caught up the chimney, nor the scuttle of a mouse in the wainscotting. A long day of rain had died into windless, silent night. I could hear quite clearly the far-off sound of the waves breaking among the rocks below the cliff. Retiring quite early, I lay back in my pillows and gave myself over to serious and practical thoughts, such as: what would be the composition of the guest list for the wedding? Uncle Gervase, certainly. And an elderly maiden aunt who lived in Polperro – these two were the sum of my surviving relations. As to friends, there were three old schoolmates and another girl who had taken the Stenographic Sound Hand course with me. I supposed that Martin and I would jointly be inviting the St Gawes 'gentry': the doctor and his lady, the Rector and his – and, of course, Nick Pendennis and Lady Amanda . . .

I was speculating whether Lady A. would be likely to accept the invitation, or allow Nick to do likewise (and I had decided, on balance, that her curiosity would far outstrip her scruples, and that she would accept with alacrity), when I heard a peal of ghastly laughter coming from outside the window!

I chilled on the instant, with gooseflesh crawling upon the whole of my body.

Twice before, the sound had come to me: the first time, on my first night in Malmaynes, when it had echoed along the upper corridors; the second time, more briefly, in the hawthorn copse at the head of the beach. It was the same laugh, coming from somewhere down in the moonlit formal garden below my window. Even as my hands flew to my ears to shut out the awful sound, it died away in a throaty gurgle. Then there was silence.

The most resolute half of my mind dictated the will to throw aside the sheets and spring out of bed – while the other, weaker half screamed to me to stay. Leaving the candle on the bedside table, I crossed swiftly to the window and, lifting the catch of the shutters, cautiously opened one side a mere sliver – enough to permit me a glance down into the shadowed garden, where Jabez's prim rose-bushes stood in line beside their enclosing hedge of trimmed box.

A figure stood down there, close by the cliff edge!

The figure of a man, wrapped about in a dark cloak, with a tall hat set aslant. He appeared to be on the short side, but that could have been due to the high angle from which I was viewing him. His back was turned towards me, though I doubt if I could have seen his face if he had been looking my way, for the moonlight was casting a deep shadow from the hat brim. Likewise, the cloak threw a semi-circle of darkness about his feet. He stood, with feet all but protruding over the cliff's dizzy edge, head bowed, staring down into the breakers far below, the whole of his dark figure silhouetted against the surging white water. And while I watched in breathless horror, the apparition raised both arms from his sides, carrying the swaying folds of the cloak like the spread wings of a bat.

Once again, the insane laughter rose in the night. The

figure flourished its wings, flapping them as if to take flight. Numbed, shocked, baffled by horror, I could only shut my eyes and open my mouth in a scream that would not come.

When, later, I opened my eyes again, the clifftop was empty, as was the formal garden; just a row of well-tended rose-bushes and a line of box hedge in the light of a moon that was still nearly full. The apparition had gone on its way.

Next morning, I told myself it was all a nightmare: that I had drifted away while pondering upon our wedding guest-list, and had seen the apparition in the twilight places behind sleeping eyes.

Certainly the view from my window had a hard reality about it, with a greyness to the sky and a gusting of wind that bent the rose-bushes and set the box hedge swaying. The motion of the sea had increased and the crash of the breakers was like the booming of great drums. Far off, near the horizon, a small fleet of fishing boats went about their task with sails reefed almost to the bare poles. We were in for a storm.

Dressing warmly, with a thick shawl about my head and shoulders, I went downstairs and out of a side door leading from the passage to the kitchen quarters out into the formal garden. Fearful of Jabez, it was the first time I had ventured there. The wind took my skirts and teased out long strands of my unbound hair, buffeted my body, stung my cheeks icily. Bowing my head against the worst of it, I passed along the line of the box hedge, through a gap, and out towards the cliff edge.

I went as close to the edge as I dared; but it was a long stride from the very spot occupied by the phantom of my nightmare – or by the man in the cloak and the tall hat that I had witnessed with my wakeful eyes. Craning my head forward, bracing myself against any sudden, treacherous gust of wind that might have swept me over to destruction, I peered downwards.

The drop was completely sheer: a falling body could not have touched the smooth granite wall, for it inclined inwards.

Nothing would have impeded such a fall, till the body reached the maelstrom of rocks and white water at the foot. I shuddered at the sight of those rocks and their humpbacked spines, sharp-edged and glistening; now covered with a new inrush of breakers, now bared.

I turned with a start, to hear a soft footfall. Mrs Challis was standing behind me. She also wore a shawl over her head, and her sunken eyes were fixed on the awful scene below.

She said something; but the utterance was snatched away by the wind. I leaned closer to her. She pointed down into the abyss.

''Twas here he fell!' she cried above the roar of the growing gale. 'From the very spot where you were standing. My Saul. They who saw it do say that he threw up his arms and leapt out with a laugh on his lips!'

Martin had arrived back at Malmaynes in the early hours of the morning, he and Challis having been relieved in their patrol duties by other men of the parish. The vigilance force had kept the parish under surveillance the whole night through. Under their shield, no terror had stalked abroad and St Gawes had slept in peace.

Except for Charity Carew . . .

Martin slept till noon and joined me for luncheon. By that time, I had definitely decided to dismiss my experience as the figment of a nightmare – notwithstanding the unnerving aftermath on the cliff edge with Mrs Challis. So I said nothing of the occurrence to Martin. He, in his turn, was in good spirits and confident – as were his fellow members of the vigilance force, he told me – that their continued presence would dissuade the nocturnal marauder from any further activity.

How wrong they were!

News travels fast in a Cornish rural community, and never so fast as in times of crisis. During the days and nights that came to be known as 'The Time of the Beast', it was scarcely possible for a dog to bark or a cockerel to crow at an untimely hour without the news reaching the most far-flung hovel in double-quick time. Two evenings later, just as Martin and I were sitting down to dinner in the great hall, there was a disturbance from the direction of the kitchen quarters: voices raised in excitement, running footsteps in the passage.

'What's amiss out there?' cried Martin, turning. 'Go and enquire what's going on, Challis.'

Challis, who was serving at table, hastened to do his master's bidding. Moments later, he appeared at the door with a man in a caped coat whom we instantly recognized as the driver and owner of the village hackney coach. Staring-eyed, the newcomer fumbled nervously with the brim of his big waterproofed hat.

Challis said: ''Tis Tribble, sir. With terrible news from the Manor!'

'From the Manor?' Martin leapt to his feet.

Nick Pendennis! The name sprang instantly to my mind.

''Tis her ladyship, sir,' cried Tribble the coachman. 'I had the news just now in the lane. Sergeant Buller, he's on his way there now.'

'Her ladyship? You mean she's been attacked?' demanded Martin. 'Is she hurt?'

The coachman nodded frantically. 'So I do hear, sir,' he said. 'Nigh unto death, so they do say.'

Martin turned to me. 'I must go and see what's happened, Cherry,' he said. 'It may be that I can render some assistance.'

'I'll come with you, Martin,' I cried.

He nodded. 'Take us there with all speed, Tribble.'

'Right you are, sir!'

Out into the blustery night, with the large moon flitting in and out of the clouds that scudded past. There was rain in the air: it rattled against the ancient leatherwork of the coach, drummed like fingertips upon the roof. I huddled inside, close to Martin, my fingers entwined in his. Tribble cracked the whip, and we set off down the drive.

'I pray that we shall not arrive at the dower house to learn that another tragedy has taken place,' murmured

Martin, close by my ear.

I squeezed his hand, suddenly having a vision of a still figure lying in the rain, one white-clad arm outstretched . . .

Tribble was as good as his word: his aged hacks drew the coach to the Manor in fine style. As we passed the main building, we observed that every window was lit up on the ground floor and that the front doors had been left open.

The dower house, which lay some two furlongs further down the main drive, was a bijou copy of the Manor house itself, with columns in front and steps up. Every light in the place must have been blazing, and hurrying figures were to be seen passing to and fro behind the unshuttered windows. A saddled horse, which I recognized to be Nick's favourite black, was tethered at a mounting-block near the steps, and there also was a dog-cart bearing along its side the inscription: CORNISH CONSTABULARY. Sergeant Buller had arrived.

It was he who greeted us in the hallway, where he stood talking to the uniformed village constable.

'Good evening to you, sir and ma'am,' he cried. 'I am glad to see you.'

'We were told of this latest dastardly attack,' said Martin. 'It occurred to me that a widespread search should be made for the scoundrel.'

'Too late, I fear, sir,' replied Buller. ''Tis a pity that we did not institute a vigilance patrol in the Manor grounds and park, but, alas, our forces are too thin to be spread everywhere.'

'Lady Amanda, Sergeant,' I interposed. 'Is she . . .?'

'Thanks to the timely intervention of her gallant rescuer,' he replied, 'her ladyship has suffered no harm, ma'am.'

'Her gallant rescuer' – I thought of the horse tethered outside. So, once more, Nick Pendennis, by his splendid heroism, had saved life. What a marvellous man he was, to be sure.

'The bravery of that lady!' cried Police Constable Pannett. 'I would never have credited it, to look at her.'

Lady Amanda – brave? It sounded unlikely. Still, there was no accounting for the human spirit in times of stress. It seemed possible – just possible – that Lady Amanda might show a vestige of bravery in the defence of her own life, I thought uncharitably.

'Where and how did the attack take place, Sergeant?' demanded Martin. 'And how was the scoundrel thwarted in the execution of his intent?'

The sergeant indicated double doors behind him. 'In the drawing-room, sir,' he replied. 'If you will come this way, I will show you the evidence of the struggle and give you the opportunity of congratulating the rescuer.'

He opened the doors and stood aside to let us pass. The drawing-room of the Manor dower house was surprisingly large, covering, so it appeared, an entire half of the ground floor. It was furnished in the Louis XVI style, with lots of pretty gilt ornamentation, white panelling, and an ornate glass candelabrum. There was an acrid smell in the room that I did not immediately recognize – till I connected it with the shooting parties to which I had occasionally accompanied Uncle Gervase on the moors above St Errol.

'The smell of powder still lingers here,' said the sergeant. 'And there, sir and madame, is the evidence of the shot that was fired by the gallant rescuer.'

He pointed up to the ceiling, where, close by the chandelier (indeed, on a second glance, I could see that one of the crystal lustres had been severed from its attachment and lay shattered on the rug beneath), the moulded white plaster ceiling was pierced by a sizeable round hole, with a spider's web of cracks radiating from it.

'By heaven!' cried Martin. 'I am not an expert on such matters, but that looks a confoundedly large ball lodged up there.'

'It is indeed, sir,' confirmed the sergeant. He reached and took up a massive pistol lying on an occasional table nearby. 'It came from this horse pistol, which, fired by a steady hand, would have carried the very head from the shoulders of our villain.'

'I thank heaven I missed! Oh, how awful it would have been, to kill a man, however wicked!' A voice from the other side of the room.

'Permit me, sir and madame,' said Sergeant Buller, with the air of a man introducing a paradox, 'to present her ladyship's gallant rescuer – the Honourable Miss Pitt-Jermyn.'

I stared in surprise. Lady Amanda's mousey cousin was seated in a deep, button-back armchair by the far window. She had a large brandy glass in her hand and her face was flushed a bright pink. She beamed delightedly in my direction.

'Why, it's the very nice Miss Carew,' she said. 'How pleasant of you to call, to be sure. Do please take a seat. The weather continues changeable, don't you find?'

Sergeant Buller gazed at her indulgently. Clearly, the Honourable Miss Pitt-Jermyn had joined the ranks of his favourite pupils.

'I declare,' he said, 'that, but for this lady's timely intervention, her ladyship would have shared the fate of the others!'

'Most commendable conduct, ma'am,' said Martin gallantly. 'Might one enquire, if the telling of it will not distress you too much, how you effected the rescue?'

The Honourable Miss Pitt-Jermyn took a swift, birdlike sip from her brandy glass, the level of which sank a surprising amount. 'It was a dreadful experience for poor Amanda!' she cried. 'Truly awful!'

'Her ladyship is at present prostrate with shock,' murmured Buller to me, *sotto voce*. 'The doctor is administering sedatives, and her fiancé is trying to comfort her. I'm afraid her ladyship does not share her cousin's fortitude.'

The object of our attentions took another sip of her brandy and said: 'It happened shortly before dinner time, which would have been about seven o'clock. Dear Amanda came down to the drawing-room after dressing. I heard her pass my room and descend the stairs. A little later, her scream of terror from the drawing-room sent me hastening downstairs – having snatched up Nicky's pistol . . .'

'Ah, the pistol, ma'am,' interposed Buller. 'That was loaned to you by Mr Pendennis, was it not, for just such an emergency?'

'Indeed it was,' confirmed the other. 'He offered its pair to my cousin, but she shrank from even touching such a thing. I had no such scruples, thank heaven. Nicky loaded it for me and showed me how to cock the hammer, in order to bring it down upon the percussion cap – as he called it.'

'Just so, ma'am. Please continue. Our friends are most interested. What did you see from the door of this room?'

'The drawing-room was in darkness,' she said, 'save for a single candle burning – over there – ' pointing to a candlestick on a table by the window – 'by the light of which, I saw poor dear Amanda struggling in the grip of the villain.'

'You saw him clearly?' cried Martin.

'Not at all,' replied the Honourable Miss Pitt-Jermyn. 'Nor, I suspect, did poor Amanda, for I believe he was masked.'

'And then,' prompted Sergeant Buller. 'What was your next action, ma'am?'

'I cried out to him to desist,' said she. 'Then I presented the pistol and threatened that I was going to fire. At this, the monster sprang away from Amanda, who fell to the floor in a swoon. I saw him cross swiftly to the window. Whereupon I closed my eyes and pulled the trigger.'

'Would that you had kept your eyes open, ma'am!' ejaculated Martin.

'The force of the discharge knocked up my hand,' said the Honourable Miss Pitt-Jermyn. 'And the terrible smoke and confusion – as well as the blast of sound which quite deafened me – leaves a blank in my recollections. The next thing I recall is kneeling by poor Amanda, while servants came running with lamps. The window was wide open, and our butler was leaning out and staring into the night.'

'You are very brave, ma'am,' said the sergeant.

'You have covered yourself with glory, Miss Pitt-Jermyn,' smiled Martin admiringly.

She beamed, and hiccuped gently. 'I think I should like another tiny brandy,' she declared. 'Would you care for a brandy, Miss Carew – or you, gentlemen? I wonder, sir, would you please be so kind as to pull the bell-cord for a footman? So kind, so kind.' She leaned her head back against the chair, closed her eyes and beamed seraphically. 'I do hope that poor Amanda is feeling better,' she murmured. A few moments later, she was snoring quietly.

We crept out of the drawing-room and Sergeant Buller carefully closed the door behind us. Looking up at the sound of a footfall, I saw Nick Pendennis coming down the staircase. He wore a bottle-green riding coat. His face was drawn and serious, and he looked thinner and paler than I expected.

'How is her ladyship, sir?' asked the sergeant.

'Sleeping now,' replied Nick. He looked at me and bowed. Then, glancing at Martin, a spot of colour appeared on each of his cheekbones. 'Your servant, ma'am. Sir,' he added with stiff formality.

Sergeant Buller turned to Martin and said: 'I wonder, Mr Revesby, while you are here, if we could discuss plans for extending the scope and duties of the vigilance force?'

'Most certainly, Sergeant,' replied Martin.

'With your permission, sir and ma'am,' the sergeant nodded to Nick and me, and taking Martin by the elbow, led him away across the hall towards an open door, saying: 'Now, what I have in mind is to double the patrols between dusk and dawn . . .'

The door shut behind them. I looked at Nick. He looked at me.

'Hello, Nick,' I smiled at him. 'How are you?'

'Well enough, thanks,' he said ruefully. 'We've had our hands full with Amanda, Dr Prescott and I, but she's calmed down now, thank heaven. Must have been a terrible experience for her, poor girl! She's rather delicate in constitution, you know, though one could hardly credit it. How are you, Cherry – may I still continue to call you Cherry? I believe Revesby is to be congratulated upon winning the promise of your hand. Lucky devil.'

'You'll come to the wedding, Nick? It's in less than a month. You'll receive an invitation, you and Lady Amanda.'

'So soon? Yes, of course we shall come, and with the greatest of pleasure.' He stared at me gloomily.

I looked down at my fingers. 'It was a terrible thing – what happened tonight,' I said. 'What a blessing that Miss Pitt-Jermyn was at hand.'

Nick said: 'I know all about her visiting you – Amanda, I mean. And I think it was unspeakable of her. What's more, I told her so!'

'Please, Nick . . .' I whispered.

'The very idea of her accusing you, of all people, of any impropriety. By jove, Cherry, I can tell you that I gave her a piece of my mind. Furthermore, when she is recovered from the shock of tonight's business, Amanda is going to apologize to you. I've told her so in round terms!'

'Nick, I promise you that it doesn't matter,' I told him.

'I – I would like you two to be friends,' he said lamely.

'Of course, Nick,' I said.

He looked down at the toes of his highly-polished riding-out boots. 'She's a good sort, at heart,' he said. 'When we're married, I shall take her away from the Society whirl. India – that's the place. I intend to follow Father's footsteps and apply for a position in the Company service. I – I think Amanda will be happy in India. Confoundedly interesting country, India. Marvellous hunting there – tiger, leopard, wild boar. Deer. Gazelle. Cherry, you really are the most beautiful . . .'

'Nick! Please!' I said angrily.

There were voices approaching. The door opened again on Martin and Sergeant Buller.

'Well, I'm glad you agree with me on all that, sir,' said the latter. 'We'll put the new system into use tomorrow night. Ah, Mr Pendennis, before I go – if you could just confirm a couple of points, please.'

'Certainly.' Nick's glance slid reluctantly away from me.

'Concerning the pistol, sir – the one you lent to the Honourable Miss Pitt-Jermyn.'

'Mmmm?'

'Now, sir, it puzzles me that you should have lent a lady – I may say a somewhat frail lady – a horse pistol of such great power and calibre. Surely, sir, in your possession you have hand guns of lighter build?'

'Indeed I have,' replied Nick unconcernedly. 'I first thought to lend Miss Pitt-Jermyn a small under-and-over pocket pistol. But, on reflection, I decided that something which made a confounded good bang and flash would be more effective to scare off an intruder.'

'But – not do him any damage!' said the sergeant, with a keen and meaningful look. 'Since, in the hands of a lady – a somewhat frail lady – the recoil of such a weapon would throw the aim impossibly wild!'

Nick shrugged, and said: 'Seregant, I should tell you that Miss Pitt-Jermyn is as blind as a bat, and, in consequence of not wearing spectacles for reasons of vanity, could not, in my opinion, hit the side of a house at ten paces with the most accurate pistol made!'

'I see, sir.' The sergeant sounded disappointed. 'Well, gentlemen and ma'am, I will bid you all good night.' He took up his hat from the hall table and crossed to the door. There, he paused a moment – and turned.

'One last point, Mr Pendennis,' he said. 'I understand from the servants that you were immediately summoned, after the incident, by a boot-boy who ran to the Manor. But you were not to be found.'

'Quite correct,' replied Nick blandly. 'I had gone for an evening ride.'

'In which direction, sir?'

'Down the Truro road – in the Truro direction.'

'Away from the village?'

'That is so.'

'And you saw no one on the road?'

'Not a soul, Sergeant. I saw no one till, on arriving back here at about half past seven, I was greeted by my butler at the gates.'

'Thank you, Mr Pendennis,' said Sergeant Buller quietly. He bowed to us. 'Good night, all.' He was gone in a trice.

Martin and I exchanged brief farewells with Nick Pendennis, and I contrived not to give him my hand. It was bright moonlight outside as we took our places in the waiting hackney coach and Tribble flicked the bored horses into movement.

'Buller is nobody's fool,' said Martin. 'His new scheme for the vigilance force is bound to be a winner. The monstrous creature we are dealing with will certainly be apprehended by our fellows if he dares to venture abroad after tomorrow night.'

I gazed out of the coach window, at the moon flickering behind the bare, tall trees of a copse, past which we were moving. The moon was well on the wane: a large slice had disappeared from its right-hand side.

It occurred to me that it would be full again about the time of our wedding!

Chapter Eight

It may have been the waning of the moon, it may have been the efficaciousness of Sergeant Buller's new organization of the vigilance force, but the attack upon Lady Amanda spelt an effective end to 'The Time of the Beast'.

There were no more attacks; but two nights after, the crazed laughter was heard coming from the churchyard. No less than ten of the vigilance force, who were patrolling the village at the time, closed in on the spot, and others were speedily summoned to join them, including Sergeant Buller. The cordon of men, all armed with guns, stout walking-sticks and cudgels, carrying lanterns, and some with dogs, formed an impassable barrier to anyone attempting to break out of the churchyard. Wisely – since it would have been impossible to distinguish friend from foe in the darkness – the sergeant passed the word round the cordon to stay put and keep watch. All through the long night from the early hours till the frosty dawn, the men of St Gawes parish – Martin Revesby and Nick Pendennis included – remained at their posts behind the churchyard wall, staring into the shadows; imagining, no doubt, all manner of things among the gravestones, the sentinel cypresses and the dark yews – but seeing nothing.

At dawn, on the order from the sergeant, they took a firmer hold of their weapons, and, climbing the wall or passing in through the lychgate, they stepped forward through the frost-spangled grass.

The vigilance force met in the middle of the churchyard.

They had found nothing but each other!

I had been somewhat concerned about not hearing from Uncle Gervase, the more so because of the momentous news that I had imparted to him in my last letter. However, I presently received a reply from Poltewan, and the first paragraph explained Uncle's delay in replying.

My dear,

Anno Domini and a flagrant disregard for the Classical precept of Moderation in All Things have recently laid me low. Nothing to cause alarm, I hasten to assure you. A touch of bronchitis, coupled with a muttering of pleurisy, brought me abed last Thursday and I have not ventured forth since. A daily woman (a Mrs Stittle – a virago, but an honest one) tends to my needs, and La Belle Mme Parnes visits me never less than every other day, bearing gifts of exotic fruits and sweetmeats. I fear that I have taken a mightily unfair advantage of Capt. Arbuthnot – and a fig for his chances! Seriously, I beg you, dear Cherry, do not disaccommodate yourself by flying to my bedside, for my afflictions, though inconvenient and humiliating to a man of my temper, are not of the sort to lay me in the churchyard.

Of your terrible news concerning the foul murder of the little bride-to-be I cannot bring myself, at this time, to write (what is the modern world coming to? – *O tempora, O mores!*), but will do so when my strength returns.

Your revelations concerning Mr Revesby, and the lengthy postscript telling me that you are now affianced, fill me with great joy.

I have troubled myself, ever since you flew the nest to take up the position of Mr Revesby's secretary, to enquire into the origins and achievements of the gentleman in question, and have come up with nothing but excellence in all respects. The son of an honest but unsuccessful tradesman of Liskeard, Mr Revesby rose from this humble beginning to cover himself with distinction. Winner of an Open Classical Demyship to Magdalen College, Oxford. First in Classical Moderations and First in 'Greats'. Winner of the Newdigate Prize for English verse. Receiving wide critical acclaim for his first published collection of poems at the age of 24. Honoured with the award of the Belgian Order of Leopold for services to European letters. Professor of English Literature at the Free University of Brussels. A record of achievement that must eventually be crowned with the very highest distinctions of the literary world. You have chosen well, my dear Cherry. In lieu of a parent, I give you my blessing upon the match.

No more now. I have to confess that I am a little tired. Have a care for yourself, and see to it that Mr Revesby (to whom please convey my warmest good wishes and congratulations) also takes care of you. It is a blessing that you live securely, with servants to look after you – and are not an easy prey for the dastardly killer who haunts the district . . .

Uncle Gervase ended his letter with the conventional endearments. I had the immediate impulse to ask Martin if he would mind my visiting the poor old fellow, who, despite the ministrations of the daily woman and the attentions of his admiring widow, might not be getting the very best of care. Then I told myself that I was fussing too much: Uncle had his fair share of self-pity; if he felt ill enough, he would swiftly be calling for my presence. I remembered him of old: a particularly self-indulgent and demanding patient – especially if cut off from the brandy decanter. Re-reading the first part of his letter, I decided that he was feeling ill, but not all that ill. And almost certainly well enough to take his daily dose of spirits. Accordingly, I wrote him a short letter in reply, telling him that he must see to it that I was informed immediately if he needed me, and that I would come post haste. I also entreated him to be well again in time to give me away on my wedding day.

The prompting to tell him about the attack on Lady Amanda and the others was very strong, but, on reflection, I decided not to. It would give an ailing old man little comfort to know that his only niece enjoyed no special protection from living securely in a mansion with servants to look after her.

What protection had these advantages afforded to Lady Amanda, who, but for her cousin's action, might have shared the fates of the others?

At the end of that week winter gales swept the West Country, scouring out the last of the dead leaves, howling in the dark eaves, adding another hard year's wear and tear upon the ancient stonework of Malmaynes.

I seldom ventured out, even for a short constitutional on the wind-blackened greensward, where the sheep huddled for shelter by the drystone walls; but I took occasional coach journeys to Penryn and Truro, to the former for fittings of my bridal gown, which Miss Faversham and her assistants were shaping very nicely. I had chosen white silk, trimmed at bodice and neck with lines of lace and tiny embroidered white flowers; the same motif being repeated on the edges of the three-tiered crinoline. The effect was one of deceptive simplicity; in fact, Miss Faversham was having to 'farm out' a great deal of the embroidery work upon cottage women of the district, and I saw as many as six young seamstresses plying their swift needles on the skirts of the crinoline during one of my visits.

Preparations for the great event took on an alarming complexity, and for this reason: quite unexpectedly, while I was mentioning to Martin that I supposed we should have a very modest invitation list of friends and relations, he declared that, as one of the major landlords of the district (the

Malmaynes estate included the ownership of more than half the village of St Gawes), it would be necessary to invite the entire parish – every man, woman and child – to our wedding breakfast!

I all but swooned at the news, but Martin then smilingly reassured me that it was not so bad as it sounded. The meal – for reasons social, practical and gastronomic – would be in two sittings. The guest list for the wedding breakfast proper – to take place immediately upon our return from church – would comprise relations and friends, the local 'gentry', and the principal yeoman farmers who were tenants of the estate; a gathering that would number about thirty-five in all. They – we – would sit down to a meal that, in Martin's phrase, 'would rival the excellent dinner-party that you first arranged for me, my dear'. The remainder of the parish – the cottagers and farm workers, everyone, right down to the poorest and humblest – would be fed afterwards, when Martin and I had departed for our honeymoon; but in rather more cramped conditions, and upon fare that was more consistent with their simpler gastronomic tastes.

Mrs Challis and I together devised the bills of fare for the two meals, and I have them still.

Wedding Breakfast for 35 Persons

First Course
Game Soup   Julienne Soup
Fried Whiting   Stewed Eels

Entrées
Curried Lobster
Filet of Beef & Sauce Piquante
Mutton Cutlets & Soubise Sauce
Sweetbreads

Second Course

Boiled Turkey & Celery Sauce   Roast Goose
Ham & Brussels Sprouts   Roast Hare & Currant Jelly

Third Course

Widgeon   Pheasants
Vanilla Cream   Iced Pudding
Mince Pies   Blancmange
Apricot Tart   Plum Pudding
Wines: Sherry wine   Claret   Hock   Champagne
Madeira   Port

That for the villagers was more modest in scope, but gargantuan as to quantity:

WEDDING BREAKFAST FOR 90 PERSONS

Boiled Cod's Head and Shoulders
followed by
Stewed Rabbit & Potato Cakes
followed by
Mutton Pudding & Bubble and Squeak
followed by
Apple Pudding & Cream
Beverages: Cider both sweet and rough. Ale

Ever since the announcement of our engagement, Mrs Challis's attitude to me had changed for the better. Knowing as I did of her resentment towards her master, and how she forever harked back to better days under the late Mr Henry Tremaine, I supposed that she saw some hope that my influence would bring about a return to the old ways. It was true that, due to her increasing response to my wishes and institutions regarding the running of Malmaynes, I had come around to leaving more and more responsibility in her hands. The mansion was better run, the meals better cooked, served on time and served hot, while such shortcomings as imperfectly washed dishes and cutlery, dusty tabletops, and soiled hands had become things of the past. I saw a time when I should be able simply to issue my requirements concerning the household, and leave them to Mrs Challis to carry out in whatever way she thought best. And it seemed to me that, after working with me for three months odd, she had come to the same happy conclusion, and that on this account she greatly approved of my forthcoming marriage to the master of Malmaynes.

In only one particular did Mrs Challis decline her full co-operation, and for what reasons I could never determine. Despite all my urgings, she continued to set her face against the employment of any living-in servants; despite the abundant evidence to the contrary, she persisted in her declaration that none of the village women wanted to live in – and nothing I could say would shake her. Finally, I came to accept the situation. The day-servants continued to arrive in a cart that brought them up from the village at five in the morning and they departed by the same means at night, after dinner had been cleared away.

I never grew accustomed to my lonely room on the third floor of the old dark house. My imagination continued to inhabit the corridor outside with sounds and shadows, and I never entered without locking and bolting the door behind me, nor snuffed my candle unless I had added a heavy chair to the defences of my threshold. In the dying weeks of the year, as the winter gales blasted the thick walls and roared in the chimney, the sea was all tossing white horses from shore to horizon, the clifftop a desolation, my nerves were greatly tried. I took heart from the thought that Martin was in the house, and that on our return from honeymoon we should be sharing a suite of rooms on the elegant first floor – for so I had prompted him, and he had agreed.

Our honeymoon . . .

True to the spirit of the lyrical love poem, it was to be

the villa of white marble above the wine-dark sea. Such an idyllic place existed, Martin said. It was situated on the tiny island of Capri, off the coast of southern Italy. He had seen it – and fallen in love with it from afar, while travelling as a penniless student. And now that he had the means to rent the selfsame villa from the Italian nobleman who owned it, we were to spend the harsh winter months in the sun of the Mediterranean: departing from Malmaynes immediately after the wedding breakfast, taking ship from Falmouth to Naples, and thence to the villa of the poem. Many was the night that I lay in the darkness, speculating upon the wonder of coming events: the unfolding of the poem into reality. And always my thoughts returned to the manner in which Martin and I had conducted ourselves, and were continuing to conduct ourselves, since our engagement began: most of the time there was scarcely any sign, in his demeanour towards me, of the ardent lover of the poem; only a tenderness and gentle consideration of my every whim, my every mood. Yet behind the bland mask of his courtship I was aware of forces which I could scarcely begin to comprehend, of intensity of feeling that must soon show itself. Sometimes I would glance up and see him looking at me with an expression of such ardour that my heartbeats quickened and I felt the blood rush to my cheeks. At such times, seeing how I was affected, Martin would immediately introduce a lightness and gaiety into the atmosphere, so that the intensity of the passing moment was dissolved in laughter.

I decided that he worried greatly about the difference in our ages, and that this accounted for his manner towards me: as if he was reluctant to dwell upon the true depths of his feelings for fear of the kind of rebuff that – so he might think – I would not have accorded to a younger man. I constantly strove to show him, in all kinds of ways, that he need have no worries on that score. As I had told him from the first, I was conscious of no disparity of age. Men, I had long ago decided, improved with keep – like vintage claret and well-ripened cheese.

My only regret was that I fell so short of his image of me as portrayed in the poem. Though proud beyond all belief for the honour he had accorded me, I was nevertheless fearful of the prospect of being pointed out for the rest of my life as the secret lady of Martin Revesby's masterwork. How, when I was old and worn, short of breath and uncertain of temper, would the world ever believe that he could have loved me so? Add to that, I was uneasily aware that, loved as I was, and with such intensity, where I should have been all fire and air, I felt only tenderness and deep admiration.

Martin had done no work since our engagement. He explained that he would now have to cast around for another theme, and that something would certainly come to him in Italy. As far as the cycle was concerned, he was well-satisfied, having all but finished the Tristan and Iseult as well as the lyrical love poem.

With nothing to occupy him, we spent much time in each other's company, taking all our meals together, spending long hours in the cosy room off the great hall, he with a book, me with my sewing. We were so engaged one afternoon a week before the wedding when we had a visitor: Sergeant Buller. He was ushered in by Challis.

'Good day to you, sir and ma'am,' he said.

Though he was not one to radiate cheerfulness, I had never seen Buller looking so woebegone. It was almost as if his bulky figure, like some huge stuffed animal in a natural history museum, had had some of the straw and sawdust taken out of it. There was a perceptible sag to his shoulders, his back was rounded, he almost bowed at the knees. And his face – that heavy, bewhiskered face that scarcely knew how to assemble a smile – was lined and creased with the weight of untold burdens.

'Do sit down, Sergeant,' I told him. 'You don't look at all well.'

'Nor he does,' confirmed Martin. 'Would you care for

a brandy, my dear fellow?'

'Thank you, no, sir.' Buller sat down on the edge of a chair opposite us and laid his tall hat by his feet. 'Strong drink has never passed my lips since the day when, as a young man, I heard Bishop Blomfield preach on behalf of the British and Foreign Temperance Society in Truro market place.'

An awkward silence followed this declaration. Martin and I exchanged glances, and to my alarm, I saw a mischievous smile playing at the corners of my fiancé's expressive lips. Knowing his turn of humour, and fearful of what comment he might make, I quickly introduced a question to our visitor:

'And to what cause, Sergeant, do we owe the pleasure of this visit?'

His mournful, regarding eyes fixed upon me. I was the favourite pupil, about to receive some doleful tidings from the lips of my kindly master.

'Alas, ma'am,' he said. 'I am taking this opportunity to come and wish you farewell.'

'You're leaving us?' I asked.

'Yes, ma'am.'

'Permanently?'

He cracked the knuckles of his great white hands.

'Put it this way, ma'am,' he said. 'Put it that we are not like to meet again in the same circumstances. I am obliged to leave, and no one could be more sorry than I.'

'You are being recalled to your headquarters?' interposed Martin.

'I journey to Truro this afternoon,' replied the other. 'To receive further instructions. I can only guess what they might be.'

'I take it, then,' said Martin, 'that you are being withdrawn from the case?'

Buller inclined his head in assent. 'My colleague Sergeant Hennick will arrive in St Gawes this evening,' he said. 'Hennick will continue the enquiries and supervise the deployment of the vigilance force. I shall be – ' he drew a sad, shuddering breath – 'otherwise employed.'

Martin said: 'I hope, my dear fellow, that you are not leaving under a cloud.'

'That, sir, would express the situation exactly,' said Sergeant Buller sadly. 'There will be hard words said about the way I have conducted the present enquiries.'

'But, Sergeant, I don't understand!' As I blurted out the words, his unhappy glance was directed towards me. 'You told me, remember? – at least you implied – that your enquiries had met with some success.'

'Did he, now?' cried Martin. 'That's news to me, my dear.'

Buller transferred his gaze to my fiancé. 'What Miss Carew is trying to say, sir, is that I informed her, in strictest confidence (which, I am not surprised to hear, she has respected), that certain enquiries which I conducted in Paris had not been entirely unsuccessful.'

'In Paris?' exclaimed Martin.

'However,' said Buller, and his sad eyes sought mine again, 'I have to admit that I was completely led astray by my enthusiasm.'

'You were mistaken?' I suggested.

'Entirely mistaken, ma'am,' he replied.

Poor Sergeant Buller. My heart went out to him as he took his final leave of us, shaking hands with Martin and bowing low over mine: the discredited teacher bidding a last farewell. I could have wished a better end to the curious bond that had been forged between us: my mentor should have been given the opportunity of withdrawing with his dignity intact.

'I hope you will find the opportunity to attend our wedding on Friday next,' I told him. 'I know you've had an invitation, for I penned it myself.'

'With much regret, ma'am, I think it unlikely,' he replied. 'Those who are set in authority above me will almost certainly ordain that I must be elsewhere. Your servant, ma'am. Mr Revesby, sir.'

He left us. On an impulse, I followed to the door and watched him go down the drive, seated beside a uniformed officer who was driving the Constabulary dog-cart; tall hat and caped coat hiding all of him, but doing nothing to conceal the fact that a great deal of the spirit and confidence had drained away from that curiously likeable arm of the law.

And then, one evening, there arrived a parcel by hand of a special messenger, who demanded a signature for its safe delivery and deposited his burden on the hall table with the sort of care that suggested he was handling a piece of priceless crystal. Martin was with me at the time, and himself signed for the receipt.

'Martin, what can it be?' I cried.

He smiled. He was already unwrapping the parcel. Within the outer wrappers was a large dress box that was emblazoned with the signature and trade mark of London's most famous and expensive emporium.

'A present,' he said. 'My wedding-present to you. Will you please turn your back?'

I obeyed him, wonderingly. There was the sound of the box being opened, the rustle of tissues as the contents were lifted out. Next, a burden of incredible softness and lightness was laid across my shoulders, and I felt a strange thrill run through me at the touch of his fingertips.

'Oh, Martin!'

'Does it meet with your approval?'

I was wearing a full-length cloak of startling white ermine trimmed with a fringe of dark-tipped tails at the hem. A garment fit for an empress. As a present, a gesture of most incredible richness and extravagance. I whirled round, delighting at the way my wonderful cloak swirled about me.

'It's beautiful, Martin – so beautiful!'

'For the Winter Bride,' he said. 'You must wear it with your wedding gown for the journey to church.'

Chapter Nine

Martin, true to tradition, did not spend the wedding eve under the same roof as his bride-to-be, but lodged with the Prescotts.

My memories of the unforgettable day when I rose in the early dawn to be a winter bride have not lost, nor will they ever lose, the slightest shade of their vividness.

I remember it all: every word, every action, every event – right down to the smallest detail.

I remember rising in the half-light and sensing a special, new chill in the air; noticing that there was an unusual brightness to the chinks of dawn that showed through the cracks of my shutters. Leaping from bed, I crossed to the window and threw open the shutters.

It was snowing. A counterpane of whiteness lay over the clifftops. The formal garden might have been carved out of cake icing. Only the grey sea was unchanged: curling sulkily among the rocks below. And the snowflakes were still descending, light as eider down in the very still air. I was to be a winter bride indeed.

There were already sounds of activity outside: a distant door banged somewhere in the kitchen quarters, and a voice called out. A rumble of heavy cartwheels from the front of the mansion sent me out into the corridor, where, from a window that gave a view of the drive, I was in time to see a massive waggon drawn by four shire horses come to a halt at the main door. On it were a dozen great oak logs the length of a man and thicker than two arms could embrace. Seated upon the uppermost log was Jabez, in an over-long coat and a battered tall hat. He was leering and gabbling at the waggoner and his assistants, who were blowing upon their frozen hands and stamping their booted feet in the powdery snow. Presently they took hold of the uppermost log, with Jabez still perched there, and, lifting, bore them both in through the main door.

The crackle of blazing logs in the great hall fireplace greeted me when I descended, in a warm dressing-gown, for a cup of coffee and a buttered oatcake. I took them by the fire, warming myself by its boisterous blaze. It was eight o'clock: plenty of time yet before I needed to get ready. The tables were already in place for the first wedding breakfast; the big refectory table at the end by the minstrel gallery for the bridal party, and three others running the length of the hall. A sea of spotless white napery was set with every piece of silver in Malmaynes and lines of glittering crystal glassware. Two of the servant girls were passing slowly from place to place, giving a final polish to a spoon here, flicking a duster there, adding a touch of refinement to a floral decoration. Everything was to be perfection. When they saw me, they curtsied and smiled a good morning. There was wistful envy in their honest, open faces for the new mistress-to-be of Malmaynes.

Mistress of Malmaynes! It was a heady thought, and one that I had scarcely examined before. As châtelaine, I had tried hard to make the place a suitable abode for the man who was certain to become one of his country's most renowned personages. In my new and vastly more exalted role, I supposed that I should be entertaining, in that very hall, some of the highest in the land: leaders of the artistic and literary world, people of high birth and title, even Royalty. It was a daunting prospect; but one which I resolved there and then to face up to with a determination to succeed. I had been chosen to be the consort of a great poet. Martin Revesby would not be disappointed in his choice – not if the former Cherry Carew, spinster of the parish of Poltewan, had her way.

The thought of Poltewan brought me to Uncle Gervase:

right till the last, till the evening before, we had lived in hope that he might turn up, to give me away. Last evening the village postman had brought a letter from him, saying that another bout of bronchitis made it impossible for him to venture out. In the letter, he enclosed a damask handkerchief edged with French lace that had belonged to his mother, my paternal grandmother. I would carry it with me to the altar.

Something old, something new,
Something borrowed, something blue.

I counted my white kid button boots as new; Janey Pinner had lent me, for my signet finger, a simple silver ring set with a tiny seed pearl; and one of my petticoats was sprigged with a design of blue roses. I should be the complete bride – but with no one to give me away. Nor any bridesmaids – for, though I had had hopes of enticing the three old school friends and the girl who had been with me on the Stenographic Sound course, the idea had come to nothing. The brief span of time between our betrothal and wedding offered very short notice for most people to travel any great distance. Martin's sole surviving relations – a married cousin and her husband who lived in Bristol – had written, regretfully declining our invitation. I did not mind the lack of bridesmaids, and a fig for the Bristol cousin – but I greatly missed Uncle Gervase.

At nine-thirty o'clock, bathed and scented like all the gardens of Araby, there began the heady business of getting dressed in my bridal finery. Janey Pinner had early plumped for the task of being my lady's maid on the occasion, and it was she who helped me into my petticoats, blue-sprigged one and all; laced the frame of the crinoline, and guided me into the voluminous skirts. While she was fastening up the back of the bodice, I glanced at her reflection in the mirror, and saw that she was crying.

'*I* shed a tear of emotion this morning,' I said lightly. 'But one simply has to tell oneself, Janey, that weddings are *supposed* to be joyful occasions.'

'I'm – I'm sorry, ma'am,' she replied, wiping her cheeks with the back of her hand. 'It's just that . . . that . . .'

I felt a chill creep across my bare shoulders, though the flames leapt high in my bedroom fireplace.

'It's just *what*?' I asked her – knowing the answer.

'You know, ma'am,' she whispered. 'It was on just such a morn, at this very hour, that poor Alice Witham was a-dressing herself in her wedding gown. That selfsame gown as became her shroud, and that she'll wear down in the churchyard till Judgement Day.'

'Really, Janey!' I rounded on her. 'I will not listen to such talk on this of all days. It's most unkind and thoughtless of you!'

I regretted my anger immediately, as she burst into heart-rending sobs, covering her face with red, work-worn hands.

'Forgive – forgive me, ma'am,' she wailed.

I put my arm round her shoulders. 'Of course, of course,' I said. 'Though there's nothing to forgive. It's quite natural that you should continue to grieve for your friend, and that my wedding-day should remind you – ' as I said the words, I caught sight of my own reflection in the mirror. By a trick of the stark, wintry light from the window, I appeared to myself ghastly pale. Corpse-like – 'should remind you of her . . . end.'

Janey's hand clutched my arm. Her eyes swollen with weeping were staring and anxious.

'Ma'am!' she whispered. 'You will be careful, won't you?'

'Janey!' I felt my anger and irritation returning.

'No, ma'am, I mean it!' she cried. 'My old gran, who lives with us. You'll remember her, I don't doubt, ma'am . . .'

'Yes,' I said. On the hideous afternoon following the tragedy, I recalled seeing an old crone in the chimney corner of the Pinners' cottage. She had seemed to be asleep most of the time.

'My old gran, ma'am. Now, she be the seventh child of a seventh child, and many do say that the future is not hid from her and that she can see and hear from afar. On the day of poor Alice's funeral, my old gran declared that it wasn't all over, that there would be other deaths before the murderer was finished with his evil work – those were her very words.'

'Was I named by your all-seeing grandmother as one of the final victims?' I demanded with considerably more unconcern than I felt.

Janey shook her head and said, 'That you were not, ma'am. Indeed, she did say that you would be happily wed afore the spring – and that was afore there was any talk of you being betrothed to Mr Revesby, ma'am.'

Pleased and relieved, I said, 'Well, there you are, Janey. If your grandmother sees no danger for me, you can put aside your fears on my behalf.'

She nodded. 'But – you will be careful, like I asked you, ma'am?'

'I will be more than careful,' I assured her. 'I will be prudence itself. Not that it will be necessary, for I shall be well-guarded. At Mr Revesby's request, Police Constable Pannett will be riding in the coach when it arrives to take me to the church, and he will accompany me all the way, armed with a brace of loaded pistols. Now, what do you think of that?'

'I am mightily relieved to hear that, ma'am,' said Janey.

'So we can now resume the dressing of the bride,' I said lightly.

The light had shifted. My complexion had returned to its normal healthy colour when next I met my reflection. But the conversation and the images that it had conjured up had cast a dark shadow.

Unbelievably, I was dressed and ready by ten minutes after ten. And, with over half an hour to wait, I decided to go down to the small sitting-room and watch from there for the arrival of my wedding coach. Janey draped my beautiful ermine cloak about my shoulders, and we descended the stairs together. A gratifying chorus of admiring murmurs greeted my arrival in the great hall, where the servants were putting the finishing touches to the tables. I saw Mrs Challis give me what I took to be an approving look, and she buttonholed me at the sitting-room door.

'It will be all right, will it, ma'am, for the women to go to the church?' she asked. 'There's a waggon calling at half past ten to take them down.'

'Of course, Mrs Challis,' I replied. 'It's entirely up to you. If they can be spared from the preparations, I should be delighted for them to be at the ceremony. What about yourself – may I hope that you'll be present?' I smiled at her encouragingly.

The sunken eyes slid away, avoiding my gaze. 'Well enough for the others to go,' she said, 'but there's too much here for me to leave, what with food still cooking. Challis and me will stay behind. Along with Jabez.'

'Very well, Mrs Challis,' I said mildly, forbearing to point out that, had she wanted badly enough to attend the ceremony, she could easily have delegated one of the more responsible serving women to keep an eye on the cooking stove.

'Thank you, ma'am,' she murmured.

I closed the door of the sitting-room and crossed over to the window. The snow had stopped, but the considerable depth of the fall could be judged from the ruts that had been made by the wood waggon. Whiteness stretched in an unbroken expanse across the greensward, to the humped figures of the sheep by the drystone wall. Beyond that, black fingers of bare trees stood against a slate-grey sky.

Out of the distance came a mount and rider, dark against the snow and the sky: a black-clad rider who resolved into the figure of the Reverend Mr Josiah Murcher. What was the Rector coming to Malmaynes for at this hour? In forty-five minutes' time, cassocked and surpliced, was he not due to join me in holy wedlock to Martin Revesby? It was most puzzling.

As they came nearer, the Rector's mount was revealed as a plump pony who seemed to make light work of the scrawny churchman, for all that the latter's button boots nearly trailed on the ground either side. The rider dismounted and, having tethered the pony, wearily climbed the steps to the door. A moment later, I heard the sound of the bell.

Footsteps in the hall. Voices. A tap on the door.

'Come in,' I called.

I had not seen the Rector's face clearly from the window, for his head had been bowed and a wide-brimmed hat had masked his features. Hatless and facing me from the open door, he presented the look of a man in a fatal sickness, with hollow cheeks, glazed-over eyes, and a yellowish complexion. I was shocked at the further deterioration that had taken place since last I had seen him, and was perturbed by his expression, which was one of extreme agitation.

My first thought was that he brought news of tragedy, and, naturally, my fear was for Martin.

'Mr Murcher!' I cried. 'What is it – what's happened?'

'Madam, I . . .' He swayed and would have fallen, but for a chair which stood near to his hand. I rushed forward to give assistance, guided him to sit down.

'You're ill, Mr Murcher,' I said. 'If Mr Revesby and I had had any idea of your condition, we never would have put the burden of the wedding ceremony upon you.'

The haunted eyes gazed agonizingly up at me.

'It is about that I have come to see you, ma'am,' he said hoarsely. 'You must find another minister to perform the ceremony. I cannot administer the sacred sacrament of marriage . . .

'I am defiled – unclean!'

I had not managed to get another word out of him, and he was sitting with his head in his hands, keening quietly to himself, when a tap came on the door and Mrs Challis put her head in. She gave the Rector an astonished glance, then addressed herself to me.

'The waggon's come, ma'am, and the women are ready to go. Janey Pinner says can she leave with them, or will you be needing her for anything else?'

'No, I shan't need her again, Mrs Challis,' I said. 'Tell her she can go, please.'

'Very good, ma'am.' She gave the hunched figure in the chair another curious glance, and shut the door.

I took a deep breath, and said, 'Mr Murcher. It wants a quarter of an hour till my wedding coach calls to take me to the church, where my groom awaits me. Will you please be so good as to tell me why you have left it till this late hour to decide that you are unable to marry us?'

There was no immediate response. He continued for some few moments to sit with his head in his hands. Then, stirring himself, he put a hand in his breast pocket and took out a crumpled sheet of paper which he held out to me – still without meeting my eyes.

'Read,' he whispered. 'Read . . .'

It was a letter. Very brief. And I experienced a sharp shock of surprise to see the familiar hand of Uncle Gervase.

Sir,

I am not known to you, but you are acquainted with my niece, Miss Charity Carew.

A protracted feverishness which has, no doubt, stimulated those portions of the brain devoted to higher reasoning, prompts me to recall certain texts from the Bible, to wit: Isaiah, chapter 28, verse 15; Exodus, chapter 20, verse 16.

Perhaps you will wish to examine your conscience in the light of these texts.

I remain, sir,
Your servant,
Gervase A. Carew
Barrister-at-law

I re-read the letter, but could glean no intelligence from it. What could Uncle Gervase be meaning, to send such a curious missive to a total stranger? And what lay behind the contents that could reduce the man before me to such a state of collapse?

'Mr Murcher!' I appealed to him. 'Will you please compose yourself and explain what this is all about?'

The black-clad figure stirred. The domed head rose. His eyes met mine – then swam away guiltily. It occurred to me that, from our first meeting, I had been struck by something odd about the Rector of St Gawes – and now I thought I knew what it was.

Here was a man with a bad conscience . . .

He exhaled a long, shuddering breath, and said: 'The letter from your relation arrived yesterday. It troubled me greatly. I was in two minds about what to do. In the end, I slept on it. I use the phrase loosely, for not a wink of sleep had I, but lay turning the thing over in my mind. In the light of dawn I saw my duty clear, which was to confess my sin to another human being. And what more suitable person, ma'am, than yourself? – you being kin to the man who shed light on my wickedness and whom I was to have joined in wedlock on this day of all days.'

'Which you now say you cannot do,' I interjected. 'Because – in your own words – you are defiled and unclean. Mr Murcher, will you please tell me, and tell me quickly, what are those texts my uncle quoted that have troubled you so?'

He took out a handkerchief and passed it slowly over his eyes.

'The verse from the Book of the prophet Isaiah,' he said, 'is addressed to the scornful man who ruled the people of Jerusalem. The prophet declares that they speak of having made a covenant with death and an agreement with hell – and ends with the words: "we have made lies our refuge, and under falsehood we have hid ourselves." '

' "*Made lies our refuge*",' I repeated. A light was dawning in my mind. 'And what else, Mr Murcher?'

He said brokenly: 'The verse from the Book of Exodus is the ninth commandment.'

I said: ' "*Thou shalt not bear false witness . . .*" '

From outside came the clip-clop of horses' hooves and the crunch of wheels on snow and gravel. Glancing, I saw a hay waggon with the serving women inside, all well wrapped-up against the cold. The snow had started again, but the manner of its falling was quite different: now the flakes were flying in wild abandon, driven on the wind; and the ruts left by the wood waggon had half drifted over. I could no longer see the trees beyond the end of the drive.

'I have been made to look into my own heart,' said Mr Murcher. 'I detest what I see there, but have only gratitude for the man who took away the blindfold of self-deception that I have worn – and worn willingly – all these years.'

I looked down at him. His eyes were tightly shut. A line of tears ran down each sunken cheek. His twice-around neck-cloth was frayed at the edges and none too clean.

'I think I follow my uncle's reasoning,' I said. 'It puzzles him, you see – and it puzzled me, also – that Mr Henry Tremaine, who never raised a hand to help the parish, should have been so generous to you. You may think me harsh towards you, Mr Murcher – and you are probably right; but it has to be said. The reason he paid for your wife to convalesce abroad – was it bribery?'

He gave a harsh intake of breath. 'Bribery – yes!'

'For identifying a body washed up by the sea as that of Saul Pendark?'

A nod – eyes still shut tightly. 'Yes,' he whispered.

'Why, Mr Murcher – why would Mr Tremaine do such a thing?'

A gust of wind blew a flurry of snow against the window, rattling the diamond panes in the iron frames. I shuddered and pulled my ermine cloak more closely about my shoulders.

Presently, and so quietly that I had to stoop closely in order to catch the words, he said: 'Because Saul Pendark was his natural son.'

In the long silence that followed between us, I think I heard every sound of movement in the old mansion: every creak of woodwork, the tap-tap of a death-watch beetle in a far-off beam, the roar of wind in distant chimneys, the tick of the French clock on the table opposite, my own heart-beats and his.

'So Saul Pendark – the Beast of Malmaynes – he still lives!' I cried.

The clergyman raised his shocked face. 'I do not know!' he cried. 'Before heaven, I promise you that I do not know!'

'How can you say that?' I demanded. 'Were you not paid to give false witness in order to conceal the fact that he had not been killed?'

A tremor ran through his gaunt frame, as if I had struck him. And then, slowly and with a fragment of dignity, he rose to his feet and regarded me. And then it was I who dropped my eyes, to avoid his gaze.

'I'm sorry, Mr Murcher,' I whispered. 'I shouldn't have said that. I had no right . . .'

'You have every right to speak what you understand to be true,' he said mildly. 'And, indeed, what you say is true – though not perhaps the entire truth.

'I was summoned by the constabulary to identify a body which had been washed up on a beach – the first to have appeared since Saul Pendark fell to his death from the cliff yonder. It was – a distasteful task. I will not dwell on it, but suffice to say that certain identification seemed well-nigh impossible. Such was my conclusion that I gave to the police.

'That evening I was visited by Mr Tremaine. He was very reasonable. Gave his opinion that it were better for all concerned if the matter be allowed to rest along with Saul Pendark, in a known grave. He put it to me: could I positively state that the body was *not* that of his son? I was able to make no such assertion. It was then that he – gently – introduced the topic of my wife's ill-health, and how it would benefit her to go abroad . . .'

I remembered his wife: the peevish, self-declared invalid. 'Mr Murcher,' I said, laying a hand on his arm, 'you don't have to go on distressing yourself any further. I think I understand.'

'She is a good woman,' he said. 'Though sorely tried by her infirmities, she has always done her best to be a loving and dutiful wife to me. Sadly, at the time of which we are speaking, the wretchedness of her condition, both mental and physical, rendered her incapable of rational behaviour. She needed rest, away from the ramshackle rectory, the poverty that is our constant state. Away from me, perhaps . . .

'It seemed such a small lie. Hardly a lie at all. More nearly likely to be the truth. Armed with that thought, I returned to the police and said I should like to reconsider my decision. Once again, I was shown the body – and do you know, I had no difficulty in convincing myself that I was indeed gazing upon the remains of Saul Pendark?' He pressed his hands to his face and groaned.

Questions were teeming in my mind; but there was so little time. I glanced at the clock: it wanted only five minutes before the wedding coach was due. In my mind's eye, I saw Martin standing by the altar rail, distinguished in dove-grey frock-coat, decoration in his buttonhole. The waiting congregation: the doctor and his wife, Lady Amanda and her cousin. Nick . . .

'Mr Murcher,' I said, 'Saul Pendark's mother also identified the body. Did she really believe it was that of her son?'

He shook his head. 'I do not know,' he said. 'No matter how I search my memory and my conscience, I cannot give you the answer to that.'

'But she loved him enough – and with a fierce and possessive love – to have concealed the fact that he was alive, that he had survived the night fall from the clifftop?'

He nodded. 'Her love for him was boundless,' he said. 'And of a kind that destroys while it nourishes. She contributed greatly to his downfall. I witnessed much of it, for I was one of the few who knew that she was Mr Tremaine's mistress: she confided in me when she brought the child for baptism. Whatever the infirmities of Saul's mind, whether caused by demonic possession, heredity, or any other means, I remain convinced that her baleful influence aggravated his insanity. From the very first, he was brought up to regard himself as different from others: a superior being, destined to take his rightful place in the world as the son of a gentleman. The future master of Malmaynes.'

I stared at him. 'She told him that?' I cried. 'That he would succeed to Malmaynes?'

The Rector shrugged. 'In ignorance, merely,' he said. 'And

certainly not on any prompting from Mr Tremaine, who, though he was indulgent to his natural son – spoilt him outrageously, indeed – knew full well that the estate was entailed and could not be bequeathed at his pleasure.'

I nodded. 'One last question, Mr Murcher,' I said. 'You said you did not know if Saul Pendark still lived. *If you saw him again, would you know him?*'

'Over twenty years ago,' he said, 'I was called upon to give what poor aid I could to a youth whose appearance, whose ravings, whose manner and demeanour, were those of an animal, a mad wolf. If I saw that creature again, I should recognize him on the instant. I believe that I have not seen him again, or anyone resembling him in the slightest degree. Does that answer your question, ma'am?'

'It does, Rector,' I replied.

The clock thinly chimed the quarter-hour. I looked out of the window. The driving snow now hid the end of the drive. The coach might well be approaching, but I could not see it.

'What is to happen this morning, ma'am?' asked the clergyman brokenly.

'Why, I am to be married,' I replied. Adding gently: 'And you are going to perform the ceremony, Mr Murcher?'

The tired eyes brightened, and a hint of colour appeared on his drawn cheeks. 'Can you wish that?' he asked. 'After what I have done? Knowing that I have lived all these years with a lie upon my conscience?'

'A half-truth,' I corrected him. 'Uttered unselfishly, to benefit another. And now confessed. Yes, I should greatly like you to marry us, Rector.'

'Then I must hasten,' he said. 'Your coach will be here any moment, though I doubt if it will have an easy passage up St Gawes hill in all this snow. It's likely that I shall have time to don my vestments and be ready at the church porch well before you arrive, ma'am.' Taking up his hat, he moved swiftly to the door, where he turned and regarded me. 'How shall I ever find words adequate to thank you for your trust and your compassion?'

He shut the door quietly, and I heard his footfalls cross

the hall. A little while later I watched the plump pony and its lean burden vanish into the swirling white world that lay beyond the scope of my vision. And I was alone with my teeming thoughts. Waiting.

'NO!'

I cried it aloud, my sudden conviction. There was no refuge to be had in the thought that the body which the Rector had identified might have been Saul Pendark after all. The rocky heel of Cornwall, jutting out into the wild Atlantic, was a landfall for every ship approaching from Biscay and from the west. A haven – and also a hazard. On the tumbled rocks of its shoreline and in its shallows, uncounted ships had perished down the years. Its waters were the grave of countless sailors: in winter months, scarcely a day passed without some pitiful human flotsam being washed ashore. It was probable – almost certain – that Saul Pendark's unmarked, unhallowed grave contained the remains of an unknown, honest sailor.

It followed, then, that Pendark was still alive. And had committed the crimes that had lately terrorized the district. It also followed that Mrs Challis had lied when she assured me that he had died down among the rocks. But, of course, she would do anything to protect him. One small lie – what was that? Yet, strangely, she had convinced me at the time. Perhaps her son was alive and living in the district, all unknown to her. I considered the possibility, and dismissed it.

My reason, my instinct, told me that if the Beast of Malmaynes still lived and breathed in the parish of St Gawes, he was in the care and protection of his mother's fierce love; a love that had no regard for prudence and reason; that kept a dangerous maniac locked away in times of the full moon and told the world that he was only 'a little soft in the head'. This day, my wedding-day, was a time of the full moon. Was Saul Pendark – twenty-odd years older, now, still homicidal and still insane – locked away in his mother's care? And, if so, where?

Somewhere in Malmaynes . . . ?

The snow was now being driven on the breath of a blizzard, so that I could see nothing from the window. My coach – even if it managed to reach the top of St Gawes hill with the men pushing and the horses pulling – was going to be very late in delivering me to the church. This brought to mind another occasion, another late bride . . . I tried to shut out the thought . . .

Did Mrs Challis keep her mad son hidden somewhere in a remote fastness of the old dark house? There were many such places – as I knew from the time when I had made my search. It was of a piece with her early promises to him that he would one day be master of Malmaynes.

But Martin was master of Malmaynes, and if Saul Pendark was still alive, the man who at that very moment was waiting for me at the altar, was in very real peril. It was no wonder that Mrs Challis resented the new master; she must have regarded him from the first as an interloper, the stranger who had stolen what she had always regarded as her child's birthright.

I turned from the window: nothing to be seen there. The first I would know of the coach arriving would be the ring of the doorbell.

Restless, fearful, I went over to the door and opened it, looked out across the great hall. As I did so – it often happens in moments of extreme agitation – the sight of well-ordered calm had a curiously soothing effect. Long tables primly laid with the glitter of glass, silverware and napery, and the scent of wood smoke mingled with the appetizing aroma of baked meats lured my senses back to the world of reality. With a sudden feeling of relief and release, I smiled at my heated imaginings and felt the need to talk to someone in order to strengthen the sensation of having returned to the commonplace and tangible. I wondered if all of the women had gone in the hay waggon, for I had not counted them. At any rate, Mrs Challis remained. To kill time, until the sound of the doorbell announced the arrival of my coach, I would talk to her about everyday things, such as how she must be careful to keep well-aired the suite of first-floor rooms that

Martin and I would be occupying on our return from Italy; and had our trunks and portmanteaux been brought down in readiness for our departure immediately after the wedding breakfast? And all the while I would look at her and marvel at the feat of overheated imagination that had made me suppose her still to be hiding her long-dead son.

I called her. 'Mrs Challis, are you about?'

There was no answer; only the hiss and crackle of logs in the great fireplace. One of the double doors leading to the kitchen quarters was ajar, and it was from there that the delicious scents of cooking were being wafted. I crossed the hall, went through into the passage and paused at the top of the steps leading down into the kitchen.

'Are you there, Mrs Challis?'

No reply. It was chilly in the passage, and I could hear the wind moaning somewhere up on high. The warm kitchen enticed. I went down, my ermine cloak billowing behind me.

Signs of the impending feasts were everywhere. The tables were piled high with cold dishes, such as iced puddings, tarts and blancmanges; while every inch of the Leamington range was crammed with bubbling saucepans and steamers, and its black-leaded sides positively glowed with the heat. There was no one in sight. Perhaps, I thought, she was in the scullery.

The scullery lay at the end of a passage leading off from the kitchen, past a row of provision rooms. Its door was ajar. A dozen paces from the threshold, some impulse prompted me to walk the remaining distance on tiptoe. Reaching the door, I peered cautiously round the edge of it – and gave a start of alarm to see Jabez.

The deaf-mute was sitting at a scrubbed table, his back partly turned towards me so that I could see only the misshapen curve of his cheek, one ear, and his domed head rising from massive shoulders. A tray of food was set before him, and he was eating – noisily, swiftly, like a hungry dog. As I watched in distaste, he tossed aside a gnawed bone and, picking up a pewter mug, threw back his head and swallowed loudly. Shrinking from the idea of an encounter, I tiptoed quietly away. It was surely time for the coach to have negotiated the hill. Best return to the great hall so as to be ready for a swift departure.

There was still no one in the kitchen. No matter; I had killed a few minutes, and was now entirely composed. It was as if the unhealthy fantasies of a short while ago had never existed. Even my encounter with Jabez had done no more than give me a brief jolt. I glanced approvingly at the rich abundance of food and wondered how even the entire parish of St Gawes were going to eat their way through it all.

My way lay straight across the kitchen to the stairs. By the side of the stairs, in an alcove, stood a small table which had not caught my attention on the way down. What I saw lying there, on the table, halted me in my tracks, with surprise turning rapidly to horrified speculation . . .

There was a plain wooden tray – a companion to that from which I had seen Jabez wolfing his meal. It was set for one person, with some pieces of roughly-sliced cold beef and a hunk of bread on a pewter plate, and a pewter mug containing beer.

Not Jabez's tray – for the deaf-mute was already provided for . . .

Then – *whose*?

I had scarcely framed the question in my mind when I heard footsteps approaching along the corridor above. When they reached the top of the stairs, I darted round the side of a tall cupboard set against the wall, from where I had a clear view of Challis as he came unsteadily down the stairs. One glance was enough to tell me that his earlier condition had greatly deteriorated: the fellow was far gone in drink, and even as I watched, he took a flask from the pocket of his butler's tail coat and drank deeply. That done, he hiccuped and peered about him. I drew back into the shadows, but need have had no fear. The short-sighted eyes behind those thick glasses, coupled with the effects of the strong spirits, rendered Challis in no condition to detect a fleeting movement. Nor was his attention directed my way; he saw what he had been seeking in the alcove and moved towards it, took up the tray and carried it back the way he had come, towards the stairs.

I waited till he was out of sight. And then I followed.

I had been that way before, had trodden the same dusty stairs and felt the cobwebs brush my face. Heaven only knew the ruination to my wedding-dress of white silk and lace and tiny embroidered flowers. My beautiful ermine cloak I had discarded on a lower landing, and would gladly have disposed of my wide crinoline, the better to negotiate the tortuous, narrow labyrinth that occupied the vast roof void of Malmaynes. We had reached there, my unwitting guide and I, by means of one of those flights of rickety wooden steps that I had remarked on my previous visit to the upper floors; and were seeming to traverse the whole length of the main wing, climbing higher all the while. Challis, by reason of his inebriated condition, moved slowly and unsteadily, and apparently lost his way from time to time, for, on two occasions, I had to slip back into the shadows when I heard his returning footsteps.

Where he was leading me, I could only imagine. But neither my terror nor my physical frailty were going to prevent me from following him to the very end. And so I stumbled on, with only the chinks of light from dusty skylights to guide my footsteps, and the howl of the blizzard outside masking their sound from the man ahead of me.

Between the terror of the present and dreadful speculations about what lay immediately ahead, I had visions of what was happening down in the village church: Martin glancing anxiously at his watch; the congregation restive, muttering among themselves, remembering a previous time when a bride had been late for her wedding; the Rector, newly vested and waiting in the draughty porch, peering anxiously through the blizzard towards the invisible hump of St Gawes hill, where, surely, my wedding coach was immovably stuck in the deep drifts . . .

I halted, seeing Challis turn abruptly and begin to mount

a steep flight of steps that must have led to the very high crest of the great roof. Reaching the top, he laid down the tray and fumbled in his pocket, muttering to himself all the time. He was perhaps ten paces from me, above, in the gloom.

Next came a jingle of keys. The scrape of a lock. The drawing back of a heavy bolt. I held my breath, leaned back against the wall and waited, staring towards the figure above me.

'Here's your grub,' came Challis's surly growl. 'Put one hand out and take the tray. Don't want any trouble like we had yesterday. No tricks, you devil. Remember the door's still on a chain and I have a loaded pistol. Right – take hold of it now.'

I could see the chain on the partly open door. There was total darkness beyond. From out of the darkness came a hand and a bare arm, reaching for the tray.

It was at that moment – when every hair of my scalp prickled and stood out with sheer horror, when my skin crawled and every nerve in my body screamed at me to run – that I felt something move across my back!

My crazed scream echoed in the dark void above. It was followed by the sharp squeal of a frightened rat as it brushed past me and scurried along the rafter against which I had been leaning. I pressed my hands to my mouth, choking the scream to a whimper – but the damage was done, I had betrayed myself. Challis turned at the sound, lurching unsteadily, so that he dropped the tray and its contents. Cursing, he took a pace forward and peered down into the gloom; put his foot beyond the top step and fell headlong down the steep flight. He landed heavily and lay very still, face-uppermost, not five yards from where I crouched. His eyes were wide and staring, with the broken spectacles hanging from one ear.

There came the sound of a jingling chain from above. Turning my horrified gaze in that direction, I saw the bare arm reaching round the part-open door; the fingers scrabbling for the attachment of the chain. Probing. Testing. Unhooking.

Staring, without the will or the energy to run, as the fascinated rabbit will deliver itself to the ferret, I saw the chain drop clear and hang there, swinging. I saw the door creak slowly open. Another hand appeared on the jamb. A dark figure loomed forward into view. Two burning eyes looked out from a mass of hair and beard: they took in the scene below them: the still, sprawled figure at the foot of the stairs; the scattered receptacles and the broken food; me.

The meeting of those eyes with mine broke the spell that held me still, the more so when the creature moved forward and, stretching out a pointing finger to me, uttered a hoarse and blood-chilling cry. I turned and fled – back the way I had come, holding high the skirts of my crinoline, with the cobwebs pulling at my hair and showering me with dust, with protruding angles of ancient woodwork and broken nail-heads tearing at my gown. Somewhere along the way, the delicate French heel of one of my white button boots was wrenched off in a crack in the floorboards, so that my headlong flight became slow and clumsy, like a draggle-tailed bird running with a broken wing.

I was immediately lost, but that scarcely signified, since flight was my only consideration. I knew that *he* was close behind me: while pausing for an instant to choose between two paths, I clearly heard the rapid patter of bare feet on wood. The creature was running – and faster than I. I was doomed to end my life, hideously and with violence, in the half-darkness and the ancient dust, with the howl of the blizzard and the wild laughter of a madman as the last sounds I should hear on earth. It was an image that set me screaming.

Screaming still, I came to the head of a staircase and plunged down it without hesitation, leaping awkwardly, one-legged on my heel-less boot; stumbling and nearly falling when my toe caught up in the hem of a petticoat. One landing came and went. Then another. And another. Yet still the hands from whose touch my whole body shrank did not reach out and take me. I had the wild hope that perhaps I had evaded my pursuer; that he was still searching for me in the gloom of the roof void. Near the foot of the next flight,

I dared to look behind me.

The face – that wild-eyed, hair-covered face – was so close that I could have reached out and touched it!

Holding high my skirts, I took the last few steps in one leap. One more flight remained. Below was the great hall: I could see the end of one of the long tables covered in snowy-white cloth. I landed awkwardly and reached out to recover my balance. In the act of doing so, I saw the creature bound past me; turn at the head of the next flight, regarding me with arms extended, barring my way. He was mouthing something, some hideous, incomprehensible gabble that my tortured wits could not begin to comprehend.

I backed away, holding out my hands to protect myself; then, when a few paces separated us, I turned and ran again. And I heard my pursuer come after.

We were on the first floor above the great hall, the elegant apartments that were to have been mine and Martin's. The painted faces of long-gone Revesbys and Tremaines looked down upon the doomed bride of Malmaynes as she fled in her ruined wedding finery. The double doors at the far end of the passage were closed – marking the end of my life. I should never have time to open them before those hands closed about my throat and began to choke me. A dozen paces more, with rich rugs yielding suavely beneath my feet. Through a passing window, I caught a glimpse of drifting snowflakes. A clock began to chime.

I reached out my hands to clutch the gilded handles of the doors – knowing that the gesture was hopeless.

Before I could touch them, they moved. The two doors opened towards me, and I was face to face with . . .

'*Martin!*' I screamed his name like a pæan of deliverance.

Martin's eyes widened with shock to see the state I was in. Then they went beyond me and saw my pursuer. Without a word, he thrust me aside, and, reaching out, took a candlestick from a nearby table. His tallness, his broad back, hid the other man from my view, as he moved swiftly forward with the candlestick raised on high to strike.

There was a strangled cry – immediately cut off by the

sound of a heavy thud. The half-naked and barefoot figure reeled into my view, took a pace and pitched to the floor, where it lay face downwards and still.

I leaned back against the wall and closed my eyes.

'Oh, Martin,' I whispered. 'It's all over. The nightmare's over. You've brought down the Beast of Malmaynes, dear Martin. That thing – that creature – is Saul Pendark!'

'Oh no, my dear Cherry, my bride,' came the reply, 'you are quite wrong. The creature to whom you refer is not Saul Pendark. He is Martin Revesby, sometime poet and littérateur . . .

'I, my dear, am Saul Pendark the Beast of Malmaynes – as you must know very well!'

My eyes flashed open to meet the unaccustomed madness in his. And his hands – those well-tended, capable hands – were already crawling up my bodice towards my throat.

Chapter Ten

He was playing with me: toying with my life, the way a cat makes sport of a mouse, tossing it in the air, patting it lovingly to death. Those strong fingers were looped loosely about my throat, occasionally tightening, cutting off my breath, checking the flow of blood, so that a blackness descended upon my world and I all but fainted away. And all the time, he talked to me: sometimes laughingly, coaxingly; sometimes breaking into unpredictable fury . . .

'Your wedding coach, my dear, when last I saw it, was slewed sideways half-way up St Gawes hill with snow up to its axle-tree, and the driver and Police Constable Pannett trying fruitlessly to dig it out. I doubt, my little bride, if you will ever reach the altar this day.

'I came back by the fields, which the wind has conveniently swept clean of snow. I went to the church, you know. Arrived punctually at the quarter-hour. The congregation all in their places, like puppets in a marionette theatre, all in their best. Waiting for the groom. Waiting for him to spring – *The Trap*!'

The last words were shouted into my face, and the fingers tightened convulsively round my neck. The last I saw before unconsciousness closed in upon me was his wild face, bared teeth, mad eyes.

The death grip slackened again, and his countenance swam back into view: no longer furious, but sneering. And the voice insinuating, full of contempt.

'Oh, you knew about the clever trap that our excellent police sergeant had devised, did you not? I take it that you are a party to the conspiracy; though, from the little pantomime I have just witnessed, you contrived to give the impression of innocence.'

I struggled to find my voice, and said, 'I didn't know who you are. I – I swear it.'

'No matter,' he said. 'It's over. Finished. And I had such hopes, such high hopes of happiness, my Cherry.' To my horror and disgust, he took one hand from my throat, and with one finger, a finger with which he had lately been half-choking out my life, he gently stroked my cheek.

'You were to have been different from the rest, Cherry. You were so open, so candid, so free of coquetry. Not like the others: the women who sneered and made mock of me when I was young and untutored in the ways of the world; and others who deceived me, threatened me. You were different – *or so I thought*!'

Once more, the hands were about my throat so that I was choking. I beat my own hands fruitlessly on his shoulders.

'Please – please – I never knew!'

'You are lying, my Cherry, but it doesn't matter any more,' he said. The grip relaxed, and I saw that tears were in his eyes – those fine, clear, insane eyes. 'For now, because you and your friend the sergeant have trapped me, I have got to go away again. Malmaynes is lost. And you with it, my Cherry, my bride. Farewell . . .'

For the first and last time, he stooped and kissed me upon the mouth. Still with his lips on mine, he tightened his fingers in a grip that could end only in my death. I passed into a limbo where I had no substance, no weight, no feeling. Still connected to life by the slenderest of threads, I was aware that the thread was lengthening, stretching, becoming ever more frail and ready to snap. When it parted, I would be dead.

But a great new light burst in upon my darkness, and the air was full of sound: shouts, crashes of noise. I reached out my hand and touched solid substance that revealed itself to be a chair. Two paces from me, the man whom I had known as Martin Revesby, whom I was to have married that morning, was struggling in the grip of the deaf-mute Jabez.

'Hold him fast, Jabez. Sit him down in that chair and stand over him. Calm yourself, Saul. Or, as heaven is my witness, I will kill you with my own hand!' The voice of Mrs Challis.

She stood by the doorway, and there was a levelled pistol in her hand. Levelled at – her son.

Jabez seemed to comprehend the woman's commands. He dragged his adversary back towards an armchair, massive arms entwined about the other's chest from behind. And there he thrust the unresisting figure in the grey frock-coat.

'Hello, Mother.' The fury was all gone. Saul Pendark crossed one elegant leg over the other, straightened his black stock and smiled mockingly at Mrs Challis. 'I'm rather afraid the wedding is not going to take place after all. Pity, don't you think?'

Weakly, bemused, gazing from one to the other of those nightmare creatures in their insane charade, I shrank against the wall, making myself as small as possible.

'A pity, indeed,' cried Mrs Challis. 'Though my eyes wouldn't have beheld it. My own son – forbidding me from his wedding. Many's the burden of sorrow and suffering you've laid upon me, Saul Pendark, for which you will one day be called to judgement. But you never did a wickeder thing than that.'

'Mother dear,' he sneered, 'would I have had you weep for joy in the congregation and betray me as your ever-loving son?'

The woman's gaunt face was bitterness in every line. 'You are no son of mine!' she cried. 'My Saul – him who loved and obeyed his mother as a son should – he was lost for ever down among the rocks!'

He laughed. 'That poor, inexperienced youth? Surely, Mother dear, you much prefer the refined and educated gentleman of the world that I have become? Come now, admit it.'

'You're fine gentleman enough,' she conceded grudgingly. 'Though you treat your own mother like a servant. But you might have improved, if you'd married her – ' the muzzle of the pistol was jerked in my direction – 'and had some offspring by her.'

I shrank closer to the wall as his gaze was turned in my direction.

'Yes, she is rather splendid, isn't she, Mother?' he said. 'Beauty coupled with refinement and sensibility. Such a pity.'

'I thought little of her at first,' said Mrs Challis. 'But she showed herself to be the right sort: the sort of woman who'd be able to take my place and look after you when I'd gone. Not like that flibbertigibbet, her ladyship, her you had your eye on.'

'Lady Amanda!' His eyes blazed and his voice rose in fury. 'She was just like the rest of them – leading me on with her soft ways and her soft talk. And then she cut me dead. It was after she came back from London. She was driving out with that oaf Pendennis, and she looked right through me. Me!'

'And for that you nearly killed her!' cried his mother. 'Fool! You nearly got yourself caught that night. I don't know what's come over you, for you were a nice enough lad when you were young – save when the black moods came on you. Now it's kill, kill, kill. That woman in the churchyard...'

'She threatened me! She had to die!'

'The Witham slut – heaven knows I've no time for the Withams...'

'She was like that aunt of hers. As soon as I set eyes on her, I saw the resemblance. I remembered how the other one used to mock me and call me soft in the head. She had to die.'

'You're a bad boy. A bad boy. I don't know what I'm going to do with you.' Mrs Challis shook her head. Her eyes seemed as crazed as her son's eyes.

He was laughing: a low, self-indulgent, insane laugh. Then he paused and said: 'Do you know, Mother, I think of all the things I did, I most enjoyed the night in the churchyard when I had them all waiting till dawn for – nothing!'

'You are a wicked boy,' said his mother. 'I don't know

what's to be done with you.'

Averting my gaze from the sight of them both, my eyes fell upon the prostrate, half-clothed figure lying on the floor beyond. In the horror of what had followed, I had forgotten Saul Pendark's latest victim. I rose to my feet and made to go towards him.

'Sit you down, miss!' snapped Mrs Challis.

'But – he may be badly hurt!' I cried.

'So much the worse for him,' she replied. 'Back to your place!' The dark muzzle of the pistol was aimed at me and brooked no argument. Reluctantly, I did as I was bidden. Saul Pendark's eyes were upon me, broodingly. Behind his chair, great arms hanging limply, head on one side, the deaf-mute was also looking at me.

I disregarded them entirely. My whole mind was directed to the hurt man on the floor. Hurt – or dead. There was little enough of him to be seen that gave any indication of the sort of man he might have been: bare arms and legs emerging from the tattered remains of a shirt and pantaloons; a mop of unkempt hair; a patch of uncovered forehead down which trickled a thin rivulet of blood that formed a pool in which his face was lying. Yet I was filled with a sudden wonder as I gazed upon him: a wonder that seemed to open out upon unknown vistas that were just beyond the reach of my imagination.

'I must go, Mother,' said Saul Pendark. 'It's finished for me at Malmaynes. As soon as the police realize I've escaped their trap, they'll be up here. It's goodbye again, Mother. I shall be out of the country by nightfall. This time for good.'

'You are a fool!' she told him. 'A fool! If you'd obeyed me and let me lock you away when the moon's full and the evil feelings come upon you, like I did in the old days, you would have been safe here in Malmaynes for ever. And now you're to be outcast again. But – no! You shall take her with you –' she pointed to me – 'take her, marry her or not, as you please. Teach her to look after you, the way I looked after you when you were a lad.'

'No!' I cried. 'No!'

Saul Pendark laughed. 'I am afraid, Mother, that the charms of poesy have faded somewhat for my former intended. A pity. It would have been such a delightful ceremony, with the feast and the honeymoon to follow – ' his nostrils twitched – 'and, by the way, Mother, I fancy from the smell of burning that you have quite ruined the wedding breakfast by your inattention.'

'Be off with you!' cried Mrs Challis.

By the shifting humours of his flawed mind, Saul Pendark was now in full command of himself: no longer frenzied killer, or tearful with a crazed self-pity, but the incisive man of action. Bounding to his feet, he embraced his mother, kissing her on both cheeks. For an awful instant, I thought he was going to accord me the same valediction; instead, he seemed to change his mind, checked himself, smiled wryly and bowed to me.

'My apologies for – everything,' he murmured. 'And be assured, in spite of everything that points to the contrary, that I have been entirely sincere with you. You did indeed become for a very short time my only hope in life.'

I said nothing.

The double doors were shut. He threw them open – and instantly recoiled as a gust of oily black smoke poured in, driven by a rushing wind that had been suddenly released by the opening of the doors.

Mrs Challis screamed.

'The place is on fire!' cried Saul Pendark. 'The staircase out there is thick with smoke and no one could get down without being overcome by the fumes!' He slammed the doors shut and looked about him, calm and incisive as any captain on the quarterdeck of his burning ship. 'The staircase at the other end of the building may still be clear of smoke. Follow me!' He set off quickly down the passage, and his mother went after him.

My only thought – and it came strongly and all unbidden – was for the unconscious figure on the floor. I rushed forward and fell on my knees beside him. I laid a hand on his back and felt him breathing. He was alive, at least. With both hands under his armpits, I turned him over. The face, almost entirely covered with hair and beard and smeared with blood, was still a mystery.

I tried to drag him the way the others had gone, but he was too heavy for me. All I succeeded in doing was to ruck up the rare Persian rug upon which he was lying. Numb with anguish, I looked around me for some better means to shift him – and met the bovine, vacant stare of Jabez. He loomed over me, massive arms swaying at his sides.

'Please help me to get him out of here, Jabez,' I pleaded. 'Please!'

After a moment's hesitation, the deaf-mute stooped, and, taking the unconscious man by the ankles, proceeded to drag him, swiftly and effortlessly, towards the double doors, through whose cracks the curling tendrils of black smoke were now issuing.

'Not that way, Jabez!' I cried, pointing in the direction the others had gone. 'There's our only hope!'

The big, domed head shook dismissively, and he growled some incoherent reply from the depths of his great chest. Next, he got down on his knees, then lay flat on the floor, still facing me and still holding the stricken man's ankles. Nodding and grunting, he conveyed to me that I must do likewise. I did so.

He reached up and opened the double doors. Immediately, a hot breath of scorching air swept over us, bearing with it a streaking black cloud of smoke that instantly filled the apartment and swept on down the passage. If I had been standing up, I would surely have choked to death within a brief space of time; miraculously, there was a small pocket of air close to the floor, scarcely higher than one's head, but free of the smoke and fit to breathe.

Ahead of me, I saw Jabez beginning to crawl painfully backwards, dragging the inert form after him by the ankles. I followed after, giving what assistance I could by lifting the limp head and pulling aside rugs that got in the way. In this manner we passed through the doors and out on to the landing beyond, where, through a narrow tunnel of safety, I could see the staircase and the dense black smoke pouring up it.

The descent to the ground floor was a nightmare. The fire, being on the increase, sent its scorching breath up the narrow funnel of the staircase, where the panelling was already too hot to touch, and the very carpet down which we half-dragged, half-pulled our burden was smouldering in places. My clothes threatened to catch alight, and I experienced the horror of smelling the unmistakable scorching of my own hair.

But still our tunnel of safety remained, though much narrower, so that, in order to suck in the hot, life-giving air, we had to press our faces close to the carpeted steps. And in this manner we descended to the ground floor, with every step haunted by the dread that the smoke and the heat would suddenly be replaced by the devouring flames themselves.

We reached the bottom. The great hall was alight in several places: a line of flame was devouring the panelling and the roof beams; the main staircase was entirely ablaze; while, at the far end, the shape of the round-topped archway leading to the kitchen quarters was picked out by the holocaust beyond.

I could see no way out for us, because the main door half-way down the hall was the centre of a raging inferno – and there was no exit at the eastern end, where we were. But the deaf-mute was again equal to the emergency. Rising to his feet into the smoke, he crossed to one of the huge windows and began to beat upon the diamond panes with both massive fists. There was a shattering of glass, and a plume of rushing air was sucked in. Building on his success, Jabez took hold of the criss-crossed strips of lead and tore them out – broken glass and all – at awful cost to the palms of his hands. Presently, there was a gaping hole above the window-sill through which the white snowflakes drifted in through the swirling smoke.

Jabez returned to me. Together, we lifted the limp form

and bundled it unceremoniously over the window-sill, out of the ragged hole in the diamond panes, and into the blizzard beyond. Next, the deaf-mute fell to his knees, indicating to me to step up on his bent back. This I did, and by some means contrived to get my legs over the sill, though my crinoline snagged itself to ribbons upon the broken shards of glass and twisted lead. Below me lay a drop of some twenty feet, to where the unconscious form of our companion lay in the deep snow. I was summoning up my nerve to make the jump when an unceremonious shove from behind sent me plummeting down.

I landed on my hands and knees in the snow, close by the bearded head of Saul Pendark's latest victim, and Jabez thudded down close by a few moments later. In the distance, above the roar and crackle of the conflagration, we heard the shouts of men coming up the drive.

Ironically, it was our own means of escape that doomed the east end of the mansion. Fed by the inrush of air through the broken window, the flames raced up the narrow staircase down which we had descended only a few minutes before, and were soon issuing from the windows of the floors above. But it was only when Jabez and I carried our burden round to the front of the building that we saw in all its awfulness what destruction was being wrought on Malmaynes.

The entire kitchen wing at the western end was afire from ground to roof, with tongues of flame licking from the windows of the attics. In the main block, the fire had reached to the second floor along its entire length, and to the uppermost floor in the centre, where the main staircase had stood. Stark against the grey, snowswept sky, the great stone hulk was being consumed of everything within it that was consumable, and its pyre of black smoke rose out of sight in a slanting line, driven on the chill breath of the blizzard.

Through the blinding snow loomed dark figures from all about us. Hands came out and took our unconscious burden. A man's heavy, caped coat was put around my shoulders. I looked down at my hands, and saw with a shock that, like my skirt and bodice and my sleeves, they were black with soot. I could only presume that my face was similarly defaced, for I heard a voice near at hand cry out if anyone had seen Miss Carew? – and the question was addressed to me.

'I'm here!' I cried. 'Is that you, Sergeant Buller?'

'Indeed it is, ma'am. What a blessing that you are safe.' The familiar bulky figure in the long coat and tall hat loomed up beside me. 'By heaven, ma'am! Are you hurt?'

'I'm all right, but I think that Jabez must have torn his hands terribly whilst breaking out of the window,' I said.

'The doctor will tend to Jabez, ma'am,' he replied. 'Come you over to the shelter of yonder coach. There's nothing that you can do here.'

He took me by the arm and guided me towards a coach that stood in the drive nearby. By the white ribbons that fluttered forlornly from its coach lamps, I knew it to be the vehicle that was to have borne me to my wedding. Next to it was a brougham, into which men were lifting a limp figure wrapped in a blanket. I caught a glimpse of a mop of ragged hair and beard, a pale brow smeared with soot and blood. Before I could start forward to run over to the brougham, the door was closed, someone shouted to the driver, and the carriage moved off swiftly down the drive.

'Where are they taking him?' I asked.

'To Truro, where he'll best be tended, ma'am,' replied Sergeant Buller.

'That man is Martin Revesby,' I cried. 'The true Martin Revesby!'

'Is he now?' murmured the sergeant without any note of surprise. 'Is he now? Well, we've all been properly fooled, haven't we, ma'am? And why did Pendark allow him to live, I wonder?'

I said, 'All I know is that he *had* to be alive, for it was Martin Revesby – and no one else in the whole wide world – who wrote a certain poem during the last few weeks.' I savoured the thought for a few moments, and added: 'And he wrote it about – me!'

*

'I fear there'll be nothing left of Malmaynes but an empty shell,' said the sergeant. 'The long drought of last summer dried the inside woodwork like tinder. See how the flames are already coming through the rafters at the kitchen end. There she goes, ma'am! There goes the roof beam, yonder!'

We sat together in my wedding coach, the police officer and I; watching the roof of the kitchen block fold in the middle and collapse into the shell of the building in a rising cascade of bright sparks. Somewhere in the middle of that inferno – already, no doubt, a mass of molten iron – was the untended kitchen range that must have been the source of the disaster. Another irony: my wedding feast had been the cause of Malmaynes's certain destruction.

The sergeant was clearly correct in his assertion. The blaze was completely out of control; not all the fire-engines that were supposed to be on their way from Truro, from Penryn and from Falmouth were going to put it out; and how much less able to do so was the line of dark figures – silhouetted against the flames like demons in an inferno – that formed a bucket chain from the well in the kitchen garden. As soon extinguish the fires of hell with one sinner's tears.

'Saul Pendark and his mother – have they been found?' I asked.

'No, ma'am,' came the reply. 'I fear they are still in there. It may be that they still have the means to get out – and will do so when they're driven to it.'

'They went the other way from us,' I said. 'Towards the main staircase.'

'Then I have doubts for their survival,' said the sergeant, 'for they went straight towards the centre of the outbreak.'

The winter's day that was to have been my wedding-day was already dying; the grey overcast fading into dusk, and the blizzard slackening. Now the snowflakes fell like white petals, mocking the violence of the inferno within the great bulk on the clifftop. I thought of the two people – the madman and his grotesquely devoted mother – who were still within the holocaust. And what of Challis, whom I had last seen lying at the foot of the staircase in the roof?

Sergeant Buller broke in on my thoughts.

'You will be surprised, ma'am, that I once suspected you of murder!' he said abruptly.

'Me?' I stared at him. There was nothing approaching a smile on his unaccommodating countenance.

'Indeed so,' he said. 'At the discovery of the body of the strange woman in the churchyard, when I was not unduly impressed by the possibility of Saul Pendark still being alive, my suspicions were directed to new arrivals in the district. To the man whom we knew as Martin Revesby – and to yourself. I was able, finally, to eliminate you from my list of suspects only after the murder of Alice Witham.'

'And then you only suspected – Martin?' I could scarcely bring myself to utter the name in connection with Saul Pendark.

'He was never free of my suspicions, from first to last,' came the reply. 'Especially after my return from Paris.'

'What happened in Paris?' I asked. 'What did you find out there?'

His reply was delayed by the strident clang of a bell and the thunder of hooves, as a fire-engine swept close past us, drawn at the gallop by four big horses. From the chimney of a polished brass boiler showered a cascade of glowing sparks. A dozen helmeted men clung to its sides: they leapt to the ground before the driver had drawn rein in front of the blazing mansion, and commenced to uncoil a length of leather hosepipe, to the cheers of the men who had been handling the buckets. Within moments, a single jet of water was challenging the inferno within the great hall.

'In Paris,' said my companion, 'it was simplicity itself to identify the murdered woman from the label on her outer garment – a coatee of green velvet that had been tailored by Vuillard et Cie of the rue Royale. From their books I gleaned that the customer was a Mme Raymond of the rue d'Artois. In company with my colleagues of the Paris police, I visited the apartment in the rue d'Artois that had lately been inhabited by Mme Raymond and her – husband. On enquiry of the concierge, we learned that Monsieur Raymond – an

Englishman – had departed on business some time at the beginning of August last and had not since returned. Similarly, the wife had gone away some six weeks or so later. We had already shown the tailor a drawing that had been made of the dead woman's features. The concierge was able to confirm the tailor's view that this was Mme Raymond.'

'And the husband?' I breathed. 'Was anyone able to identify him?'

'Monsieur Raymond was described as a man in his late thirties or early forties,' said the sergeant. 'In every respect, he resembled the man I knew as Martin Revesby. In every respect save one: Raymond was bearded – an item which I completely disregarded. Armed with this information, I returned to Cornwall with the hope of making an early arrest.'

Memories were flooding the dark areas of my mind with the light of realization. 'You came back to arrest the man who called himself Martin Revesby,' I said. 'But you were prevented from doing so by the evidence of the poetry that I showed you!'

'Immediately on my return,' he said, 'Saul Pendark killed again. But I could not believe that any man who was able to pen such verses – and I have said before, ma'am, that I am not one for poetry, nor any judge of same, but I know fineness of sentiment when I come upon it and I know nobility of mind when I come upon it – I could not believe that such a man could slay defenceless women with his own hands.'

'Nor did he, Sergeant,' I said. 'Nor did he!'

And my thoughts went to the man, the almost complete stranger, who was being borne away through the gathering night in the brougham. I wondered how we would look at each other and what we would find to say to each other, when next we met.

The inferno still raged. Save for a part near the east end of the main wing, the flames had everywhere reached the upper floor and smoke was pouring even from attic windows. Another fire-engine had arrived to join the first; another puny jet of water to be mocked at and devoured by the indestructible flames. The intense heat had forced the other men to abandon the bucket chain and withdraw to a safe distance. One of them detached himself from his companions and came running over to the coach where we sat. Despite his scorched and smoke-blackened face, I recognized Nick Pendennis in his ruined wedding frock-coat. He put his head in through the window and took my hand in his.

'They told me you were safe, Cherry,' he said. 'And thank God for that.'

'What's the opinion of the firemen, sir?' demanded Sergeant Buller. 'Do they think there's hope of saving any of the building?'

'Not unless more engines arrive,' replied Nick. 'There's nothing left of the two lower storeys but red-hot stonework. Do you hear that? Do you see the sparks rising? There goes the third floor! The flames will be up to the roof in no time now. I'd best get back. The engine that's just arrived is pumped by hand and we're taking it in turns. Bless you, Cherry, and I thank heaven that you've been spared.' A squeeze of my hand, and he raced off.

'There was a time, after the attack upon Lady Amanda, when I suspected that young man,' declared the sergeant. 'That was when the evidence of the poem had seemed to prove the so-called Martin Revesby's innocence. However, I couldn't square the age difference between Mr Pendennis and my Monsieur Raymond.'

'Nor with the age of Saul Pendark,' I said.

He cast me a wry glance and cracked the knuckles of his big hands. 'I have to admit with some shame, ma'am,' he said, 'that I never was one for the Saul Pendark legend, though I have been proved to be sadly amiss in my assumption of his death. You see, I believed that the Rector was telling the truth when he gave evidence as to identification.'

'It was a half-truth,' I said. 'Told in good faith, for the best of intentions, and unselfishly.'

He stared at me anew. 'And might I ask how you come to know that, ma'am?' he demanded.

'The Rector confessed as much to me this morning,' I

told him. 'He did not try to secure the promise of my confidence, and I am quite sure he will repeat his confession to you.'

His regard was all admiration. I was the favourite pupil again. 'Did he admit that to you, ma'am?' he said. 'Did he indeed? Now, do you know, at first I had a mind to squeeze a confession out of him – if confession were there to be had. I had in mind to give him a fright, submit him to a long period of cross-questioning without rest or respite. There's not many who can hold back the truth after such treatment. It was something that Dr Prescott let drop that stayed my hand.'

'And what was that?' I asked.

'He let drop that the Rector's a very sick man. Pressed further, when I told him of my intention towards the old man, he declared that I must do no such thing, because the Reverend Murcher has a fatal illness, and is not long for this world.'

I said: 'I am sorry to hear that. Poor old man.'

'Yes indeed, ma'am.'

We sat in silence for a while, watching the men grouped by the fire-engines. A cascade of bright sparks rose from the roofless kitchen block and died high in the air.

Presently I said: 'I am puzzled, Sergeant. The last time I saw you, you told me – you told *us* – that you were leaving for good, that you had been dismissed from the case in disgrace, and that your enquiries in Paris had come to nothing.'

'In that, ma'am,' he said, 'I was less than truthful. Indeed, I may say that I played the deceiver.'

'To deceive – him?'

He nodded. 'By then, I had information that ran so strongly counter to the evidence of the poem as to make it almost certain that he was the man I sought. I called at Malmaynes for two reasons. Firstly, to convince him that he was safe from detection while I set about laying a trap for him. Secondly, because of my bad conscience concerning yourself, ma'am.'

'Concerning me? I don't understand.'

'If, as I believed, I had the means to destroy him, it could only bring you the greatest pain. For that I was – and am – deeply sorry. So I came to say farewell. I had thought, ma'am, that you would never wish to speak to me again.'

Dangerously close to tears, I said, 'You prevented my marrying a monster. Could I now have any other feeling towards you but the deepest gratitude?'

'There was the poem, you see, ma'am. Which suggested to me that, despite all, the man was capable of finer feelings. Feelings which – you will forgive me for speaking frankly – might well have – have . . .'

'Made me fall in love with him?' I looked out into the darkness, away from the blazing mansion, searching my own heart. 'I think I can now say with complete certainty that I never loved the man I knew as Martin Revesby. I may have loved the image of the poet. For the man, I now know that I conceived a powerful and fatal attraction. And that, as you must guess, has turned to horrified revulsion.'

'Furthermore,' said Sergeant Buller, 'he was not the author of the poem after all. And I am ashamed to admit that it never once occurred to me that it was written by another.'

I made no reply to that, since it opened fields of speculation that I was not yet prepared to explore myself, let alone in the company of my extraordinary friend and confidant.

So I said: 'You spoke of laying a trap for him, Sergeant. He used the same term. Everyone was waiting in the church, he said, for him to spring a trap.'

'The evening before I called upon you,' said my companion, 'I had received news from my police colleagues in Paris that they had unearthed two relatives of the deceased woman: a father and a brother. Not men of very high character: one an unemployed waiter, the other an unsuccessful singer on the music halls. They knew their sister's husband well enough and thought little of him. I myself went over to persuade them to come to England and identify him.'

I exclaimed, 'So that was what you meant when you said you were leaving?'

'Yes, ma'am. I went over to Paris again and questioned

these two gentry. They were truculent. Suspicious. Their English brother-in-law, they said, was a liar and a boaster. Boasted of a fortune that he would one day inherit. He had deserted his wife, but she had found letters among his belongings by which she had been able to trace him. Letters from his mother.'

'From Mrs Challis!' I cried. 'So she was in communication with him all those years?'

'Undoubtedly, ma'am. Armed with the address, Madame Raymond was able to follow her wayward husband to England. To St Gawes. And with what dire results we are aware. Up to this point, the father and brother had not been told of Madame Raymond's death. I broke the news to them – and had little difficulty in persuading them to come to England and denounce her murderer.'

'At my wedding!'

'The thing had to be done publicly, ma'am. And all the better for catching the scoundrel on an occasion when he was completely off his guard. As it happened, he saw the bait. I should have foreseen it. There was no one at the church porch, for the Rector was late in arriving. He must have spotted the two Frenchmen immediately, sitting in the front pew, where I had placed them for the greatest effect.'

'And he returned at once,' I said. And, with a shuddering breath, added, 'Here – to settle with me, before he fled. For he thought that I was a party to the trap that you laid for him.'

'Ma'am,' cried Sergeant Buller, 'I would not have placed you in the slightest danger for all the world. Why, the way I had intended it, he was to have been arrested and removed before you even arrived at the church.'

'It would have been a very doleful arrival,' I said ruefully. 'Poor bride. Poor me.'

'Ma'am!' he cried. 'Soon or late, I would have prevented that wedding ceremony, I promise you. I swear by all that's holy that I would as lief have seen my own daughter give herself to that madman as you. And that's the truth of it!'

'I believe you, Sergeant,' I assured him. 'I know that

you have my welfare at heart.'

He looked broodingly towards the blazing mansion. "Twas a tragedy that you were ever caught up in that brute's career, ma'am,' he said. 'A tragedy and an ill chance that should never have happened. The second coming of the Beast of Malmaynes could never have gone its full term. He had left too wide a trail behind him. Boasted too much. Made too many mistakes. His new identity as Martin Revesby, poet, was doomed to be short, brutish and a failure.'

'Possibly,' I conceded. 'But he convinced me completely. Though I see now that he couldn't possibly have gone on to do all the things he boasted of: becoming the idol of Society like Lord Byron, taking London by storm. Martin Revesby's brilliant academic career, the many friends and acquaintances he must have made at Oxford and elsewhere – all that condemned Saul Pendark to a world of fantasy that could never have extended far beyond the walls of Malmaynes and the parish of St Gawes.'

'True, ma'am. Very true.'

We sat in silence – a long silence that was broken by a chorus of shouts from over by the fire-engines, where men were pointing upwards and gesticulating to each other.

'By all that's holy, ma'am!' cried my companion. 'See up there!'

I followed the direction of his pointing finger. High on the steeply-pitched roof of the doomed mansion, two figures were emerging from an upper dormer window.

'Saul Pendark and his mother!' I cried.

'They have retreated before the flames all this while,' said the sergeant. 'Whether trapped or not, they went ever upwards till they can now go no further. And now they are trapped indeed!' He opened the coach door and got out. 'I beg you to remain where you are, ma'am,' he urged me.

I was close at his heels. The early winter's night had descended and the snow had stopped. Not a voice was to be heard above the heavy crackle of the flames and the hiss of the water jets from the two leather hosepipes, the clank of the hand-pump, the rumble of the steam-engine. Everyone was staring up at the two figures, which, having emerged from the dormer window, were picking a careful way up the steep side of the roof, hand in hand, towards the high ridge, the man leading.

The smaller figure slipped upon the slates, which, due to the heat of the fire, were wet with melted snow. This brought a concerted gasp of horror from the crowd – surely the whole populace of the parish of St Gawes – that was massed in the darkness beyond the glare of the blazing mansion; but the leading figure remained steady and, stooping, assisted the other to an upright position once more. Hand in hand still, they continued on their perilous way to the very summit of Malmaynes.

I was now close to the smaller fire-engine: the one with the hand-pump, which had two men bearing their weight on each end. I saw Nick Pendennis working next to Edgar Portwell – Edgar Portwell the tragic bridegroom. They were both staring over their shoulders at the two figures high above.

'Do you not have a rescue net?' I recognized the voice of Sergeant Buller.

'We have a good stout sheet of canvas for rescue work,' came the reply. 'But 'tis useless at such a height. And the more so now that they're up beyond the roof edge. Why, if they let themselves go, there's no telling where they'd fall to earth.'

'Just so, just so,' replied the sergeant.

A few feet only separated the leading figure from the ridge of Malmaynes's roof, etched against the night sky like the keel of an upturned man-o'-war. One hand out-thrust, one more step, and the ascent was made. There was a discernible sigh of relief from the watching crowd. Such is the instinct of humanity – even towards the inhuman.

It was at this moment that the fury of the inferno seemed somewhat to abate. It may have been no more than a slackening of the flames at the ground floor, where everything but the stone walls must have been entirely consumed; on the other hand, it is possible that the efforts of the firemen and their engines were beginning to make some headway against the conflagration. In any event, there was a distinct lessening in the terrible volume of sound, a fading of the ruddy glare, even a reduction of the intolerable heat which we had been experiencing even at some considerable distance. For the first time it seemed – to me at any rate – that the fire-fighters were making some inroads upon the flames.

I stared up into the night, narrowing my eyes. Saul Pendark and his mother had safely gained the roof ridge. She, the smaller figure, was hunched there, seated on the ridge. He was standing up, arms folded, legs straddled, gazing out into the immeasurable distance above our heads: over St Gawes, the bay, the headlands, the wide seas, and all the world beyond.

'*Curse you, Saul Pendark!*'

All eyes turned to regard the man who had shouted the words. It was Edgar Portwell, eyes staring with emotion. Releasing one hand from the pump-handle, he shook his fist at the figure high above him.

'For what you did to my Alice, may you perish this night!' he shouted. 'And may you burn for ever in hell's fire!'

The response to that awful utterance will remain with me till my last day, for above the roar and crackle of the flames, high in the night sky, we heard an answering peal of mocking, demoniacal laughter. I clasped my hands over my ears to shut out the sound. Because of that I did not hear the coming of the mighty wind, which, as was whispered afterwards, blew from out of the sea and across the headland. I knew nothing of this wind till I felt its buffeting, so that I had to reach out and take hold of the wheel of the engine for support.

The great wind acted like a mighty bellows upon the sullen flames, rekindling every smouldering particle anew. A white flame roared through the hollow shell of the mansion, devouring in one searing breath all that remained: dormer attics, rooftops, chimneys – all.

When the wind had died away, nothing remained but four stark walls. Malmaynes was gone, and the Beast with it.

Chapter Eleven

The snow had thawed. It lay in banks of dark slush by the sides of the streets as I was driven through Truro to the public nursing home where Martin Revesby was being treated.

I was greeted in the warm hallway by a pleasant-looking woman in a mob-cap who introduced herself as Mrs Giles, the proprietress of the establishment. With her was Dr Arthur, the same surgeon who had rendered aid to Nick Pendennis after he had been tossed by the bull.

'Good day to you, ma'am!' cried the doctor cheerfully. 'Called to see the patient, eh? Well, ma'am, I am happy to inform you that the concussion to the brain, though of a serious nature, has dispersed nicely. Mr Revesby is well on the way to recovery.'

'He is a very good patient,' said Mrs Giles. 'Beautiful manners, he has.'

Beneath his brash cheerfulness, the doctor was all curiosity. The woman made no secret of her own morbid interest, but ogled me unashamedly. For was I not the tragic creature who had all but married a maniac killer? Scarcely a week had passed, but the news of Saul Pendark's end was the sensation of the whole county. In the quiet hostelry in Truro, where I had gone for refuge, the very maidservants vied with each other for the pleasure of bringing the meal trays to my private suite: I had not the courage to use the public dining-room. I was celebrated. Notorious. And I detested the experience, but had no means to combat it. I longed to go far away from Malmaynes; but could not summon up the enterprise, even, to journey as far as Poltewan and see Uncle

Gervase. Instead, some compulsion kept me in Truro, where, for a week, I had waited to be told when Martin Revesby would be well enough to receive his first visitor. The occasion had arrived.

'Is he – in good spirits?' I said, conscious of the absurdity of the question, but reaching for any straw to break the awkward silence, to have them stop staring at me.

'Oh, very cheerful!' cried Mrs Giles hastily, seemingly relieved at having been given something to say. 'He has us all in fits. So clever. So witty. And a real gentleman.'

'Considering the rigours of his incarceration,' said Dr Arthur, 'he has retained his equilibrium to a very remarkable degree. Mmm – truly remarkable.'

His 'incarceration' : I had computed that the secret captive of Malmaynes – bearing in mind that his letter from Brussels offering me the position of secretary had been written shortly before his departure to England – must have been locked up in the dormer attic for over four months. And in all that time what hope of eventual freedom could ever have seemed possible while Saul Pendark was still at large?

'Perhaps you'd like to come this way, Miss Carew,' said Mrs Giles, disappointed, perhaps, that I had made no comment on the doctor's observation.

I followed her down a parquet-floored corridor that smelled of beeswax, and up a flight of stairs. She knocked at a door on the second floor. A voice said to come in. My guide opened the door and stood aside to let me enter. I waited till she had shut it behind me before I turned to look at Martin Revesby and see what manner of man he was.

' "East, West, home's best," ' said my Uncle Gervase. 'If I may be permitted the triteness of the observation. It is uncommonly pleasant to have you back again, my dear.'

'I'm pleased to be back, Uncle,' I told him. 'And glad to see you looking so well.'

He shrugged. 'My excellent physician presented me with a stark alternative, the logic of which could not but appeal to a man of legal training: "forswear the bottle, or the bottle will surely forswear you." I have not touched a drop in a month, but I would be deceiving you, my dear Cherry, if I were to give you the impression that I am as contented within as I am healthy-looking without.'

We were at breakfast, I having arrived by dog-cart from St Errol station late the previous evening. Now I was presiding in my accustomed place at the table over the coffee-pot and the cream jug. Uncle Gervase was eating fried eggs on oatcakes with every sign of enjoyment. Through the cottage window, I could see a fishing-boat rounding the little stone-built harbour wall, with a mass of seagulls wheeling noisily above it. I was home. And feeling curiously contented and at peace.

'And how is the widow-lady?' I asked.

'We have been sorely deceived, the gallant captain and I,' replied my uncle. 'Whilst seemingly testing the both of us for suitability in the matrimonial stakes, milady has also been trailing her cloak elsewhere, the jade. She has, we now learn, been pursuing no less than the Lord-Lieutenant of Cornwall this last twelvemonth, and finally she has allowed him to catch her. They are to be married at Christmas.'

'That must be a tremendous relief to both you and Captain Arbuthnot,' I smiled.

'We shall miss the thrill of the chase,' he said. 'And the amusement of trying to determine who was the intended quarry.' He pushed aside the empty plate and dabbed his lips with his napkin. 'Enough of all that, my dear. To return to serious matters. It was a bad business, a terrible experience, that you went through.'

I said: 'People stared at me in the streets of Truro. It's very odd, Uncle, but that's what troubles me most. I hope they won't do it in Poltewan.'

'I am very much afraid they will,' he said. 'And the more so – and with added zest – for having known you before the tragic occurrences in question took place. You will have to steel your resolve, my dear, and console yourself with the thought that all things pass. And now, if you will be so kind as to replenish my cup, please, I should be grateful – if it don't upset you too much in the telling – for a more rounded-out version of the brief account you gave me late last evening.'

'Of course,' I said. What I needed, what I longed for most of all in the world was to tell of what had happened. And what better person to confide in than the wise, cranky, wayward old man seated before me?

'Not the events on the day of the fire,' he said. 'I've read all that a score of times in every newspaper to be had. What of the aftermath? You met Revesby. The true Revesby. What manner of fellow is he, now, eh?'

Describe Martin Revesby? How to begin? My mind went back to the room on the second floor. The figure seated in the high-backed armchair, his head turned away from the window with its drawn blinds. A profile, dimly-lit . . .

'As unlike Saul Pendark as it is possible to be,' I said.

'That is not to be wondered at,' said Uncle Gervase drily. 'Considering one was a raving maniac and t'other's a Scholar of Magdalen College – not that I haven't met some pretty rum Oxford men. But pray continue.'

'And yet,' I said, 'while totally unlike Saul Pendark, Saul Pendark was curiously like *him*. I said as much to him, and he was able to explain why.

'They saw each other constantly. The gaoler visited his prisoner daily and talked with him for hours. A curious bond was forged between them, half-way between detestation and something like affection.'

'It is not an unusual phenomenon,' said my uncle. 'It has frequently been observed in penal establishments that a turnkey will conceive an almost maternal affection for one of his charges, while still holding him in the deepest contempt. Conversely, the prisoner, though continuing violently to resent the gaoler, will grow almost to love him, listening with beating heart for the sound of his approaching footsteps.'

'It was like that at Malmaynes,' I said. 'Martin Revesby grew somehow to like and admire Saul Pendark. He found him a highly intelligent man, with an uncanny gift for assimilating knowledge, ideas, poetic concepts. Martin talked to him: told him the story of his own life, his early struggles, his academic successes, his determination to write great poetry. Saul absorbed it all. Gradually, without the other being aware of the process till it was accomplished, Saul took upon himself a very considerable part of his captive's character. I said as much to Martin. I said: "I met the man who played the role of Martin Revesby, and I thought he was real, but he turned out to be a puppet. Now I feel that I have met the puppet-master who pulled the strings." '

'To digress,' said Uncle Gervase. 'How was Revesby's incarceration accomplished? You briefly intimated, last evening, that they first met in Brussels.'

'Saul Pendark confided every detail of his plans, past, present and future, to his prisoner,' I said. 'What happened was this: Saul learned of Mr Tremaine's death from his mother, who wrote and told him that Malmaynes was to pass to a nobody, an outsider, who lived in Brussels. He, fed from birth by his mother's talk of the estate that should rightfully be his inheritance, determined to make it so. He abandoned his wife and went to Brussels, where he contrived to scrape up an acquaintance with the poet Martin Revesby. They were fellow-Cornishmen, you see, and Saul had the advantage – after feigning surprise and interest in Martin's new inheritance – of being able to describe Malmaynes and its late owner with great familiarity; telling his intended victim that he was the son of one of the local landowners, who had frequently dined at the great house. What more natural than that Martin should invite his new friend to accompany him back to Cornwall and be his first guest at Malmaynes?'

'The exchange of characters took place where?' asked my uncle.

'Literally on the threshold of the mansion,' I replied. 'The two of them had been brought from Truro station in a hired dog-cart driven by Mrs Challis's husband – a weak, drunken dupe who paid for his shortcomings with his life. Martin was struck down from behind, and remembered nothing till he came to in a narrow room high in the roof void of the great house. A room with a boarded-up window, a pallet bed and a few utensils.'

'Why was he not killed? Simpler, far simpler, to have killed him there and then!'

'Saul had ambitions,' I replied. 'In Brussels, he had seen something of the tremendous admiration with which Martin was received everywhere he went. A poet already honoured, and marked for fame. Saul resolved to have all that – or as much as he could – for himself.'

Uncle Gervase fussily ruffled his fine head of flaxen-white hair – a habit he had when perplexed. 'But I don't understand,' he cried. 'Are you telling me that Saul confided all this in Martin, and that, aiding and abetting his gaoler's insane ambition, Martin continued to write poetry, thereby furthering that ambition?'

I remembered the face of the man in the high-backed chair, I remembered his manner of speech. I could almost hear the tone of his voice when he answered the self-same question when I had put it to him . . .

'Martin Revesby,' I said. 'Martin Revesby, the artist, the poet, would have agreed to anything – any condition, however unreasonable and humiliating – in order to have been given writing materials and the opportunity to set down the images which were crowding into his mind. To him, despite his surroundings, the act of poetic creation was life itself. To be deprived of it was worse than lifelong imprisonment, worse than death.' I looked down at my hands: they were trembling.

'I concede the point,' said Uncle Gervase. 'Being supported by excellent evidence as regards character. I refer to the character of the creative artist. Please continue, do. Tell me, if you will, what happened to upset this mutually advantageous arrangement? Why – and here we must disregard the activities of the excellent Sergeant Buller, not to mention my own not inconsiderable efforts, which together would have set this arrangement to naught in any event – why is Martin Revesby not still composing deathless poetry in a narrow cell in the roof of Malmaynes, and the false Martin Revesby not still taking the credit for their composition – albeit only from yourself?'

It was a question that had to be answered very carefully, after consideration of all the evidence – as my uncle would have put it. I answered it on the impulse, with the immediate image that sprang, unbidden, into my mind:

'Because, one day, Martin Revesby chanced to see that there was a knot in the thick boarding that covered the window of his cell-room . . .'

'Yes – and . . .?' Learned Counsel gave some encouragement to the hesitant witness, while affecting not to notice that she was fighting against her emotions.

'Using the spoon, which was the only eating utensil he was allowed, he carefully worked at the knot till he was able to remove the hard plug and replace it at will.'

'So that he had a secret eye on to the outer world, so to speak.'

'Yes. And, one day, through it he saw . . . *me*!'

The winter's night had fallen, with new snow, over Poltewan and all the wild Western Land. The cottage windows were shuttered with a whiteness that obliterated all. That afternoon, we had gone for a short walk along the quay and had seen ice floes in the harbour. Inside our small parlour, we were cocooned in a cosseting warmth from the coal fire that burned in the iron grate; each in an armchair at either side of the hearth. There was a row of chestnuts roasting on the edge of the grate, tended by Uncle; from time to time one would pop and split its skin, then he would take it up with the fire tongs, peel it, break it, half for him and half for me.

'It was a wonder,' said Uncle Gervase, 'that Pendark received you into Malmaynes in the first place. I suppose your letter advising Revesby of your imminent arrival threw him into something of a quandary. Then, on second thoughts, he decided that you could be useful to his plans.'

I had a vision of Malmaynes now a gaunt and burnt-out shell standing high above the winter sea.

'He was there when I arrived,' I said. 'Watching me from an upper window. I heard it from Martin Revesby, in whom he confided everything. He thought I looked appetizing – that was the word he used. That night he had one of his maniac fits. I heard the terrible laughter, and never properly accounted for it.'

'You say he confided everything in Revesby?' asked my uncle.

'Everything – in his own good time,' I said. 'And similarly, Martin confided in him. Later, he told Saul about having seen me; confessed about his secret Judas window. Saul was indulgent. Amused. It pleased him greatly when Martin turned from the Tristan and Iseult to a poem that was an expression of his feelings for me: the woman he saw – briefly and occasionally – through his small window out on to the world. Saul encouraged the composition of the poem. It served him in his campaign to entrap me.'

'The monster found you useful as secretary and châtelaine, but speedily grew to covet you for his bride!' cried Uncle Gervase. 'By heaven, my dear, when I think of the hellish fate that you so narrowly escaped! But did Revesby know nothing of this? Did Pendark not confide in him that he was to marry you?'

'First, he told Martin that I was going away,' I replied. 'This he did for some perverse reason on the day that was to have been poor little Alice Witham's wedding-day. Martin saw me leaving for the church, and it provided him with the closing theme for the poem: the departure of the unknown lady.' I closed my eyes, pressing my fingers hard against my brow. 'And while Martin Revesby wrote those verses, Saul Pendark killed!'

'Cherry, Cherry . . .' Uncle Gervase reached across and, taking my hand, squeezed it comfortingly. 'My dear, it's all past. The dead can't be recalled, nor the evil undone. You live. Revesby lives. And the poem . . .'

'It survived,' I said. 'My copy – the one I kept in the tin box – was found, though badly charred by the tremendous heat, among the ruins. I took it to Martin when I visited him at the nursing home in Truro.'

'It will live for ever,' he said. 'Do you not see, my dear Cherry, that at least one great good has come out of all this?'

'The poem was nearly the last thing that Martin Revesby ever wrote,' I said. 'When Saul Pendark told him of our forthcoming marriage – taunted him with the news – everything changed between them. Gone was the strange relationship that was half-hate, half-affection. Martin swore that he would find a way to kill his captor. And he refused ever to set pen to paper again. From that day forth, he was marked to die. Saul Pendark gave him to the New Year. If, by then, he had written no more, he was to have been left to starve to death up there in the roof.'

'Horrible!' breathed Uncle Gervase. 'Horrible and unspeakable! It is beyond all belief that that creature stalked the earth, his condition undetected, for twenty years. How was it accomplished, I ask myself. How?'

'Saul claimed to have been cured,' I said. 'He boasted of it to Martin many times: how he had been treated by a Paris professor who was an adept of mesmerism.'

'Mesmerism!' cried Uncle Gervase. 'Ah, the mysterious science of "animal magnetism". Yes, that may well have brought about a temporary remission of his condition. Sufficient, at any rate, to have succeeded where poor Reverend Murcher's exorcism failed. And I take it that it was the natural father, the late Mr Henry Tremaine, he of the tight fist in matters of charity to the village, who supported Pendark all those years?'

'From first to last,' I said. 'When Saul survived that awful fall into the waters below the cliff, he moved heaven and earth to get him safely out of the country, to be treated with the mesmerism, and financially supported for the rest of his life. All Mr Tremaine could not bequeath to his natural son was the thing that Saul most craved for.'

'Malmaynes! And he would have given him that, I don't doubt, if it had been in his power to break the entail.'

'I've no doubt,' I said.

'And all for a raving maniac – because he was his son!'

I pondered for a while, and said: 'There was more to it than that, I think. Henry Tremaine had a strange quality of compassion towards the deformed, the outcasts, the spurned ones of normal existence. He rescued Jabez from a life of misery and degradation. I think he had the same compulsion to save Saul Pendark, son or no son.'

'Yes, you may be right,' said my uncle. 'It may be that the character of the late Mr Henry Tremaine lies at the heart of all this business. Indeed, as you will remember, it was his inexplicable action of paying for the Rector's wife to go to Baden-Baden that first set us thinking. You were speaking of Jabez – by heaven, you have much to thank that poor unfortunate for, my dear.'

'He saved my life,' I said. 'I think Saul Pendark was intent on killing me when Jabez and Mrs Challis came upon the scene.'

'Yet he was in league with them, this Jabez?'

'He knew a little,' I said. 'But not all. When I first came to Malmaynes, Mrs Challis set Jabez to keep an eye on me, to make sure I saw and heard nothing. He followed me everywhere – ' my mind went back to the events, and an involuntary shudder ran through my frame – 'I heard him cough in a hawthorn thicket and thought that the Beast of Malmaynes was close to me. On another occasion, when I was searching the mansion, he deliberately frightened me, I think, to warn me away from prying too much. By that time, I fancy Mrs Challis – who had by then decided that I would make a good wife and keeper for her son – had revised Jabez's role to that of my protector. She disapproved of what Saul had become, you see, and mistrusted him. She resented the education that he had picked up on the Continent, the adoption of superficial trappings of gentility that came so easy to him, the manner in which he treated her – like a servant. In truth, the son whom she had loved – the young lad with a demon from hell on his back – perished, for her, in the maelstrom below Malmaynes.'

Uncle Gervase nodded, but made no comment. We sat in silence for a very long time, and I imagined pictures in the red-hot coals. Faces and places: Malmaynes in the light of dawn and dying in flames; the features of my mother as I remembered her from the mists of childhood; Nicholas Pendennis's face; another face – a profile that I first saw by the dim light coming through drawn window-blinds . . .

Nick Pendennis came to see me a few days before Christmas, breaking his train journey from Truro to London. We went for a walk together along the quay. He had entirely recovered from his wound, and was in a fur-collared covert coat and cap. He was also in high good humour, though it seemed to mask an undercurrent of unease in his manner.

'I have brought Amanda to heel,' he said. 'The wedding's fixed for the first week in January and we depart for India at the end of that month. Amanda has quite resigned herself to the prospect of being wife to a John Company official. Y'know, Cherry, it was the attempt upon her life that changed milady's way of thinking. Concentrated her mind no end upon the realities of existence. No more talk of the London Season and all that rot. Ascot and Henley Royal Regatta might never have existed.'

A seagull watched us, head on one side, from the top of an iron bollard at the quay's edge. As we drew closer, it flapped clumsily into the air and soared away across the icy waters of the harbour, above the dark boats massed at their moorings.

'I think, rather, that she has awakened to the fact that she loves you, Nick,' I told him. And I had a rueful recollection of the time when Lady Amanda had warned me off her man. 'Many things could have contributed towards helping her do that,' I added.

'I'm very firm with her,' he said. 'Have been, ever since that time she roundly insulted you, Cherry. I haven't insisted that she apologize to you yet – but I will, next time I think of it.'

'It doesn't matter, Nick,' I told him. 'It's all forgotten now.'

'Deuced nice of you to say so, Cherry,' he said.

We came to the end of the quay, where there was a big

Russian schooner which had taken refuge in our harbour against the icy gales of the previous days. A row of pale blue eyes watched the two of us from the vessel's taffrail as we turned about and set off back.

Nick said: 'Cherry, I want to put a few things to rights. There are things I've said to you – what I mean is – devil take it, I'm not much of a hand at putting my thoughts into words!'

'What you want to say, Nick,' I interposed helpfully, 'is that you made several rather indiscreet declarations to me, which, though sincerely intended at the time . . .'

'Yes, yes!' he cried. 'Made with the deepest sincerity, I promise you, Cherry. I'm not one to trifle, I assure you!'

'Though sincerely intended, were rather impetuous . . .'

'Impetuous! Yes, that's the ticket!'

'In view of your coming nuptials, you wish to do the honourable thing, both by me and by your intended, and withdraw the said indiscreet declarations. Do I have it right?' I smiled up at him encouragingly.

His broad, handsome face was furrowed with doubt.

'Damned nice girl, Amanda,' he said. 'Don't want to start off on the wrong foot. Especially since one's taking her so far away from everything she's been used to. Wanted to put it right, you understand? Wanted to start with a clean slate.'

I took his gloved hand in mine: squeezed it hard.

'You're a very nice man, Nick,' I said. 'And I hope you and your Amanda will be very happy.'

'And you, also, Cherry,' he cried. 'From the bottom of my heart!'

I kissed him on the cheek, as sister to brother.

'I'll write to you often,' he said. 'We'll both write to you from Cawnpore.'

'Goodbye, Nick.'

'Goodbye, Cherry.'

He set off along the road to the railway station at St Errol: a big handsome bear in his fur-collared coat. At the first bend in the road, he turned and waved back to me.

I never saw him again.

Chapter Twelve

A week later I received from Martin Revesby the briefest of letters. The sight of that familiar handwriting had the power to evoke memories of many sorts: some that I would gladly have put out of my mind, some that made my heart sing for joy.

He was still at the nursing home, he informed me, doing very nicely, but not yet declared fit by Dr Arthur. Notwithstanding which, he was hoping to be out soon.

'I would call upon you at St Errol, but for my present incapacity,' the letter concluded, 'for I have a communication of some importance to make to you that can scarcely wait. I wonder, my dear Miss Carew, if you are in or about Truro in the course of the next week or so, if you would be so kind as to call upon me here . . .?'

It was a request that I could not have refused if my life had been at forfeit. The following day, I took coach to Truro, and let my mind wander upon Martin Revesby, while the dark hills of mid-Cornwall rolled slowly past my window.

I remembered that Uncle Gervase had asked me what quality of man was Martin – the real Martin Revesby; and how I had stumblingly tried to explain that I had earlier fallen in love with – no, conceived a tremendous attraction towards – a man who was the marionette on the end of the strings that the real Martin Revesby had manipulated; the creature who had been a shadow only of the real substance of the man. Merely by playing the role of Martin Revesby, by partaking of his thoughts, his inner feelings expressed in conversation, in poetry, the insane Saul Pendark had absorbed sufficient grace, enough stature of mind, to make himself from time to time – and I would remember the occasions till my dying day – almost irresistible to me.

We came to Truro, and the coach delivered me almost to the door of Mrs Giles's nursing home, where that cheerful and inquisitive body raised an eyebrow to see me, and gave me to understand that Mr Revesby had made a point of informing her that he was hoping – *greatly* hoping, she added – for a visit from Miss Carew, and would she, Mrs Giles, make a very special point of ushering Miss Carew straight in to him, be he awake or be he asleep. That was the way of it, she told me, nodding knowingly.

I found my own way down the corridor, up the stairs to the door on the second floor, at which I knocked.

'Come in,' said the voice I had learned to shape by its pitch and its timbre in my dreams and in my waking hours.

Uncle Gervase had asked me if Martin Revesby was impressive, and I had found it a difficult question to answer. Was he an Adonis in appearance, Uncle had persisted, and of looks to match the stature of his mind and intellect? I had had to smile at that. Hardly an Adonis, I thought. Saul Pendark playing the role of Martin Revesby had been much more the Adonis. Martin himself was less dramatic in appearance. His face, with the beard taken off, was remarkable only for its repose.

It was in repose when I entered the room and approached him, seated in a chair by the window.

'You came!' he said simply, and took the hand that I extended. He then gestured for me to take the seat that was set beside him.

'How could I do other?' I replied.

He nodded. 'I have thought much of our last meeting, and have arrived at a conclusion.'

'Yes?' I breathed, all attention.

'You will recall,' he said, 'that I spoke of my feelings for you; feelings which, notwithstanding the fact that I had only seen you from afar and in brief glimpses through a tiny Judas window, are of a most profound nature.'

'You were very frank,' I told him. 'Very straightforward. You made no demands upon my emotions. You evoked nothing in your support – not even the wonderful poem that you wrote for my sake. You simply presented yourself to me as a stranger who had seen me from afar, asking nothing but to be heard and demanding nothing in reply.'

He nodded. 'The time has come when I must go somewhat further than that – no, my dear, I am not asking for a reply from you now. Hear me out, I beg you.

'I am going away. Soon. As soon as my strength is returned sufficiently, and it cannot be a matter of more than a few weeks, days even. The villa in Capri – the one in the poem – truly exists. At the end of a year of wandering the world, I shall go there; stay there, perhaps, for the rest of my life. A year from now, if you are of a mind to see me again, I beg you to send a line to the Villa Rosina in Capri, and I will come to you. There, that is what I have to say. I commit you to nothing. How could I? What right have I?'

I gazed at him through the gathering tears – this man who could have swept me off my feet for the asking; but who, by interposing a year for waiting and consideration, was demonstrating both the sincerity of his feelings for me and his honour as a man.

In that moment, I knew the truth of the matter, the truth about myself and Martin Revesby, and it was this. I had seen him only thrice, and briefly; but it was as if I had been part of him, and he of me, all my life. And the prospect of living through a whole year before I would see him again was more than I could bear.

My hand reached out, as if of its own accord. And his hand was waiting.